Outer Limits

Outer Limits

Armageddon Dreams

Kevin J. Anderson
Harlan Ellison

QUADRILLION
MEDIA LLC

BSV
Publishing

Contents

6

OUTER LIMITS

Introduction: Working Beyond My Limits

Harlan Ellison

Hurtling back down that shaft of memory, it is the sunflowers I remember most clearly. The sunflowers, and the still-charged recollection of being grateful that it wasn't raining as they threw me out the front door, onto my knees, on the sidewalk.

I'm getting ahead of myself.

I know this private detective down in New Orleans, name of Lew Griffin (actually, I know his daddy, Jimmy, better), and one time Lew said, "Mostly what you lose with time, in memory, is the specificity of things, their exact sequence. It all runs together, becomes a watery soup. Portmanteau days, imploded years." He likes to talk that way.

But I think he's got it right, that it all blurs around the edges. Oh, I can remember driving into Los Angeles on New Year's Day, 1962, driving that smashed-in Ford I'd bought from Bill Hamling in Chicago, with literally nothing in my pockets but a dime, and my second wife, Billie, and her son from her first marriage, Kenny, and the three of us hungry and exhausted and almost out of gas, and we were on the Hollywood Freeway, and I knew nothing of the town, but I saw the Capitol Records Tower off to the left, and so I swerved hard onto the Vine Street off-ramp, knowing that I'd hit Hollywood, one way or the other. Yeah, I can remember that clearly. But the soup gets thick when I try to remember the early afternoon of a day in the fall of that year when I got pitched out of the offices of Daystar, the production company, then readying for ABC network debut of a series they had decided to call *The Outer Limits*.

The memory I've held for close to forty years is wrong. I know that now. Because, to write this Introduction I've had to do a little research and, with the help of my friend David Schow—who co-authored *The Official Companion to The Outer Limits*—I've revived some facts that make what I've held in my head since 1962, the soupy memory, come back into focus.

And as I hurtle back down yesterday's shaft of recollection, I am astonished at the importance in my life of that simple little television series. The cross-connections. The synchronicity. The offshoots of The Outer Limits that have had such a pronounced effect on my reputation, my well-being, and even (this is hard for an atheist to parse) my basic existence.

In substantial measure, I am where and who I am today, as I write this Introduction damn near the cusp of the millennium, because I was involved with The Outer Limits in 1963-64. Not just because one of the Daystar Productions executives was a guy named Ralph Riskin, who was married to my third wife just before I fell into that disastrous 45-day marriage to her that miraculously redounded to my benefit and future; not just because my fourth wife wound up marrying Joe Stefano's son, and Joe had been the producer of *The Outer Limits*; not just because that egomaniac James Cameron ripped off *Soldier* as the basis for his film, *The Terminator*, and I had recourse to attorneys resulting in me getting a nice chunk of money, and a credit on the millions of videotapes that were sold; not just because the first AD on the series was Bobby Justman, who became my friend and later recommended me to Gene Roddenberry as a writer for Star Trek before it even went on the air; and not just because of all the significant nourishing rivulets and trickles and streams that flowed from the original liaison...

I'm getting ahead of myself. Let's go back to that fall afternoon in 1962 when the producers of the not-yet-premiered *Outer Limits* booted my ass into the street.

Close on forty years after the event—now casually "ancient history" to kids slurping up their adolescence in a world of internet and video immediacy where anything older than yesterday ain't worth knowing—you have to understand how the TV business was run. There were no staffs of writers who worked the shows in gangs, who these days accept Golden Globes and Emmys in packs that look more like hunter-gatherers than literary creators. It was the world of the freelancer. Writers who went from show to show, series to series, picking up an episode here, a two-parter there, and sticking with a series only as long as nothing juicier came into view. September was the beginning of the new season, and so during the preceding spring, through summer, and into the early days of autumn here in Los Angeles, like ragamuffin wayfarers, we freelancers wandered from studio to studio, from production office to story meeting, attending the "cattle call" showings of pilot episodes, cajoling and hustling and conniving our way into the exalted presences of story editors, producers, executives and agents who might have an inside angle, so we could "pitch" a story.

I'd been brought out from the Midwest and the East Coast by Alfred Hitchcock's purchase of my autobiography, MEMOS FROM PURGATORY, the story of my time spent undercover with a kid gang in Brooklyn when I was an aspiring, unpublished writer...and the brief stint I did in jail subsequently. I'd been mustered out of the US Army in 1959–two-year draftee—and had gone to work in Chicago for Hamling. Then I'd gotten divorced the first time, escaped Hamling and returned to New York where I'd remarried on the rebound, gone back to Chicago against my better judgment, and finally fled Hamling and the frigid environs of Evanston and the Loop, just in time to head toward Hollywood with Billie and Kenny, as that second, ill-fated, marriage was ending.

We got to LA, and I've told this story elsewhere a hundred times, with only ten cents in the till, and virtually no connections; not to mention never having even seen a script, much less knowing how to write one.

But I bluffed my way into the game, got an agent, got a few gigs, and spent the next eight years trying to climb out of the morass of debt and ruined relationships I'd sloughed into, as I pretended to be an adult.

In April or May of '62 I'd heard about a pilot for a proposed ABC series called Please Stand By. My friend Robert Bloch who had written the novel PSYCHO on which the Hitchcock film was based, told me that the pilot script had been written by Joseph Stefano, who had been the scenarist who'd adapted Bob's brilliant suspense thriller for the screen. Bob told me this series was right up my alley, as I'd already created something of a reputation for myself as a writer in the genre of science fiction/fantasy.

So I looked up the address of the producers of the show, Leslie Stevens's Daystar Productions, and I got my agent, Marty Shapiro, to finesse me an interview.

Well, they put it off for a couple of months, and if I recall correctly (which I'm sure I don't, as we will soon see) it was August or even September before they got around to seeing me.

Now here's where the recollections go wonky. (As the fine poet Olin Miller tells us, "Of all liars, the smoothest and most convincing is memory.") For nearly forty years I've "remembered" and told anyone who gave a damn, that I was tossed out of the offices of *The Outer Limits* by Joe Stefano. (Which was why it blew me away when my fourth wife, Lori, married Stefano's son.) But I was wrong. That smooth and convincing liar had put a wrong image in my head.

Where I went for that story interview, to pitch my way onto a promising new series, was a small building right at the abutment point where Beverly Hills ends at its easternmost edge, and the Sunset Strip begins at its westernmost edge. Dave Schow refreshes my memory that the venue was the old Bing Crosby Building at 9028 Sunset Boulevard, now long-ago razed. I know that was it, because it was on the same side of Sunset, and only about a block further east of a then-famous Los Angeles eatery, the three-star Cock 'N Bull at 9170 Sunset. The Cock 'N Bull served excellent English fare, and I didn't have enough money to eat there until 1972.

The offices for Villa Di Stefano were on North La Cienega, a mile or so away. I was never there. So it couldn't possibly have been Stefano who kicked my ass into the street; it had to have been Leslie Stevens and his minions. I apologize, Mr. Stefano. I'd call you Joe, but I hear you go semi-ballistic when someone mentions how good my two Outer Limits scripts were. But I digress.

Most I remember of the meeting itself, which had to've been with Stevens and/or Lou Morheim (the story editor) was that in my arrogance, relying on my credentials as a published sf author, surfeited with an absolutely imperial hubris, I told these guys that they didn't know owl shit about what sf was supposed to be, and that this reliance on monsters would demean the productions irreparably, (ABC had made it clear to Stevens and Dom Frontiere and Stefano and anyone else who would pay attention to them, that every episode had to open with "a bear on the beach." That is to say, a monster—AKA a bear). Their absolutely inflexible Obiter Dictum was this: "When that show opens, we want anyone looking at it to ask, 'How did that bear get onto that beach!'" So no one working *The Outer Limits* could do anything about the dopey monsters that crept, crawled, slithered, capered and otherwise ambulated through every episode, even my own "Demon with a Glass Hand."

And so there I sat, in either Stevens's or Morheim's office, all puffed up like a banjo player who had a big breakfast, telling them how to run their show, which was already in production.

I remember the two largish guys who bookended me down the hall, and through the little foyer reception area, and opened the doors that gave out onto Sunset Boulevard, almost directly across from the alternate Schwab's Drug Store (the main one was over on Sunset at Crescent Heights), and one of them got extra cute and gave me more of a shove than was necessary, and I went pinwheeling off the front stoop, and onto the sidewalk, on my knees.

And here's the part of the memory that is absolutely sharp and correct. This was a small, bungalow-like building, the old Bing Crosby, and it was planted all around with grass and flowers. And I remember these huge sunflowers on both sides of the front doors, as I went whirling past them. And I remember being grateful that it wasn't raining because I was so goddam poor I only had this one suit, which hung on me like the rags on the Scarecrow of Oz because I was down to something like ninety-five pounds, and I had to pull my belt to the last notch to keep the pants from falling down, and I had to keep the jacket buttoned so I wouldn't embarrass myself with the pants being all gathered and flapping at the ass...and I was thankful it wasn't raining, because if it had been, I'd have soiled the knees of that brown shantung suit, and I'd have had to go get the suit dry cleaned, which I couldn't afford to do. So I remember, weirdly, being grateful it wasn't raining.

What I wasn't so damned grateful about was that when the sonofabitch booted me out the door, and I fell, I ripped the right knee of my pants, and skinned myself good, and bled onto both legs of the pants, and I had to borrow some money from a guy I knew, John Kulhanek, so I could get the suit cleaned and pressed and repaired.

The memory was askew, with the onus put on Joe Stefano, who had nothing to do with it, but the basic recollection remained sharp. For forty years. And it was the beginning of the nexus that I shared with *The Outer Limits*. A nexus that has changed my life so profoundly.

Turns out it wasn't Stefano who wrote the pilot episode; it was Leslie Stevens himself. But by the second year, Stefano was gone, Stevens had become an absentee landlord sort of exec producer, and ABC had hired Ben Brady as producer, with Seeleg Lester as story editor. Bobby Justman was still first AD and/or production manager. And I stormed the barricades a second time. Can't remember now if it came about because Marty Shapiro heard the palace guard had changed and the new management might not have heard that I was a rampaging lunatic...or because I'd become a hot writer in just one year because of my scripts for the enormously-popular *Burke's Law* series. (About one of those scripts The New York Times said something olympian like, "Ellison's script is a blissful combination of Agatha Christie puzzler and urbane Oscar Wilde drawing room comedy." Something close to that.)

But either way, I wound up meeting with Ben and Seeleg, and pitching them the idea for *Soldier* which I had written already as a 9100 word novelette, published in Fantastic Universe, a science fiction digest magazine, back in October 1957. They had paid me the going rate for genre fiction in those days, a penny a word, I got a big-time ninety bucks whoop-dee-doo, and it was published with the idiot title *Soldier from Tomorrow*.

So now, here it is seven years later, I've been in the brain-draining Army for two of those years, I hate the damned military, and instead of pitching Seeleg the story as a pacifist tract, I give it a Skinnerian twist, and sell it as a conundrum of the heart and soul of the killer elite, trained for death and nothing less. Ben Brady stayed pretty much out of the way, and let Seeleg work with me to the best of his abilities, which was an early high-water mark of excellence in my TV career.

Just to give you a taste of what I sold to them, little old just-turning-thirty me, here is the teaser that preceded act one of the treatment I submitted on 28 April 1964:

```
THE OUTER LIMITS
"Soldier"
written by HARLAN ELLISON
TEASER:
FADE IN a nightmare landscape. A battlefield seen in
chiaroscuro, shadows and light sharp and distinct. Illu-
minated moment to moment by a spider-work tracery of
light beams across the sky. Beams that flicker on and off
like a lattice against the blackness. Piles of rubble
bulk huge against the skyline; twisted members of some
foreign machines; smoking shells of bombed-out struc-
tures. Nothing moves on this battlefield, though the
sounds of warfare—the sizzling of the beams, the distant
whump! of explosions—come through clearly. A high shot.
```

As camera begins to come down toward a dark figure hunched over in a shallow foxhole, VOICE OVER:

"Night comes too soon on the battlefield. For some men it comes permanently, their eyes never open to the light of day. But for this man, fighting this war, there is never total darkness: the spidery beams of light in the sky are the descendants of the modern laser beam. Heat rays that sear through tungsten-steel and flesh as though they were cheesecloth."

Camera comes down to a medium closeup of the soldier. First we see his odd helmet, equipped with antenna and night-vision glasses; then his heavy cape; then the metal harness he wears, supporting a strangely-constructed rifle. He pulls a cigarette from the metal tin and, holding it like a kitchen match, he scratches the end of the cigarette on the side of the pack. It ignites, and he waits, smoking, as VOICE OVER continues:

"And this soldier must go against those weapons. His name is Qarlo (pronounced: Kwar-lo), and he is a foot soldier. Trained from birth by the state, he is geared for only one purpose: to kill The Enemy."

Camera has now moved in tight on Qarlo, catching him in profile the battlefield beyond him. There is the sound of a sharp electrical buzzing in his helmet, and we hear a tiny voice in his ear say, "Attack! Kill!" and the cigarette drops from his mouth unnoticed as Qarlo leaps up and charges across the open, empty field of darkness. As he runs, we cut to another high shot looking down on the battlefield. Another man comes running—broken-field—from the opposite direction, and camera holds high as they race toward each other, blaster rifles at the ready.

As they near each other we sharp cut to a medium long shot of the warriors approaching each other, empty space between them. Each lifts his rifle to fire as we suddenly sharp cut back to a high shot and two thick laser beam rays spear out of the sky, zero down, directly on Qarlo and his Enemy. They are instantly bathed in a coruscating aurora of flickering lights and searing sound. There is an insane electrical cackle, like a thousand arc lights burning out.

Closeup on Qarlo, arms flung up, still gripping the rifle, as he screams soundlessly, twisting in the eerie light bath. Closeup on the Enemy as the same happens to him. And then...

They wink out of existence. They are gone. The light flickers off, and the battlefield is empty once more.

Sharp cut to a modern-day subway platform. An old man, walking with a cane, is about to put a penny in a gumball machine. It is obviously present day, as we can see from the clothes of the commuters standing in groups nearby. Suddenly, right in front of the old man, Qarlo winks into existence with a flickering of light, then total presence. Instinctively he hefts his rifle. The old man's face twists, he clutches his heart, and falls dead at Qarlo's feet. A woman turns in the waiting group, just in time to see the old man fall down, and her scream spins everyone around: "He killed him! He shot him!" There is screaming, and confusion for a moment as two burly men in grey flannel, with attaché cases, start toward Qarlo.

Seemingly without effort he lifts them and hurls them from him. They skid across the platform and crash into stanchions. Qarlo looks trapped, and for the first time we see his face clearly. He is not an unattractive man under his strange helmet and in his metallic suit & harness, but part of his face is badly scarred, as though from radiation.

The crowd panics, starts to flow away from Qarlo as a uniformed police officer pushes his way through. He herds the people back and advances on Qarlo. Qarlo panics. He raises the rifle. The people are streaming up a stairway to the upper floor as he fires. The laser beam flashes out, and the metal girders underpinning the stairway vanish. The stairway groans with the shriek of strained metal, and falls, tumbling people back onto the platform. The cop pauses for a moment, then pulls his gun. Qarlo aims at him.

At that moment an express train roars into the station, its sound so loud and jarring it overcomes all other sounds. Qarlo's eyes go wide, he claps his hands to his ears and sinks down on one knee. The cop charges, and without preamble brings the butt of his revolver down on Qarlo's neck. The soldier slumps flat-out. Camera comes down for a closeup of his unconscious face, and dimly, through his helmet, we hear the whispering metallic command, over and over, "Kill! Kill! Kill!" as we fade out.

Soldier was shot at what was then called Paramount Sunset. It was off the greater Paramount lot. It had once been a slave unit for Warner Bros., what was called the old Warner Bros. studio on Sunset and had even been a 52-lane bowling alley at some vagrant point in its venue. It faced across a wide, broad lawn, with old canopied trees, to Sunset Boulevard itself. And if you ever see a videotape of *Soldier*, at the point in the story where they discharge Qarlo from the "military installation," and they open the front door onto the street, that is Sunset Boulevard traffic you're looking at, circa June 1964.

Trivia fact: Jack Poplln's per-show budget for sets in the second season of *The Outer Limits* was a ridiculous (even for those days) $6000. Astonishingly, for that piddleshit amount of money he created not only all the standing sets for the episode, but also the war zone landscape, which was so bloody elegant and effective, that when James Cameron came to rip off *Soldier* for *The Terminator* film, he copied it down to the detail. Just for amusement, sometime take the two videos—both readily available—and run first one, then the other. But just the first five minutes. No more than that. And you'll see why Mr. Cameron and Hemdale Films had to pay up when I went after them. But, I'm getting ahead of myself.

The series hadn't done at all well in the ratings. That it should now—thirty-plus years later—be such an icon that has been resuscitated in a contemporary incarnation, and has become enormously popular, is one of those inexplicable twists of human behavior that defy logic. Series like *The Outer Limits* and *Star Trek*, that were so-so flops in their initial runs, have had time and taste catch up with them...so they now loom as large, or larger, in our pop entertainment mythos, as the shows that were great hits when they were dominating the prime time sweeps. But where is the recurring groundswell of nostalgia for The Dukes of Hazzard, or Mork and Mindy, or The Defenders, or Route 66, or Burke's Law, all of which were monsters in their day? Gone.. And not likely to return.

But *The Outer Limits*, as with a few others, kept breathing; and now I sit here, almost forty years older than when I sat down to write *Soldier*, typing out an Introduction to a book containing a new story set in the war world of Qarlo...and not even a story I wrote, but which was written by an excellent and best-selling author, who was smitten with the original in sufficient measure that he got a publisher to commission this new chapter in the ongoing battle.

Let me be absolutely candid with you, which at this point is not getting ahead of myself, it is catching up with where we started. Let me be perhaps more truthful than the good publisher might wish. But then, both he and you know what I'm like.

I have never written a sequel to any one of the more than 1700 stories that have been published under my name since I became a full-time professional in 1956. Yes, there are three sections of BLOOD'S A ROVER, the novel-in-progress that includes the 1969 Nebula award-winning novella known as "A Boy and His Dog," from which the Hugo award-winning movie starring Don Johnson and Jason Robards was made. But those aren't sequels. They're sections of one long novel. The first three sections have been individually published, and "A Boy and His Dog" has won awards, has a life of its own, and continues to exist in peoples' minds erroneously as a stand-alone novella..but it ain't. It's part of the long history of Vic and his dog Blood and a female solo named Spike (but you haven't read about her yet, because I've never released that longest, 100,000 word final section of the novel). But I do not digress: I don't like, and I don't write, sequels.

I despise all those windy trilogies and tetralogies and infinitologies in which mediocre writers re-chew their cuds till all that finally gets regurgitated is boredom and the maggots of things that will never become butterflies.

It only took Tolstoy one volume to write WAR AND PEACE.

Would that authors who should know better were able to resist the ballyhoo and blandishments of commercial hustlers who are as comfortable with the concept of Art as a bluebottle fly is roomy, stuck up the ass of a dray-mule.

So why have I permitted Kevin Anderson to write what some joker will inevitably refer to as a "sequel" to my *Soldier*?

I will not obfuscate and pretend that Posterity demanded it, or that the time was right to re-examine the concept or cobble up any disingenuous rationale. I have read Kevin's "Prisoner of War" and it needs no defense from me. It's a solid, neatly written story and it stands on its own. That Kevin has done me the courtesy and the respect to set it in the world of *Soldier* is half homage and half recycling of a good thing. But it isn't a sequel, any more than setting a story during the French and Indian Wars is a sequel to THE LAST OF THE MOHICANS. (However, considering the number of volumes in Cooper's Leatherstocking Tales, perhaps that's not the very best analogy I could have used. Ah, well...)

Kevin Anderson writes most excellently, and I'm pleased as I can be that "Prisoner of War" works as dramatically and thoughtfully as it does. But make no mistake, folks, I allowed Kevin and the publisher to use the world of Qarlo the Trooper because they paid me an exorbitant amount of money.

And because I didn't write a sequel, but merely let others sharecrop my little acre of story-plot, I feel no sense of remorse or guilt. (Have you ever noticed, one is frequently required to operate at a demanded level of integrity that isn't even remotely approached by the moochers and squawkers who rush to point out how much of a hypocritical sellout you are, when the truth of the matter is that they're just pissed off because nothing they've produced is anywhere good enough for them to be offered even a peek at selling out. They demand a nobility from everyone else that is way beyond their own capabilities.)

I am respectful of Kevin's writing, and I am quite smug that he has used a device of my imagination to help spark his own independent and utterly commendable conception.

And, finally, my dream remains as pure and unsullied as ever it was, as good or bad a piece of writing as ever it was, and I am not only enormously celebrated, talented and fecund, but I'm financially quite well off. When I was thirty and wrote *Soldier* that was something to strive toward. Now I'm over sixty, and it is a reality. Necessity is the mother of making sure you don't wind up in the Poverty Ward.

So don't give me no stuff, Homes.

I have been shunted and shifted, moved and manipulated, altered and activated by my association with *The Outer Limits*. I had no idea such was the case, until I sat down to write this introduction. But had the linkage not remained cold-steel forged, I'd never have noticed. And so, I have been paid top dollar to pass along Qarlo's world for another creator's attentions, and the justification presents itself as having become an exercise in self-examination, rumination, clarification and maturation. We are all tourists in our own lives, and it is only after we've returned home and emptied the suitcase of dirty socks and souvenirs, that we get those snapshots developed and discover, with amazement, where we have actually been.

I have been to the Limits, and had I not been offered this opportunity to revisit Qarlo's world, I'd never have discovered what bizarre synchronicity has manipulated my existence.

This has been my story. Now read Kevin's.

18

Introduction to
The Human Factor

WHEN I WAS A KID, I HAD A BOARD GAME based on THE OUTER LIMITS. It had simple rules—basically "Go Fish"—each card showed a piece of a monster, and once you collected all four pieces, you could lay down an ugly picture of the Galaxy Being, or Andro, or an Ebonite, or a Zanti Misfit. One of the nastiest beasties was the Ice Creature from the episode "The Human Factor" which looked like a golem made out of icicles, with glowing eyes and a nightmarish expression. The prop department had dubbed the sculpture of this monster "Chill Charlie."

Chill Charlie was created by the director and special effects advisor Byron Haskin, who had also directed George Pal's magnificent film version of *War of the Worlds*. Unfortunately, though, the horrific Ice Creature never made it to the broadcast episode, replaced instead by a much more human-looking guy in a suit covered with patches of snow. Maybe the original design was too...chilling.

Without the monster, my childhood self found the episode a little slow, dealing more with psychological concepts than alien creatures. But when I revisited it, I encountered a compelling story about cabin fever and guilt set in the midst of Cold War paranoia. The science fiction twist is a mind-transference device developed in an Arctic research station and DEW-Line defense outpost. Identity swapping is also the basis for my science fiction novel HOPSCOTCH, which I have completed at about the same time as this book; but this story uses a completely different take on the idea.

As a side note, "The Human Factor" episode was written by David Duncan, who also scripted the classic SF films *Fantastic Voyage* and *The Time Machine*.

The Human Factor

From a script by David Duncan

THE MILITARY CARGO JET ROARED INTO THE LONELY NORTH, slicing through high veils of ice crystals as it homed toward the Greenland coast. In the narrow, cold cockpit the pilot searched his topographical maps and sent out a coded transponder signal.

"Point Tabu Base, this is Roger Zulu Eight Five Niner, please respond." He waited a beat; communications personnel hidden on the ground would be checking out his identity. "Could really use some navigational assistance, Point Tabu. Got an important package for you, but can't see a thing. Over."

Below, along the perimeter of the Arctic Circle, the DEW line—Distant Early Warning—formed a net of vigilant eyes where American military personnel kept constant watch for a Soviet sneak attack of Intercontinental Ballistic Missiles.

It was 1963, and no one in the world felt their future was assured.

High above, the pilot stared out the frost-scratched cockpit windows, searching the rugged wastelands below, but saw only stark crags and plains of unrelenting white.

With the arrival of the military jet—though scheduled and expected—the uppermost extremity of North America became a gigantic coiled trap. Large satellite dishes tracked the movement of RZ 859, while servicemen in underground command-and-control bunkers plotted the cargo jet's course on vertical glass maps, using grease pencils to compare it to expected flight plans. Defensive missiles rose from their silos according to standard procedure, ready for any unexpected engagement.

Everyone knew the Soviet attack would come one day, and everyone stationed on the DEW Line prayed simultaneously, *Just don't let it be today!*

"This is Point Tabu Base," came a rasping voice in the pilot's earphones, half-drowned by the roaring whistle of air around the cockpit.

"Continue on present course, Roger Zulu Eight Five Niner. You've got five miles before you reach the coast. We've plowed and prepped the airstrip for you. It's the big white flat area—you can't miss it. Over."

"Yeah, right," the pilot said, looking at the featureless white all around him. "Over and out."

The mountains stood like a wall along Victoria Channel, whose straight course marked the Baffin fault. For centuries, intrepid explorers had sought a Northwest Passage, a clear channel of sea to pass above North America through to Asia. But the way was blocked by the rocky thread of the Hecla Isthmus. The offending barrier prevented American nuclear submarines from prowling under polar ice to the other side of the Arctic Circle.

But for the Army Corps of Engineers, even those assigned to grim and frigid Greenland duty, mere mountains no longer caused much trouble—not when they had nuclear warheads at their disposal. The pilot carried enough in his cargo hold to take care of that obstacle.

Finally, the jet crossed over the last line of mountains, reaching the coastline's uneasy, icy truce with the dark Arctic waters. Along the flattened strip of land, he spotted a cluster of half-buried buildings. Many were low Quonset huts, half-cylinder buildings, wooden structures nearly covered by windblown snow; most of the base was underground.

"Got you in sight, Point Tabu." The pilot found it hard to believe that some two hundred people could make this their permanent residence. "Beginning my descent. Please have the unloading crew meet me immediately. Over."

The cargo jet touched down in a flurry of spray, skidding and slewing toward the end of the runway. After finally coming to a halt, he shut down the engines, using controls in the cockpit to open his craft like a beetle splitting at the seams.

Heavy vehicles on snow treads came to meet him, and the pilot swung down, tugging a hood over his head and a metal-covered clipboard out of his flight pouch. He strode out, crunching in the snow and wincing at the bitter cold, in search of the duty officer in charge.

"Hey! Do me a favor and let me sleep easy tonight," he shouted to a man wearing sergeant's stripes. "Get all those atomic warheads off my plane! They're your problem now."

Outside of Point Tabu, two men labored in the Greenland night, hauling a heavy sledge across the white clearing toward the low buildings. A glare of low floodlights pierced the veils of wind-blown snow.

Their boots slipped on the ground, but the men trudged toward the armored door where a pair of guards stood at attention, rifles pointed toward the sky. Seeing the workers approach, the guards opened the first set of doors in a sally port entrance, under which an ominous sign read "KEEP OUT. FISSIONABLE MATERIAL." Inside the lead-shielded vault, it would be warmer, but not necessarily safer. Two majors and the colonel were waiting for this ominous package.

As the two workers dragged their burden into the atomic storeroom, Major Giles heaved a sigh of relief and loosened his jacket. He was a broad-shouldered Black man with a calm face and intelligent eyes. His rank was genuine, his education impeccable, and he liked to think he was many miles from prejudice and racial slurs.

Giles tugged off thick mittens while the other man beside him, Colonel Campbell, moved with greater reluctance, watching the long and detailed unloading process. Suave-looking and tall, with a pencil-thin moustache riding like a line of mascara on his lip, Campbell wasn't sure he wanted such dangerous weapons on his base.

From the edge of the room, the third officer watched the proceedings like a vulture waiting for a lost traveler to die in the desert. Major Frank Brothers was a dark-eyed, dark-haired man. He took short, quick breaths, scanning for shadows, looking for unexpected movement, though no one else was authorized to be inside the atomic storeroom. Giles and Campbell gave him his distance, intent instead on the newly arrived warheads.

Major Giles gestured for the two enlisted men to bring the heavy case to the center of the cold floor, where critical separation lines had been painted in blue on the concrete. "Carry the cartridge over here, and I'll perform the formal receipt and inspection." His voice was firm and confident, like a well-seasoned judge's.

"By the book, Major. No shortcuts," Colonel Campbell said. He brushed his thin mustache into a frown. "I know it's necessary to have the atomics here to excavate the Isthmus, but this is my base, and I want to make sure all due precautions are taken." He looked over at the other stored warheads with mild apprehension. The haulers positioned the atomic case precisely in the center of the safe zone.

Along one concrete wall of the storage bunker, metal cabinets and an instrument panel stood under a PA speaker. Other atomic cartridges from the recent delivery sat within the blue-painted criticality zones.

Dismissing the two men, Giles stepped to the dolly holding the newly arrived warhead and ripped off a tape fastener. The padded blanket fell from the case, revealing a lead-plated atomic cartridge, its forward face studded with controls.

Giles gave his uneasy commanding officer a quiet smile. "These cartridges are completely accident-proof, Colonel." He held out a Geiger counter from one of the metal work tables, directing the detector wand close to the cartridge. They heard only a slow clicking. "You see, sir? The lead shielding keeps the radiation down to a safe level, barely above background."

Silently, Major Brothers watched his every movement like a hawk. His breathing increased, and a sheen of sweat glistened on his upper lip.

Ignoring his strangely furtive counterpart, Giles reached to a horizontal bar parallel with the top edge of the cartridge. "The fissionable components are separated by graphite neutron absorbers, and there can't possibly be a detonation unless the absorbers are withdrawn. And that has to be done intentionally."

Campbell straightened, trying to maintain his composure. He was, after all, the commanding officer here. "I trust that *won't* happen, Major Giles?"

The Black major gave him a look of long-suffering patience. "Not until the cartridges are installed at the Hecla Isthmus, sir. For now, the bar is locked securely in place."

Major Brothers, his face strained and moody, stepped forward, as if ready to rupture with his barely restrained anxiety. "We must get those warheads delivered as soon as possible. We've already waited too long. My mission is to clear that isthmus!" His voice carried far more agitation than the circumstances warranted. "Do you know how much paperwork it took to get these atomic cartridges here in time? We've got to hurry!"

Campbell and Giles looked at their companion, gave him a moment to cool off, then the Colonel turned his attention back to the warhead case. "And the keys to that lock, Major? Is it secure? No tampering possible?"

The weapons officer maintained his reassuring demeanor. "There's only one key, sir, and I have it. In safekeeping."

Major Brothers stepped forward briskly and extended a hand toward Giles. "Then I'd better have that key, Major." His voice was like barbed wire. "I won't let it leave my possession."

Both Giles and Campbell gave him sharp puzzled glances, but were too professional to think the worst of their fellow officer—yet. However, they had both seen the symptoms of cabin fever even in well-respected personnel.

Though his dark eyes continued to dart back and forth, Brothers exerted superhuman control to make his voice quietly firm. "I am the project engineer. The Hecla Isthmus must be destroyed. Hand over the key, Major Giles. There's been too much delay already."

Finally pushed too far, Colonel Campbell responded in sharp bewilderment. "Major Brothers, you're overreacting. Clearing the channel is a priority for our submarines, but it's not as if we've got a ticking clock. With these nukes, we'll make a clean, fast cut of it." His voice became sterner. "Unlike what happened last time."

Brothers flinched, then shrugged off the accusatory tone in his commanding officer's voice. "Yes, the atomics can do it. Warheads for civil engineering purposes."

Under the umbrella name "Project Plowshare," nuclear weapons researchers had proposed using atomic explosions for major excavations, blasting reservoirs, cutting canals, scooping out new harbors from flat coastlines. By the same principle, Major Brothers and his corps of engineers could finally breach the offending isthmus.

"The Soviets won't dare attack once we've got our nuclear submarines in place," Brothers continued, his eyes dark and frantic. "But until that happens, we're at extreme risk! All of us. The Isthmus must be destroyed before..."

He broke off and looked wildly toward the ceiling as a low rumble like the growl of a prehistoric beast echoed through the storeroom. The overhead lights rattled and shook, making shadows pounce. Brothers backed away.

Colonel Campbell grabbed Major Giles as they steadied each other. The floor rocked and swayed. The atomic cartridge in the holding area slid to one side. Campbell looked at the warhead in alarm, but Giles seemed much more concerned that the ceiling would fall on top of them.

Major Brothers wheeled and took two steps toward the cartridge, trying to flee something unimaginable, but instead he stumbled and careened to the floor, face-first. His forehead struck the warhead casing square on.

As the shaking and rumbling continued, Brothers lifted himself onto his hands and knees, scuttling across the concrete away from the atomic warhead. He felt no pain, so lost in fear that he was unaware he'd hit his head. He murmured fearfully, unintelligibly.

After an interminable ten seconds, the tremors stopped. The overhead lights continued to sway, painting the walls with a stuttering yellow glow. A crack shaped like a lightning bolt spread from floor to ceiling at the rear of the bunker, disappearing behind the PA system speaker.

Major Giles hurried over to Brothers, grabbing the man's shoulder and helping him up. Brothers groaned, and a splash of blood appeared on his smashed forehead. Colonel Campbell removed a flashlight from an emergency kit on the wall and made his way to one of the control panels.

An authoritative voice spoke over the PA system, calm and expert. "Attention all personnel. We have just experienced a minor earthquake."

Tearing free of Major Giles, loud and fearful, Brothers screamed, "No! That wasn't an earthquake! It's here! It's finally awakened!"

Reaching the controls, Colonel Campbell turned the PA speaker volume up as high as it would go, drowning out the cries of Major Brothers. "Our instruments indicate that the epicenter is near the Hecla Isthmus. Minor aftershocks may be expected. Please take appropriate precautions."

Brothers bolted for the doorway of the atomic storeroom, heading for the freight elevator. "It's going to get us!" The other two officers exchanged frightened, puzzled stares.

Brothers dove into the elevator, pulled the heavy door shut, and started the motor. Campbell and Giles ran after him, but the elevator closed in front of them.

Inside the compartment that should have offered him safety, Major Brothers backed against the wall. He stared at the doors, expecting to hear pounding fists, bending metal—a monster trying to force its way in.

Finally, reaching surface level, the elevator came to a stop. The doors opened into a small prep room and dressing area for base personnel before they headed out into the frozen landscape. Furtively, Brothers peered out into the prep room, then emerged from the dubious safety of the elevator.

Emergency generators maintained a low illumination from light bulbs in protective cages. He crossed the prep room, drawn by the doorway leading outside. Perhaps he could escape out there...perhaps he could be free.

Major Brothers flung open the metal doorway into the howling wind of Greenland. In front of him, through the whirls and eddies of snow, he looked out into the ever-twilight sky. Stepping on a small white drift, Brothers forced himself to be brave. Cowardice was worse than guilt, and cowardice would kill him just as surely as his own weighty conscience would.

As he was about to emerge into the open cold, breathing steam from his mouth and nose, he saw a wrinkle in the air, an image, a shadow taking substance.

"No! Go away! Leave me alone!"

It was the figure of a man, encrusted with ice and snow, skin turned gray and blue, frozen solid. The face was crushed, cheekbones and chin in distorted, *wrong* places. The spectre wore some sort of padded uniform, torn insignia, a cracked helmet and blood-soaked scarf. Only its eyes were blazing blue-white fire, alive with a heat of damnation.

Brothers opened his mouth and staggered back into the prep room. He could make no sound. The Ice Creature advanced upon him, raising one long arm, extending a finger like an executioner delivering a sentence.

Finally, Major Brothers was able to scream.

The base at the far ends of the Earth was not merely for American defense. Tiny, dreary, enclosed Point Tabu served as a microcosm for other studies, a sample of the human race under high-pressure conditions.

Dr. James Hamilton's experimental Human Factors Section was exactly where it needed to be. Surrounded by the Arctic wilderness and driving cold, nights that lasted half a year, and tense soldiers waiting for a nuclear attack, Hamilton had more material to work with (and fewer prying eyes) than he could ever have found as a mere professor back at the University of Indiana.

Inside the base lab, he stood in front of his equipment racks and looked over the oscilloscopes and generators and cables; experimental apparatus far more extensive than *any* university would have funded. The U.S. Army had provided it all without blinking an eye.

Hamilton reveled in the privacy and the hours of quiet time here above the Arctic Circle. He was a mature man, lean and dignified with a philosophic mien that was barely offset by a kindly humor in his eyes. His face was seamed with lines of thought, enhanced by bushy eyebrows.

"Did you know what the letters in Point Tabu stand for, Dr. Hamilton?" Ingrid Larkin called from across the room. His assistant sounded nervous, trying to kill time and make light banter while the psychologist finished preparations on his experiment.

He looked up at her, distracted. "I never gave it much thought." She always liked to offer trivia to him, as if she needed an excuse to keep a conversation going with him.

Ingrid smiled. "A young soldier—Private Gordon—once explained to me that TABU stood for *Total Abandonment of Better Understanding*."

Hamilton chuckled. "Well, Ingrid, with this new equipment, I hope we can bring better understanding to everyone." He paused as a troubled expression crossed his face. "Private Gordon? Isn't that the poor soldier who died in the accident?"

Ingrid nodded. "Yes, out on the Hecla Isthmus." At twenty-two, she had a pleasant, intelligent face that made no overt attempt to be beautiful, but succeeded in its own way. As one of the few women stationed on the Greenland base, makeup would have been a waste of time anyway.

"Ah, I thought so." Hamilton made a distracted sound, then finished adjusting the dials and cathode-ray tubes. "I think we're ready. If this machine works, it'll be possible for two minds to communicate directly with each other."

He had made a lot of assumptions, far too many leaps of faith—but isolated out here, working for the Army, Hamilton didn't have to publish academic papers, didn't have to meet the approval of his peers. He just had to *be here*, available for the troops who experienced cabin fever or seasonal depression or paranoia. Colonel Campbell didn't care what the psychologist did on his own time.

Ingrid sat in a creaking desk chair, her back to Hamilton, as he raised up a headset of straps and electrodes, which he affixed over her hair, pressing contacts against her temples and the base of her skull. His hands were sure and firm, like a mechanic's, without the delicacy of a lover's caress. He'd never actually asked if she wanted to volunteer...just assumed.

Hamilton continued chattering without a pause, enthusiastic about his own subject. "With this linkage you and I should be able to share the same thoughts and emotions simultaneously."

Ingrid tried not to show her tension. "You mean, of course, only the *intellectual* thoughts and emotions?" She leaned back in the chair to look into his expressive eyes.

Hamilton gave her a bemused grin. "Intellectual emotions? To psychologists, the intellect is a useful but devious friend." He paused again. "By the way, Ingrid, I really appreciate your help in this. Did I remember to thank you for not being a nosy-body while I was working on the apparatus?"

"No, Doctor." She allowed herself a nervous smile, but Hamilton didn't notice. He hadn't answered her question about emotions.

Distracted again, he checked Ingrid's headset and its connection to the cables that linked it to the bank of equipment. Then he picked up the counterpart headset, adjusting the size to fit over his own head. "This machine will let me know what a subject is really thinking and feeling, way down underneath the intellect. It'll be a great boon for diagnosis, and for understanding the human mind. A psychologist's miracle worker."

Satisfied that Ingrid had been adequately hooked up, Hamilton turned to his equipment. The electroencephalograph dominated the main bank of controls next to an oscilloscope, brain-image screen, and a rotating drum for recording brain waves on a strip chart.

Humming to himself, the psychologist took the leads from Ingrid's scalp and plugged them into his equipment rack. After a loud flick of one of the power switches, the apparatus began to buzz. A night-skyline of blinking lights flickered, and the central screens brightened.

Ingrid felt nothing for a moment, then gentle spider-fingers traced ticklish tracks through her scalp. She swallowed, desiring very much to assist Dr. Hamilton . . . but having a hard time pushing back her reluctance. "I'm not sure I want to go through with this."

Hamilton dismissed her fears, without understanding them. "Be a good girl. What do we have to hide? Take a look at the oscilloscope."

Ingrid did as she was told, watching the dancing waves. "You can't tell much from that. Can you?"

"Not *too* much...but I haven't connected the magnetic-tape recorders, or my counterpart headset. Relax. In a moment, I may know what you're really feeling." He tried to sound nonchalant, but it only made her more uneasy and miserable. Yes, in a moment, he would learn what should have been plain to him anyway, if he'd only paid more attention.

Hamilton sat on the opposite side of the gray Army-issue table and started attaching electrodes to his scalp. He went through the motions as if he had practiced a hundred times before.

"I amplify those waves shown on the screen and feed them back into the machine, through recorders and processors, into a *terminal instrument* capable of translating them back into the thoughts and emotions that produced them. And that instrument is my own brain." Smiling, he tapped the side of his head. "During the experiment, our two minds will be joined. To put it simply, your thoughts will be in my head."

Her face showed increasing tension which the learned psychologist, the studier of human nature, entirely failed to notice. Ingrid closed her blue eyes. "And yours will be in mine, then?"

"Right. Relax, now. I'm bringing up the power."

Hamilton twisted a dial. Nothing was marked very well, but he seemed to know what he was doing. The humming grew louder, its pitch rising and falling. Banks of tiny lights flickered, and two sets of waves appeared on the oscilloscope. On the brain-image screen, a pair of fuzzy oblong patterns, shadowy brain silhouettes, moved closer from opposite sides of the field, seeking a common position.

The pens on the strip chart scratched across the moving paper, etching a record of the two different minds merging. Hamilton's hand turned the dial, increasing the power.

Finally, the two brain images overlapped, one superimposed on the other. The ululating sound of the machinery abruptly smoothed into a single high note. On the oscilloscope, the two wave patterns finally became one strong line tracing its roller-coaster across the cathode-ray tube. The magnetic tape reels captured it all.

Ingrid closed her eyes, breathing harder, fighting back the strain and dread. Then, like a whisper among her thoughts, and eventually a strong voice, she heard Hamilton's mind, his presence, all his past and his secrets.

And Ingrid knew he was experiencing the same thing from her.

Looking across the cluttered, serviceable lab table at him, Ingrid saw Hamilton's eyes widen. He *knew* her thoughts, her feelings. Intent on his research, single-minded in his journey of discovery into the human mind, he was completely unprepared for the mine field into which he'd stepped.

Ingrid had hoped to find the same feelings in his deep thoughts, the same attraction for her. Instead, she found a naiveté and innocence; no harsh thoughts and no scorn...but no place for her, either. He'd never even considered the possibility of romance, despite all the months they had worked so closely together, hour after hour in this Arctic concentration camp.

The psychologist stared at Ingrid, his expression in the no-man's land between surprise and consternation. Their eyes met, but their shared thoughts carried an intimacy far deeper than any matched gaze. They didn't say a word to each other, didn't need to.

Hamilton switched off the machine, shutting down the power generators and halting the magnetic recorders. The high note whined down the scale into silence—a deep and uncomfortable silence more stifling than the long polar night. He yanked off the flexible headset, disconnecting the electrodes.

Deflated, Ingrid remained in her creaking chair, eyes closed, not wanting to see what Hamilton might be thinking of her audacity, her dreams and fantasies. Twin tears trickled down her cheeks. She hated herself for crying, especially now.

She felt his large hand on her shoulder. He seemed about to speak but couldn't find the right words. At last, Ingrid opened her eyes and looked up at him. "I'm sorry, Dr. Hamilton. You've had a shock, haven't you? Not exactly what you expected to discover during your little trial run. I wasn't the ideal test subject. I...I'm sorry I ruined it for you."

Hamilton gently pulled the electrodes from her head. "I simply...had no idea you thought of me...in that way."

"Oh, I know that, Doctor," she said. "I know." Ingrid stood up, tossing the headset on the table. She feigned a smile, bright and professional. "Congratulations, the experiment was a total success." She walked away, turning her back on him. "I'll...arrange for a transfer right away."

Trying to sidetrack his own feelings, concentrating on something he could understand, the psychologist studied his electroencephalograph, pleased and triumphant. Then, like a pebble through mud, her words finally penetrated to him.

"Transfer? Ingrid, why?" He blinked, uncomprehending, then started toward her as he got an idea, finally saw a problem he needed to deal with. "Now just a moment. Let's look at this objectively. You don't happen to be a patient, but when I *do* have a patient, a big part of my job is to help him discover those secret wishes and fantasies. And when that's done . . ."

She resented his analytical assessment of her love, just wanted to run, when the base telephone on his desk rang like a baby's wail. *Saved by the bell.* Ingrid broke away from him to answer it.

"Human Factors Section...yes, Colonel." She looked up at Hamilton, trying to regain her professionalism, desperately wishing she could just erase the entire experiment and return to the way things had been. "He's right here." She handed the phone to the psychologist.

Hamilton took the phone, avoiding Ingrid's eyes, and turned to address the commanding officer with good cheer, as he would a friend. "Yes, Colonel Campbell. What can I do for you?"

After a long glance at him, Ingrid slipped quietly away. For so long she had wanted him to notice her. Now, she wanted Dr. Hamilton to ignore her entirely, to forget about what he had learned of the secrets in her heart.

Colonel Campbell leaned against the side of his desk, looking through the glass of his closed office door to where a very agitated Major Brothers squirmed on the waiting room sofa. Two security men stood vigilant in the outer office to *encourage complacency* from the Major.

Campbell lowered his voice as he spoke into the telephone. He didn't often have occasion to call on the Human Factors section, didn't need a psychologist so long as his men did their jobs. But the bizarre behavior of Major Brothers required extraordinary action.

"I hate to lose my top engineer, Jim," he said into the phone, frowning; his pencil moustache added a black line of emphasis. "Especially with the work that needs to be done at the Isthmus, but right now I'd call Brothers a very sick man. Extreme symptoms, paranoia, agitation, persecution, guilt. Might be cabin fever. I don't know. That's what you folks are for."

Hamilton's voice came over the telephone, sounding relieved to have something to do. "Can you brief me?"

"It might have been the bump on the head he got last night during the earthquake. The Major insists the base is being invaded by some kind of alien being, an *ice ghost* or something. Never heard such a preposterous thing." Worried, he glanced down at the papers on his desk, then at the postcards of Hawaii and Fiji on his cork board. "When can you see him?"

"I can see him right away."

The Colonel hung up the phone and crossed to the door. Major Brothers practically jumped, startled at the commanding officer's sudden appearance. "Hamilton's in. Go have a talk with him. Now."

Brothers glared at his commanding officer. "*Talk?* Talk won't drive it away, Colonel. Our only hope is to discover where that thing is hiding—and destroy it!" Nervously, he snatched a few sunflower seeds from a crackling cellophane packet before stuffing the packet into his fatigues. A gauze bandage covered the injury he'd received from striking his head against the atomic cartridge the day before.

The Colonel's manner betrayed both impatience and uncertainty at dealing with an aberrant man, especially someone of such high rank and in charge of such an important project. "Fine, Major. You just go explain all that to Hamilton." He could see Brothers stiffen as he returned to the orderliness of his inner office and closed the glass door.

The Major flashed a dark-eyed glance at the two security men who would babysit him all the way to the Human Factors Section, then headed out the door, moving with determination. Without a word, the two MPs accompanied him.

Hamilton hung up the phone, suddenly confronted with two large problems. He was a psychologist, certainly, but not in a clinical way. At isolated Point Tabu he'd been prepared to treat mental disorders, but never had he expected the thunderstorm of feelings from a woman he thought he'd known so well. Ingrid Larkin had certainly proved him wrong.

He finally glanced up from the silent black telephone, realizing that Ingrid was no longer in the laboratory with him. He heard her voice wafting through from the reception desk.

He stepped out, searching for her, so they could analyze what they had discovered about each other. Ingrid sat at her desk where she normally did her paperwork, but at the moment she spoke intently into the telephone. "No, it's Dr. Hamilton I'm thinking of, not myself. He needs someone who's intelligent and efficient and...unemotional. Yes, by morning. Thank you, please see what you can do to find a replacement."

She saw him out of the corner of her eye and hung up abruptly. Hamilton advanced to her desk, more uncertain and off-balance than he'd ever been in his life. "Ingrid?" He tried to be reasonable, to discuss their problem objectively. He used his best psychological technique. "Secret thoughts have a way of...losing their effectiveness...when they aren't secret any more." He searched for a further explanation, a deeper diagnosis.

Ingrid stepped around her desk and looked into his eyes. Her tone was quiet and sincere, but very determined. "I'm not leaving because I'm embarrassed or ashamed, Doctor Hamilton. I'm not." Shucking out of her lab coat, Ingrid grabbed her dark blue jacket from its peg by the door, which led out into the cold underground passages between barracks. "But I'm not what you would call a masochist, either." Ingrid smiled wistfully at him. "While I was experiencing your thoughts, I felt your wisdom, your courage... gentleness... many lovely things..." She zipped up the coat, as if fighting a cold she felt on the inside as well as in the air. "But no love, only dedication and curiosity and devotion. All for your work. You don't need anything, or anyone, else."

Before he could think of any reply, any way to counter what she'd said, Ingrid tugged open the door and strode out into the connecting corridor. He took one tentative step forward, but she closed the door in his face.

The two security guards thought they were oh so intimidating, with their weapons and their formal uniforms and their grim demeanor. Major Brothers marched ahead of them with quick assertive steps, taking charge. These two men had no idea what real intimidation was, what real terror could do to a man.

They hadn't seen the Ice Creature, the spectral thing that had emerged from the accident site on the Hecla Isthmus. They hadn't seen the thing raise an accusing finger, its eyes blazing with vengeance.

After that, how could Brothers find a couple of guards intimidating?

Grudgingly, he made his way to the Human Factors Section, where he would talk with the psychologist, explain his thoughts and fears. Maybe he could get through to the man. Maybe he could force this doctor to see the ominous threat that hovered like the Grim Reaper over Point Tabu.

Hearing short clicking footsteps from the corridor ahead, Brothers stopped, fearing who it might be. One could never be too careful. The two MPs looked at him questioningly, but he paid them no attention.

Ingrid Larkin came toward them, walking in a shroud of her own thoughts, as if she saw nothing and no one else. As she passed the men in the corridor, she slowed, noting the fixity of the Major's gaze. "Good afternoon, Major Brothers."

He didn't respond, but continued to watch her with narrowed eyes as she edged past and hurried on her way. That woman was hiding something, he could tell. Other secrets, maybe knowledge of the danger facing them all. Brothers wondered if he should make her tell him everything she knew.

One of the guards urged him forward with a nudge. Major Brothers glanced at the MPs, shook off the offending hand, and walked toward the closed metal door to the Human Factors Section.

"All right, Doctor, do your worst." He stepped inside, taking charge.

Within the reception room, a flustered Dr. Hamilton wandered back toward his laboratory area. The psychologist turned around, startled. "Hello, Major." His manner was friendly but professional. "Colonel Campbell told me you were coming."

"The Colonel *ordered* me to come, since he doesn't want to listen to me himself." Brothers threw a disdainful glance over his shoulder at his companions. "He even provided me with an escort, like to a school dance. Rather strange, isn't it, for a man with my record of accomplishments to be brought here as though I were under arrest?"

Hamilton frowned, sensing something unusual about the situation, but he maintained his easy manner. "Well, you're not under arrest, Major. And if you don't mind losing your escort, the two of us can be alone in the laboratory, where we can talk."

He opened the lab door as he spoke, gesturing inside to a more private area. Major Brothers didn't want to be in any closed room where he couldn't escape, in case the Ice Creature returned, but it seemed the only way to get rid of the two guards. He drew a deep breath, raised his chin high, and strode into the other room without even a glance at the

MPs. Maybe he could make this man see after all, explain what was really going on at the base.

Behind him, Hamilton looked at the two uncertain guards, nodded in reassurance, and left them in the outer hall behind the closed door as he followed Brothers into the laboratory.

The Major turned around, scanning the furniture, the homey touches; framed paintings on the walls and colorful photographs on the bulletin boards, all of which attempted to drive back the dreariness of the standard-plan military base.

What caught his attention, though, was the apparatus on the far wall, the recorders and strip charts and oscilloscopes. He was a crack engineer, accustomed to seeing the military's best devices. He knew how to analyze the world, study it, and build or change things to meet the Army's needs. He'd never seen any gadget like this before, though.

Brothers faced Hamilton, stiff and alert despite the doctor's insistence.

"Have a seat, Major. Relax." The psychologist gestured to a Naugahyde sofa.

The Major eyed him, suspicious, then sprawled on the sofa, attempting to appear at ease. He had to make this man *see*, but he would get nowhere if he didn't cooperate. "It seems someone on this base wants me declared mentally incompetent, Doctor." He smiled, then sat up sharply. "But I'm not, as you'll learn! Go ahead, throw a few tests at me. Calculus? Tensor analysis? Round the rugged rock the ragged rascal ran."

He scrambled to his feet again, then repeated the tongue-twister with an exaggerated rolling of his r's. "Round the rugged rock the ragged rascal ran." And again, faster. "Round the rugged rock the ragged rascal ran! That used to be a test for sanity. People with dementia couldn't say it."

Hamilton glanced at him with a flicker of concern, as if he'd been given a tough nut to crack. Could the doctor himself be in on the plot? Did he already *know* about the ice creature and its destructive need for revenge?

The psychologist managed a friendly smile and went to a hot plate, removing a coffee pot. "Let's cross that test off, then, Major. Nothing wrong with your speech centers." He poured himself a cup. "Care for coffee?"

Brothers drew a quick, cold breath. "I don't drink. I've given up all habits that might affect my nerves or weaken my mind and body." He removed the cellophane bag of sunflower seeds from his uniform pocket and tossed a few into his mouth. "These are a lot healthier."

"Well, as the old lady said when she kissed the cow, *each to his own taste*." Lifting a notebook, Hamilton took a seat where he thought he was out of Brothers' direct gaze so he could make an occasional mysterious note. He took out a pen. "Now, just why do you think anyone on this base wants you declared mentally incompetent?"

Brothers said with no hesitation, as if delivering a report before Congress, "This is a world of cowards, Doctor Hamilton. Every man is afraid of his brother. But most men try to hide from that awful fact." He stood straighter, becoming more strident. "The men here are even afraid to see the evil that's here on this base. And *they're* responsible for it!"

Not responding to the increased urgency in the Major's voice, Hamilton said, "Responsible in what way?" He gripped the pencil, ready to write clear answers.

"If they'd let me finish my job in time, the base would be safe now! Point Tabu would be guarding the free world from the Communists!"

Hamilton scribbled something, but he still didn't seem to understand. Major Brothers despaired of ever getting through to this man, or anyone. "And your job was to remove the Hecla Isthmus, right?"

"Remove it? No, *annihilate* it! Blast it out of existence, with atomic explosives if necessary."

Brothers dropped to his knees in front of the sofa, snatching a small blanket from the armrest. "Look here and I'll show you." He spread the blanket, pulling and wrinkling it until the folds became a crude relief map of the area.

"This is the Victoria Channel and over here is Baffin Strait. This ridge separating them is the Hecla Isthmus, a mountain about a half mile long. Once that mountain is gone, there'll be a channel all the way west to Alaska. The Northwest Passage! Our nuclear subs can then keep the Soviets at bay."

He crushed one of the large fabric wrinkles, metaphorically removing the mountain. "That was my job, Doctor, to get rid of that mountain *and the thing on it*. The shafts for the atomic cartridges were drilled a month ago. Everything was ready. But now it's too late!" He tore the blanket off the sofa and hurled it down in a misshapen wad.

Hamilton noted the gesture with concern. "Why is it too late, Major?"

Realizing that he had displayed a streak of irrationality, Brothers sank down on the sofa again. He didn't answer the question.

Hamilton changed the subject. "You said something I didn't quite understand, Major. You said the mountain and *the thing on it*."

Sulking, Brothers continued quietly. He knew it was a lost cause now. "That's why it's too late. Because the creature that should have been blown up with the isthmus is now *here*, on the base."

The psychologist still looked puzzled. *Could it be possible that he really didn't know?*, Brothers wondered.

"Thing? A creature? Can you describe it?"

Or is he just checking, just testing me?

"Was it human? Alive?"

Do I dare answer?

Without a response from Brothers, Dr. Hamilton tried a different approach. "Why don't you tell me about the accident last night, Major—when you hurt your head during the earthquake."

At the doctor's mindless refusal to face facts, Brothers flared out. "It was no earthquake!"

Hamilton continued to sound reasonable. "Of course it was a quake, Major. You're an engineer. You know the signs. After all, Point Tabu is only a few miles from the Baffin fault. We often experience minor shocks."

Brothers shook his head vigorously. "You think that, do you? Don't you realize that all our preparatory work on the isthmus was probably destroyed? The warheads just arrived last night, and all the shafts must be in right when we were ready to plant the atomic cartridges!"

Hamilton struggled to follow the train of logic. "But that's exactly the type of damage one would expect from an earthquake."

"It was no earthquake, I tell you. It was that *thing*—moving—splitting the crevasse—coming out from its prison of ice. And now it has to be destroyed before it attacks the whole world." Brothers took a deep breath, determined. "And to prevent that from happening, Doctor, I'll gladly sacrifice my own life. I mean that." He noted Hamilton's troubled gaze with disgust. "You don't believe me, do you?"

"I believe you," Hamilton said in a perfectly professional tone.

Brothers couldn't hide his surprise. "You believe I saw...the thing?"

Hamilton tossed his notebook on his desk and looked thoughtfully at the array of apparatus against the laboratory wall. "Self-sacrifice is a rare thing, Major. None of us swears it lightly. You must have a very valid reason to be willing to take such...extreme measures."

Hamilton stood up, leaving his notepad behind, and moved to his electroencephalograph. He regarded the apparatus. "I want to know that reason and understand it. I need to know exactly what's on your mind. And I have an idea how to do that." He looked piercingly at the Major. "Would you be willing to participate in a rather sophisticated experiment?"

After his embarrassing test run with Ingrid, Hamilton knew that the apparatus worked and he was perhaps too self-protectively eager to use it for its intended purpose. This time, it would not be just an experiment, not an unexpected confessional for a woman who was in love with him.

He was a psychologist, and Major Brothers appeared to be a very sick man who suffered from paranoia and delusions. The possibility of an instant and accurate diagnosis made Hamilton realize the full potential of his mind-reading machine. And, still stinging from what had happened with Ingrid, he wanted to show its worth. He wanted to do a *real* test.

Brothers stepped toward the experimental station, frowned down at the electrode headset. "What is it, a lie detector?"

"A little more than that. But it would help me to really believe what you're telling me." Hamilton paused at the power generator, then saw a better way of getting this man to cooperate. "What's the matter? Are you afraid of it, Major?"

"No!"

Hamilton flipped on the power switch, changed the recording tape, and even contemplated destroying the magnetic reel that held the private thoughts Ingrid had shared with him. But he couldn't do that. "It's no crime to be afraid."

"It's a crime to run from fear. Even as a kid, I never did that."

Hamilton indicated the chair. "Then you won't do it now?"

Brothers responded to the challenge and slumped into the chair.

Hamilton placed the flexible headset on the other man's tousled dark hair. "Just relax. I'll do the rest." He adjusted the electrodes at the Major's temples, behind the ears, checking for good contacts and avoiding the bandaged injury on his forehead. Brothers fidgeted during the process, obviously not as brave as he had claimed to be.

"I'll make an overall analysis first," Hamilton said. " If anything shows up, we can concentrate on the individual brain centers. Are you right-handed?"

"What's that got to do with it?"

Hamilton adjusted one of the electrodes. "It means that your speech center, where you do most of your thinking, is a little on the left side."

Satisfied with the headset placement, Hamilton took the thin cable and plugged the lead into the machine. The low humming grew louder, and a highly irregular wave pattern appeared on the oscillograph alongside a shadowy brain image. Hamilton studied the pattern for a moment, trying not to prejudge his patient.

Brothers narrowed his dark eyes as he listened to the warbling hum. The sound grated like fingernails on a chalkboard. "What's happening?" He reached into his pocket and snatched out the packet of sunflower seeds, popping three into his mouth.

"Just adjusting the controls."

Hamilton attached the counterpart electrodes to his own scalp, snugging the headset tight. On the apparatus, all the components worked just as before, the magnetic tape reels, the strip chart, the flashing lights. The hum grew louder, more intense.

After plugging his headset into the machine, Hamilton turned up the amplifier and watched the results. He waited to hear the whispering voice in his mind, the second presence. His wide eyes noted the oscilloscope displaying two sets of waves: one highly irregular, one calm and even. On the brain screen, two blurry cerebral outlines drifted over each other.

Brothers sat in the chair, looking wildly at the apparatus, flicking his gaze from side to side. His face twitched with an unfamiliar sensation. "Is this...going to hurt?"

Hamilton finessed the readings until they were perfect. "No, Major. I'm only increasing the amplification."

On the oscilloscope, the two wave patterns overlapped, becoming entwined. The pair of brain images showed better definition as they drew closer to an exact overlap.

The thoughts began to flow.

Like a muffled echo in his mind, panicked and barely controlled reactions clamored for attention, like a frightened child's. He sat across from Major Brothers, leaning closer on the tabletop. Their eyes met, *locked*. Everything became clearer.

Hamilton turned up the power, and the two wave patterns merged into one. The pair of fuzzy brain images coincided into a single reading.

Hamilton's eyes widened with surprise and deep concern. Major Brothers looked at him with the same expression, the same thoughts.

Then another, more ominous sound joined the high-pitched humming of the apparatus. A violent rumble, like grinding teeth that grew louder until it was a roar that filled the room, the ground, the entire base.

The equipment banks rattled, the lights swayed. Even disoriented with the flood of Major Brothers' thoughts in his head, Hamilton knew it was another earthquake, an aftershock of the previous night's spasm.

Alarmed as the intensity of the quake increased, Hamilton struggled to reach the controls. He had to switch everything off before the system overloaded but the lurching and twisting floor threw him back into his chair. He became totally disoriented, trying to work two bodies at once.

The equipment racks rocked. The metal struts and support tiedowns protested with shrill whines and beepings. The flurry of diagnostic lights went wild, and suddenly sparks sprayed out like flares. Dual arcs of electricity shot from either side of the machine, surging through the cables and blasting the headsets of the two men.

The overload hurled both of them from their chairs, and the tumble ripped the electrode nets from their heads. With the current broken, the machine went dead with a long descending whine.

Dr. Hamilton fell to the floor as the earthquake rumblings faded. Everything in the laboratory became motionless and black and silent. Absolutely silent.

His eyes slowly opened. His head buzzed, his vision blurred. Still dazed from the power surge, the quake, the blast of unconsciousness, he glanced around warily from a prone position before rising to his knees. He hated to be out of control. He wondered how long he had been unconscious. While he'd lain there helpless, the Ice Creature could have gotten him.

Papers lay strewn on the cold floor, and some of the ceiling tiles had cracked. He could smell burned electrical insulation, a few blown fuses. A reddish glow of emergency lights burned in the air, like the fires of banked coals. He crawled on his hands and knees, keeping a furtive eye on the now-dark machine against the wall as he got to his feet.

He called out querulously, "Dr. Hamilton, where are you?"

He rubbed his head, still fuzzy, and in passing he felt his forehead, puzzled to find no bandage there, no sore injury from the previous day's tumble. He took a step forward and noticed his cellophane bag of sunflower seeds on the floor. Recognizing his own nervous habit, he bent and picked it up, tossing a few seeds into his mouth.

Then he stopped abruptly when he saw a fallen man's shoes and khaki pants on the opposite side of the table. Strange, he remembered the psychologist wearing a white lab coat, not fatigues and Army boots. He called again, "Dr. Hamilton?"

He stepped around the table and saw the body of *Major Brothers* on the floor, his mirror-familiar face slack, his dark hair mussed, his bandaged forehead now bright with renewed blood. He rushed forward, dropping to his knees as he stared in disbelief at Brothers' face, *his own face*. For a full five seconds he gawked, haunted, then rubbed his cheeks, his heavy eyebrows, his thinning brown hair...but it was all wrong.

He scrambled around the laboratory for something to use as a mirror. Finally, he stopped at the now-dark screen of the oscilloscope, bending close to peer at his reflection. His new reflection. He saw the large, expressive eyes of Dr. James Hamilton, the seamed visage, the thick eyebrows. He blinked, and the image blinked with him. Still unable to comprehend what had happened, or not wanting to believe, he traced the leads of the apparatus that had been attached to his head, following them from the electrode mesh to the machine, then he stared at a similar empty headset where Hamilton had sat.

He breathed in as a gleam of comprehension stole through his mind, an expression of triumph, the hint of a mad smile. He was in Hamilton's body, but his mind remained his own. Major Frank Brothers. "Hamilton-B" accepted the situation immediately, then struggled with how he might make use of the fact. It was, after all, no more fantastic than the Ice Creature coming out of the Hecla Isthmus to haunt him.

Hamilton-B moved back to his still-unconscious counterpart's body and looked down at the features, knowing that the real Dr. Hamilton would be just as confused when he regained consciousness. But he could take advantage of that for now.

Groaning, the other man rolled to an elbow, struggling to wake up as he faced away from Hamilton-B. He blinked and looked around, then touched the blood-wet bandage on his forehead. With sincere concern, he called into the red-lit dimness, "Major Brothers? Are you all right?"

Coldly triumphant, Hamilton-B said, "I'm right here, *Dr. Hamilton*."

The man who now looked like Major Brothers scrambled to his feet. Hamilton-B faced him.

The dark eyes of Major Brothers stared back at him more with wonder than horror. His manner had changed; his eyes were calm and rational, albeit amazed. After only a brief hesitation, he seemed to understand what had happened. He had the features of Brothers, but his own mind, the mind of Hamilton. "Incredible! Our two minds were merged during the experiment, and they were separated when the machine short-circuited during the aftershock," Brothers-H said. "But they respectively returned to the wrong bodies. Don't you see?"

He moved closer, studying his duplicate and rival. "Amazing!" He scrutinized his callused hands, his khaki clothing, then turned back to the electroencephalograph. He picked up the electrodes that had been attached to the original Major Brothers' head, jiggling them. He said with the calm demeanor of an unflappable scientist, "All right, Major. Get back in the chair. We'll try to undo it. There doesn't look to be too much damage to the apparatus."

Hamilton-B stared coldly at him, then strode to the reception room door and yanked it open. "Guards," he shouted into the corridor.

Brothers-H looked after him, perplexed, still holding the electrodes. "What are you doing?"

Hamilton-B stepped aside as the two MPs, ruffled from the tremors, rushed in. The man in the white lab coat gestured toward Brothers-H. "Please take Major Brothers to the hospital and see that he's locked in a safe room. I'm very concerned about him. I'll call and authorize a strong sedative."

Nodding, the security men advanced on Brothers-H. They grabbed his arms, but he struggled away. Taking one step backward, he put out a hand bidding them to stop. "Wait, officers. I'm not Major Brothers at all. I'm really Dr. Hamilton." He spoke calmly and reasonably to them. "I was exploring Major Brothers' mind when the earthquake caused a power surge, and our minds became reversed."

The MPs looked at each other without comprehending. One rolled his eyes. Hamilton-B gave them a reassuring, patronizing nod. "I'll check on him tomorrow."

Brothers-H didn't know what to do as the guards grabbed him again, more forcefully this time. "I can prove what I say. Let me conduct a few tests. Send for Colonel Campbell."

The two MPs propelled him toward the door, stony-faced. The displaced psychologist's calm began to desert him. "But I tell you, I'm Dr. Hamilton! I was born in Billings, Montana. I attended the University of Chicago, and served my internship at the Menninger Clinic! You can check on everything I say!" His voice rose, growing more frantic, more like the paranoid old Major Brothers had been. He struggled to point at the other man who watched them calmly. "And that man plans to destroy everyone on this base!"

The guards had heard enough, and they'd heard it all before. They hustled the man in military fatigues out of the doorway toward the base hospital. Hamilton-B stood alone and in triumphant possession of the Human Factors laboratory. With no one to watch him, the mad light returned to his eyes.

He rehearsed his new identity. "I was born in Billings, Montana and attended the University of Chicago." He wouldn't have to convince anyone for long, just enough to accomplish what he needed to do. He paused and smiled as he added, "And, yes, I am going to destroy every person on this base."

The base hospital was a set of stark rooms not designed for creature comforts. The walls were plain, the bedsheets white, the lights harsh. Glass bottles of pharmaceuticals lined up like little soldiers behind the doors of locked cabinets. Here at Point Tabu Base, personnel did not come in for long convalescences or unnecessary care; they waited to be rotated home.

Desperate, Brothers-H struggled on a gurney, held down by two orderlies while across the room Dr. Soldini prepared a sedative for him. She was a stern woman of forty-five, with all the bedside manner appropriate for a physician exiled to a small base at the ends of the world. But she played a great game of chess, as Dr. Hamilton knew well enough. Her assistant, Medical Sergeant Peterson, assisted her with the hypodermic, rolling up the sleeve on their patient's khaki uniform.

Brothers-H, still disbelieving the incredible circumstances in which he found himself, continued his attempts to get someone to listen to him.

"Dr. Soldini, I know you well. Just listen to me for a minute. I know your two sons, Joe and Lou." He thought of something else. "I...I played chess with you last week, and you trapped me with a knight sacrifice on the seventh move. Ask me anything you want to know about Dr. Hamilton and I'll tell you! That's who I am."

Soldini prepared the sedative and approached the man on the gurney. Her assistant muttered, not caring whether Major Brothers heard or not, "He's sure made a thorough study of Dr. Hamilton."

Soldini smiled in a detached, professional way. "During one of our chess games, Dr. Hamilton told me he once had a patient who thought he was Albert Einstein. This person not only knew every detail of Einstein's private life, but could talk lucidly about the theory of relativity." She shook her head. "The human mind is an amazing piece of machinery."

When Medical Sergeant Peterson rubbed the skin on Brothers-H's forearm with an alcohol swab, the man on the gurney began to struggle more violently. "Dr. Soldini, I have to stay awake! Someone has to listen to me. The man you think is Hamilton is really Major Brothers. He's sick with guilt and thinks the entire base should be punished." His voice rose to a shout. "He'll destroy us all!"

Soldini deftly ran the hypodermic into a forearm vein, then stepped back to wait for the fast-acting tranquilizer to work. Already lost, Brother-H ceased his struggles, his face set with hopeless resignation.

Soldini said to the medical sergeant, "Put him to bed. He'll be out until morning."

Outside during the half year of night, the wind soughed mournfully, driving eddies of snow before it like frightened ghosts. The sky itself was clear, and high overhead a pale aurora probed the stars with long fingers of light. One of the large radar antenna dishes searched the remote distance for an enemy, never letting down its guard. No Soviet nuclear attack tonight.

Colonel Campbell continued to work in his underground office, sifting through the usual paperwork, civil defense preparations, and a month-old newspaper brought up in one of the last regular supply runs.

His sergeant stepped into the office to retrieve the material in the OUT box. "Dr. Hamilton's here to see you, sir."

Nodding, Campbell rounded his desk to meet the psychologist. Unusual for the scientist, Hamilton wore his military uniform instead of his customary white lab coat. "Morning, Jim. Come in and sit down. Sergeant, bring Doctor Hamilton his coffee."

As Hamilton-B took the offered chair in front of the desk, he thought about the coffee with distaste. He didn't want to pollute his body, not even *this* body that didn't belong to him. "No coffee, thank you. I...I came to talk about Major Brothers."

Campbell returned to his chair again, businesslike and concerned. "How is he? What's the professional opinion?"

"Not much hope," Hamilton-B said, maintaining the charade.

The Colonel sighed. "I was afraid of that. Well, I'll have him invalided home on the next plane. I suspect he needs a lot more treatment than we can give him here."

Hamilton-B answered quickly, not wanting to let go. "Before you do that, Colonel, I'd like to investigate a little further, try to get at the root causes of his problem. I understand he struck his head against an atomic cartridge?"

The staff sergeant entered with a mug of black coffee and put it on the desk near Hamilton-B, who refused to look at it.

Campbell slid papers aside so he could put both elbows on his desktop. "I was right there and saw it. During the quake night before last."

Hamilton-B continued urgently, leaning closer to the Colonel. "It occurred to me that Major Brothers might have received a strong dose of radiation at the same time, directly into the brain. We know that ionizing radiation can cause serious damage to other organs, and there's no reason why the brain should be immune."

Campbell replied skeptically, not wanting to second-guess the esteemed doctor's opinion. "Might be...except that there's very little radiation from these cartridges. I had Giles check that in particular, and I trust his opinion."

Hamilton responded in a firm voice. "In view of Major Brothers' condition, though, I'd like to see that atomic cartridge myself."

Now Campbell seemed even more perplexed, unable to make the connection. "If you think that's necessary, Jim. But, now that I've had reason to think on it, I realize that Brothers has been a sick man for some time."

Hamilton-B started, then narrowed his eyes. He took great offense at the supercilious man's off-hand comment. Yet another narrow-minded officer who couldn't see the real threat to the people under his command, a man who wouldn't do what needed to be done—

Campbell continued, "And he's been getting sicker."

"That's not true!"

"Look, Jim, I'm not trying to be the doctor here. I only mean that I've worked with the man a long time and have seen him change." Campbell paused, indicating the mug in front of the psychologist. "Your coffee's getting cold."

But Hamilton-B still ignored the steaming cup. He felt like a cornered animal. "Change? How?"

"Started about six months ago. He was out with a small surveying party on the isthmus, and one of his men didn't come back. Private Walter Gordon. You must remember the incident."

Hamilton-B swallowed hard, trying to drive the horrible memories away. "Yes...yes, I remember."

Campbell turned from his desk to look at the tropical postcards on his bulletin board, sunny places where he'd never be stationed. "Apparently poor Gordon fell into a crevasse, and it was impossible to get him out. At least that's the way Major Brothers reported it."

Hamilton-B spoke defensively. "It was true! Wasn't it?"

Campbell shrugged and faced the man across his desk. "I wish I knew. Brothers was quite upset when we halted work on the project to investigate. Called it an unnecessary delay, said he *had* to remove the isthmus. It's an obsession with him."

Hamilton-B drew a deep breath. "The delay would have served no purpose. The United States needs that isthmus gone. The security of our country is at stake, by God! You don't think the Commies halt work for an instant because of a simple industrial accident? A tiresome investigation would have set everything back and it wouldn't have done any good."

The Colonel removed a cigarette from the box on his desk and tucked it between his lips. He extended the box to Hamilton-B, who tried not to recoil in distaste. He masked his frown as the acrid cigarette smoke coiled around them, polluting the air. How could people do this to their bodies? Coffee . . . cigarettes . . . alcohol. He needed his mind to be sharp and clear.

Campbell nodded, taking another long drag. "By the time a rescue party got there, fresh snow had covered everything, so we had to take Brothers' word for it. But during the investigation, one of his men said they'd wanted to attempt a rescue but Brothers wouldn't permit it. Absolutely refused."

Agitated, Hamilton-B sat too-rigid in the chair. "Well, the man in the crevasse may have been dead. In fact, it was likely after such a fall. An officer must think of the welfare of all his men and not risk their lives on a slim chance like that."

Letting the cigarette burn in his fingers, Campbell looked at him in surprise. "That's exactly what Brothers said. How did you know?"

Hamilton-B panicked at coming so close to exposing himself, but he recovered. "I...heard it from him when he was in my office yesterday. We had quite an extensive discussion."

Campbell looked relieved. "Oh, yes—of course. I forget that you psychology fellows can find out anything. It's your job." He chuckled. "Anyhow, Brothers left Private Gordon down there to freeze in the crevasse. Technically speaking, as an officer he may have done exactly the right thing. But there are times when it's more important to be a *man* than an officer. If I'd been there, I'd have gone into that crevasse myself if I couldn't find volunteers. I don't care if they broke me back to private. I wouldn't leave one of my men down in that ice as long as there was a whispering chance of getting him out alive."

Beads of perspiration stood out on Hamilton-B's forehead. His eyes burned with a hatred toward Campbell and his pompous self-righteousness.

"What's wrong, Jim?" Campbell asked. "You look sick."

Hamilton-B ran a handkerchief across his wrinkled forehead to hide his face and his volatile emotions. "Nothing. You...you keep your office too warm."

Campbell laughed in disbelief. "You usually complain that I keep it too cold." He returned to his chair. "Anyway, after that disaster Major Brothers began to change. He started talking about courage and devotion to duty and complaining about even the slightest delays. It was as though he wanted to destroy the Hecla Isthmus because that's where Gordon's body lay." He grabbed some papers from his IN box and spread them out on his desk, implying that the interview was over. "And that's why I don't think bumping his head a day ago had anything to do with it. But, of course, if you think otherwise, you'd better look into it."

Hamilton-B stood up, eager to go. "Yes. I want Major Brothers to have every chance. I'd like to inspect that atomic cartridge as soon as possible."

Campbell sighed in resignation. "I'll call Major Giles and tell him you have my permission."

Hamilton-B rose, mission accomplished. "I think he should be there to explain things, too. I'm...I'm not an expert in that field."

Campbell gave a long exhale of smoke. "He'll have to be there, Jim. Security regulations. We don't just let people poke around with nuclear warheads."

"I'll get what I need to carry out a few...experiments and meet Major Giles in the atomic storeroom." He nodded stiffly and exited the room.

Campbell sat a moment, puzzled and vaguely uneasy. He stared at the doctor's untouched coffee, then he shrugged again and picked up the phone.

Engrossed in maintaining his new identity, Hamilton-B hurried back to the Human Factors laboratory. He had so much to do, so many preparations to make. He grabbed the doorknob and heard a rapid-fire clicking from inside, a typewriter at the reception desk.

He found Ingrid Larkin transcribing the notes from Hamilton's session, perhaps from his experiment with Major Brothers. Seeing him enter, she paused and looked up at him with a rush of affection, half-rising from her chair. The young woman struck him as a little sad, but also with a trace of good humor that seemed natural to her.

"I've slept on it, Doctor Hamilton, and for some reason it was the soundest, most peaceful sleep I ever had. I...I've withdrawn my request for a transfer. You were right about secrets seeming less...effective when they're out in the open." She hesitated, waiting for some reaction from him, then said, "Or maybe they're more effective."

She gave him a lovely, provocative smile but Hamilton-B didn't know what she was talking about. What had happened? What did the doctor and this woman have between them?

Ingrid continued to wait for him to say something but before he could think of appropriately noncommittal words, he felt a shimmer in the air, a presence of deathly cold. *No! Not now!*

Behind Ingrid Larkin he saw the snow-clotted, crushed and frozen-blue spectre with blazing eyes, a humanoid shape that had once been a man in a uniform. The Ice Creature appeared at her shoulder, drifting closer, accusing, pointing at *him*.

As he stood speechless with terror, Ingrid saw his expression, not even sensing the thing that stood directly behind her. "What is it?"

Couldn't she see it? Couldn't she feel the thing's blood-freezing power? Hamilton-B staggered backward and pointed a finger in Ingrid's direction. "Get out!" His voice rose to a shriek. "Go back where you belong and stop accusing me!"

Ingrid leaped to her feet, dizzy with shock. "What?" She looked like a trapped, frightened rabbit. "Dr. Hamilton!"

Moving as if he had wooden limbs, Hamilton-B forced himself to take a step toward the silent, vengeful spirit. "Go! It was your fault, not mine. There was nothing I could do! Get out!"

Ingrid looked at him, stricken and utterly overcome by the bitter-sounding words.

The spectre finally drifted to one side, keeping its cold-fiery gaze nailed to him. Hamilton-B followed it, wary and terrified, until he was no longer staring at Ingrid. The icy demon held on for a moment more, just staring, and finally dissolved back to where it had come from.

With a start, Hamilton-B became aware of Ingrid's presence. Trying to divert his terror, he snapped at her. "What are you doing here?"

Ingrid was too confused to make a coherent reply. Realizing that his behavior had aroused her suspicions, Hamilton-B turned from the reception desk and stalked into the laboratory, slamming the door behind him.

Inside, he opened cabinets, drawers, desks, ransacking the psychologist's possessions. He found coffee, packaged food, notebooks, old scientific journals, supplies, a few spare vacuum tubes and fuses, but not what he was looking for. He moved the chair, slammed another drawer.

Finally, Ingrid opened the door, baffled and hurt by his behavior. She had removed her lab coat and took a warm jacket, as if she intended to leave the office and go somewhere else. She blinked at him, unable to comprehend Hamilton-B's behavior.

He whirled. If she was the real Hamilton's assistant, she would know the answer! He stopped pawing beneath papers and slammed the cabinet shut. "Surely I have a service revolver? This is a *military* base! Where do I keep it?"

"I . . ." Ingrid frowned with deep concern, then stepped to a small closet and slid the panel aside. Behind the panel hung a dark parka and thick mittens. On the shelf lay an Army-issue revolver in its holster and leather belt. "Here. But, Dr. Hamilton..."

"Thank you. That's all." Hamilton-B pounced on the weapon, his only defense if the looming Ice Creature should return. When Ingrid studied him in exasperation, he repeated, "That is *all*."

Without another word, she fled into the outer reception area.

Single-mindedly, Hamilton-B checked the gun to find it not loaded. Rummaging around on the shelf, he located a box of cartridges. His hands trembled as he fed shells into the revolver.

He donned the parka, then thrust the loaded gun inside the deep pocket. Prepared now, he marched to the telephone and grabbed it. "Miss, uh, Larkin, get me Major Giles on the line. Now."

When Major Giles's voice came over the phone, Hamilton-B spoke quickly, his pulse pounding. "Can you meet me at the entrance to the atomic storeroom? Colonel Campbell must have called you by now." He listened, then nodded. "All right, in about ten minutes."

Without further pleasantries, he hung up, his mind racing through what else still remained to be done. As he pondered, Hamilton-B pulled the half-empty cellophane packet of sunflower seeds from his jacket pocket. Ravenous, he dumped the remaining seeds into his hand and ate them, then wadded the crackling bag and threw it aside.

With one hand inside his parka pocket, feeling the revolver, he strode through the reception room. Ingrid still sat at her desk, pretending to work. Hamilton-B didn't even notice her until he reached the outer door, then he finally paused to give her a long, searching glance. She forced herself to endure it, but neither of them spoke.

Hamilton-B didn't wonder what she was thinking. He had more important things to do.

When the door slammed shut with finality, Ingrid felt even more cut off than she had the day before, after she and Hamilton had trespassed in each other's minds. She had learned things about him then, surprising things and deep disappointments, but now he seemed a total stranger to her, a different person. Perhaps she didn't understand him at all.

As soon as he had left her, Ingrid rose from her desk, waited a second to make sure he wouldn't return, then headed for the lab. She went to the closet and with dismay ascertained that he had taken the revolver; the empty box of shells proved that he had loaded it, too.

What was he doing? Why would Dr. Hamilton ever need a weapon? Why had he treated her this way?

On the tabletop next to his mind-reading apparatus, she found the notebook he had used to keep track of his experiment. Curious, she bent under the desk lamp and leafed through the pages, finding the analytical description of his trial run with her. Ingrid wasn't sure she wanted to read what he had recorded about the experience. Then she glanced at the last entry—and came to a full stop.

Dr. Hamilton had done it again. This time, without her.

"Major Brothers...arrived at lab four-fifteen. Behavior pattern of deep guilt...feelings of persecution mixed with delusions of grandeur...'every man is afraid of his brother.' Does he mean 'Every man is afraid of Brothers?' Nervous habit of eating sunflower seeds...But what is the thing he sees? A ghost of some kind? Guilty conscience? Question: should I link my mind with his to find out? It worked with Ingrid."

Suddenly cold, Ingrid stopped reading and slid the notebook into the pool of light from the desk lamp. She glanced toward the electroencephalograph. *What had he done?*

She noticed a small cellophane bag crumpled on the floor where Dr. Hamilton had just tossed it. She stooped to pick it up. Unwadding it, Ingrid read the Army supply printed words. *Salted Sunflower Seeds.*

Her mind reeled as impossible questions rose up in front of her. The ringing telephone startled her out of her thoughts, but she lifted the receiver cautiously, as if it might bite her.

"Yes? No, he isn't here at the moment." It was the hospital, Dr. Soldini reporting on the patient's condition. Ingrid listened. "Oh. I'm glad to hear Major Brothers is feeling better this morning." Then the words sank in. "What do you mean he's stopped insisting he's really Dr. Hamilton?"

Ingrid listened a moment more, then lowered the phone to its cradle, staring at Dr. Hamilton's strange and provocative device, then at his incomplete notes.

Dr. Hamilton *never* left incomplete notes.

Abruptly, she headed out of the lab.

It was supposed to be a hospital room, a place to heal and recover—but with the locked door, the small screened window, the food tray slot, and the recessed unbreakable lights, the chamber was obviously a cell. Dr. Soldini must have sent him to sleep off the tranquilizer in the brig.

Brothers-H sat awake on his cot now, holding his knees and staring at the barrier of the door. Alternately torn by despair, resignation, frustration, and rage at an intolerable situation, he used all of his psychological knowledge, all the tests and information and studies he had read, but none of them were of practical use. Nothing in all of his training had prepared him to deal with a crisis like this.

He'd been taught how to react to a paranoid patient's delusions, how to treat them, how to bring that person back from his unrealistic worldview and make him see reality again. But what happened when the paranoid delusions were real? How could he make anyone believe him?

At the sound of approaching footsteps in the outer corridor, Brothers-H forced himself to assume a calm attitude. Panic and insistence would get him nowhere. Rationality was his only hope.

The face of Medical Sergeant Peterson appeared at the screened window in the door. "Morning, Major Brothers." He slid the lower panel aside, then clattered a metal tray against the opening. "How about some breakfast?"

A platter of ham and eggs slid through the opening. Savory smells drifted up to his nose, but Brothers-H was about as interested in food as he was in South American butterflies. But he set the tray on the bedside stand, still dissembling his true feelings. He had to look normal, had to appear reasonable...had to get everyone in the right frame of mind to *hear what he was saying*.

"Say, Sergeant, what I need first is a little exercise to work up an appetite. How about letting me have a brisk walk?" *Calm, friendly, personable.*

"Sorry, Major." Peterson gave him a knowing smile.

"Just to clear my head?" He tried not to sound too insistent. "After that sedative I'm still feeling foggy."

"Wish I could, Major, but Dr. Hamilton gave strict orders to keep you here until he talks with you again."

Brothers-H pressed his face closer to the opening. "But don't you realize that may be never? What if he ..."

"Don't you worry about Dr. Hamilton. He never deserts a patient."

Simmering, Brothers-H finally lost his tenuous control. "Then get him here! Find him and get him here—before it's too late!"

The Medical Sergeant reacted to this outburst by slamming the food slot shut again. "Enjoy your breakfast, Major."

Brothers-H pounded on the door then leaned against it in despair as Peterson shook his head, walking away.

Inside the hospital reception area, Ingrid chatted with the nurse at the counter, trying to appear nonchalant as her inner turmoil spun her thoughts around and around. On a base as small as Point Tabu, the head nurse was also required to perform the functions of receptionist, switchboard operator, and medical records clerk.

Ingrid's request sounded innocent, but the nurse shook her head. "Sorry, Miss Larkin. Sergeant Peterson has to okay any visits with Major Brothers."

Ingrid tried not to let her disappointment show, but before she could insist, the Medical Sergeant walked into the room, tossing the key ring on the counter. "Let me have Major Brothers' chart, please." He gave Ingrid a curt nod of greeting.

"Excuse me, Sergeant," she started, spilling her words, making them up as she went along, "Doctor Hamilton asked..."

When the nurse handed him the chart, Peterson interrupted. "Sorry, just let me make these notes before I forget what he said."

Ingrid watched as the nurse retrieved the keys and hung them on a hook near the switchboard. Her mind churned, but she couldn't remain silent as Peterson continued writing. "I hear he was insisting that he's Dr. Hamilton?"

Not looking up, Peterson said, "Oh, he stopped that. Saw that it wasn't getting him anywhere."

"Is he calm enough for me to talk to him?" She held her breath, met the Medical Sergeant's curious gaze. "Dr. Hamilton asked me to."

"Just give me a minute." Peterson made notes on the chart while Ingrid swallowed hard, feeling an indefinable sense of impending doom.

Huddled and cold against the northern wind and snow, Hamilton-B stood next to Major Giles, slapping his mittens together and waiting for the weapons specialist to unlock the atomic storeroom. Two armed sentries stood guard, more alert for an external Communist attack than for any threat from within Point Tabu itself.

After swinging open the heavy outer door, Giles motioned for him to follow. The armed sentries accompanied them. Hamilton-B paused, intimidated, and turned to snap at both men. "Stay at your posts. Major Giles and I won't need you."

The sentries halted, as if wondering why this mere psychologist would bark orders at them. The two looked questioningly at Giles, and the Black Major frowned at Hamilton-B. "Regulations, Doctor. No one—not even myself—is allowed in the storeroom alone."

"You won't be alone. I'll be with you. So, you men remain outside." He turned back to the entrance, expecting his commands to be obeyed.

Giles turned a perplexed gaze at the psychologist. "What difference does it make, Doctor? They won't be in the way."

"I've asked them to remain outside." Suddenly, Hamilton-B realized that his attitude was out of character for a meek psychologist, not what the other three expected from him at all. For now, though, they were merely puzzled, nothing more. As he hesitated under their combined gaze, Hamilton-B searched for an explanation. "It's simply that I see no reason why more than two of us should be exposed to...to the dangers of radiation."

He narrowed his eyes and saw that his reply had rid Giles of any apprehensions. The weapons officer gave a reassuring smile. "Always thinking of the welfare of others, Doctor? No need to worry—no danger at all. Come along."

He stepped along the passageway that led down into the underground storeroom. Frustrated, Hamilton-B could think of no further grounds for protest and could only march behind him. The sentries followed, still suspecting nothing.

Unconcerned, Medical Sergeant Peterson sauntered down the hall to the locked hospital room. Ingrid followed, mentally urging the man to hurry but unable to think of an acceptable reason to push him. She had her doubts and suspicions, but she somehow couldn't believe what might have happened.

She would *know*, though, as soon as she looked into the eyes of the man listed as Major Frank Brothers.

"He's in there," Peterson said. "You'll have to talk to him through the grill, though. Can't let you inside."

She nodded and stood firm, waiting for the Medical Sergeant to leave; if he intended to eavesdrop, she was clearly going to disappoint him. With an embarrassed clearing of his throat, Peterson found other pressing business that called him away.

Alone with the prisoner, Ingrid advanced to the little barred aperture in the door. Tense and uncertain, she peered in. On the far side of the small cell, Brothers-H sat on the cot's rumpled blankets, unaware of being observed. His back was turned; from his hunched shoulders and deflated demeanor, she could see he remained despondent.

Testing, uncertain, she moved her face away from the screened window so that the prisoner couldn't see her. "Tell me who I am."

At the sound of her voice, Brothers-H lifted his head and sprang to his feet like a flower blooming in spring. He hurried to the door aperture, eyes bright. "Ingrid? Ingrid!"

Finally her face became visible, lit by the garish corridor lights. "What did I tell you yesterday?"

He didn't hesitate at all, sensing someone who might believe him at last. "That you love me." Brothers-H paused, then said more urgently, "Look into my eyes." They stared at each other through the screen, trying to recapture the moment when they had shared minds the day before. Frustrated by the obscuring screen, he ducked to the bottom of the door and stared at her through the food slot.

Ingrid stared into the depths of his pupils, saw the features of Major Brothers...but deeper inside them she saw the man she knew so well, the deeply caring and sensitive eyes of Dr. Hamilton. His eyes were sane, compelling. His face pleaded for recognition.

Ingrid stepped back, breathless and convinced. "Dr. Hamilton! I'll tell them!"

She turned to rush off, to speak with Dr. Soldini, but Brothers-H pressed his face close to the grill. "No, no, they'll never believe you. I've tried to tell them, and they won't listen, and there's no time to lose. Major Brothers' mind is in my body, and he means to destroy the base. He's paranoid and delusional, and willing to sacrifice himself. Because everyone thinks he's me, they won't suspect anything until it's too late. *You have to get me out of here yourself.*"

"How?" Ingrid turned back, feeling overwhelmed.

"The keys. You have to get the keys."

The sentries dutifully remained beside the armored doors within the atomic storeroom, while Hamilton-B and Giles stood before the atomic cartridges.

Giles waved the end of a Geiger counter in front of the warhead casings, smiling up at the psychologist. "You see, Doctor? Even in direct contact the radiation level is low." He pressed the end of the wand against the atomic cartridge.

Hamilton-B drank in every detail, his dark eyes dancing. "But this control bar—suppose Major Brothers struck his head against it hard enough to jar the neutron absorbers. Couldn't that have produced a temporary burst of radiation?" He was more interested in how the device worked, how to override the safety controls, but he had to maintain the charade no matter how ridiculous his psychologist's speculations sounded.

Laughing with self-confidence, Major Giles grasped the bar in one dark hand and tugged to demonstrate its immobility. "It can't move. The safety controls are perfect."

"No controls are perfect!" Hamilton-B snapped. "How is the bar released?"

"With a key." The weapons officer shrugged. "At least, we call it a key."

Hamilton-B glanced at the sentries who hovered at the door, then at Giles. "A key?"

A chain of keys hung above the hospital receptionist's desk, beside the switchboard. Anxiously, Ingrid wondered how she could distract the nurse. The receptionist looked up at her and smiled. "So, how did you find him, Miss Larkin?"

Ingrid maintained her composure. "I believe I'll have to talk to Dr. Hamilton. Would...would you mind calling his office for me?"

"Not at all. What's his extension?" The nurse reached toward the base's small switchboard.

"It's two six . . ." She stopped, pretending to have forgotten. "Imagine that, forgetting my own number! Here, I'll look it up for you."

Ingrid moved around to the nurse's side of the counter and pulled out the thin Point Tabu directory from a cluster of Army manuals. The receptionist could have done it herself, but she thought nothing of the assistance. Ingrid moved closer to the set of tantalizing keys as she riffled the pages in the base directory. "Ah, here it is! Two-six-nine, of course."

The nurse plugged in the line and dialed. While she was distracted, Ingrid moved closer to her, pretending to look down in anticipation as her hand reached for the keys. Only a few more inches.

"Mind handing those to me, Miss?" A male voice startled her. One of the hospital orderlies leaned on the counter.

"Hand you what?" asked Ingrid, keeping her voice firm.

"The keys." The orderly waited, suspecting nothing wrong. The nurse looked at him and dismissed him as she dialed Dr. Hamilton's office.

"Oh...yes, of course."

In dismay, Ingrid took the keys, clutched them a moment in her sweaty palm, then passed them across the counter to the orderly. "Thanks." He walked off with the keys jingling in his hand.

Ingrid watched him go, then looked at the receptionist, still preoccupied with tracking down Dr. Hamilton, whom Ingrid knew to be away, both the impostor and the real scientist.

The orderly went down the hall to a locked storeroom, opened it, and stepped inside the small room. He yanked the pull-chain light on the closet ceiling. He left the keys dangling in the lock. *The keys.*

Hamilton-B scowled, desperate to find some loophole that would give him the access he needed. "If this lever bar is released by a key, then it can't be absolutely motionless. There has to be some play." He leaned closer; sweat glistened on his forehead. "Maybe microscopic, but when you're dealing with radioactive materials, even a micron too much can be deadly."

Condescending, Major Giles stepped back. "You don't seem to understand very much about safety devices, Doctor. It's not the kind of a key that you *turn*. It's a magnetic key that fits into those two openings there and releases the controls by magnetic force. See, no movement at all."

"What does such a key look like?"

Finally, Major Giles looked as if he'd had enough. "I can't see what bearing that has on the case of Major Brothers." Hamilton-B did not relent, but fixed him with a fiery gaze. Giles sighed. "But if you're interested, I can show it to you."

The weapons officer reached inside his coat and brought out a neat oblong box. Hamilton-B's eyes were wide and intent as Giles groped in another pocket.

The weapons officer smiled like a showman. "First I need the key that unlocks the key."

Hospital keys dangled from the lock in the closet door, tempting her. She had no choice. *The keys!* She needed them if she meant to prevent Major Brothers from destroying the base.

The orderly came out with a stack of clean sheets, humming to himself as he stacked them on his cart. Then he went back into the closet, oblivious.

The moment he ducked out of sight, Ingrid slipped forward to grab the precious keys. Whistling at his work, the orderly saw her at the last instant as she slammed the door, locked it, and took the keys, dashing down the hall.

The orderly pounded on the locked door, his voice muffled through the base walls. "Hey, what are you doing? Open it up!"

As Ingrid ran down the hospital corridor, Brothers-H peered through the screened window in his cell door. Ingrid arrived breathless; she said nothing as she started trying the keys to find the right one. Finally, the lock clicked.

Brothers-H burst through the door, looking sidelong at her but intent on getting away. "I've got to do this—now!"

He ran down the corridor and charged into the reception area. Panting, Brothers-H saw the alarmed nurse, ignored her, and grabbed a warm coat from a rack by the door. He rushed off, trying to get outside the hospital. He already knew where the impostor would have gone.

The receptionist grabbed the phone at her station. "Call security! Put out a general alarm. Major Brothers has escaped from his room, and tell them he's dangerous."

Major Giles held the oblong box in his hands, opening it to reveal the peculiar key to the atomic cartridge: two oppositely polarized prongs like a tuning fork with a small dial at the end of the stem.

Hamilton-B bent closer, fixated on the magnetic key, fighting back his compulsive urge to seize it. The guards, still not suspicious, nevertheless hovered in the background.

Giles held the key to the holes to demonstrate. "These two magnetic poles fit into these holes on the cartridge."

Hamilton-B struggled to control his tension and eagerness. "And if that were done, then the cartridge would be turned into...an atomic bomb?"

"Not quite. It's a very detailed and complicated process. Just to prove to you how perfect these safety devices are—watch." As he inserted the twin prongs into the two small holes, he pushed the magnetic key down all the way to its stem. "There, even now you still can't move the bar. Try it."

Hamilton-B stared at him a fraction of a second. Then he grabbed the bar and gave it a mighty tug, to no avail. He shoved down a second time, on the verge of exposing his frustration. He released his grip, staring at Giles.

The weapons officer seemed amused by the situation. "You see? The chances of the thing going off accidentally are non-existent."

"Then how *do* you release the controls?"

Hamilton-B's tone became so intense that Major Giles looked at him sharply. Then his hand went to the little dial on the tip of the key stem. "It's a matter of turning this dial to release the safety." But instead of turning the dial, he drew the entire key out of the cartridge.

Hamilton-B lurched out to grasp Giles' wrist before the weapons officer could raise the magnetic key higher. "Wait! I didn't see that."

Giles drew back and stared at the psychologist, finally sensing something wrong. The two guards looked at each other, then took an ominous step forward.

At that instant Colonel Campbell's sharp voice came over the PA system. "Attention all personnel! Major Frank Brothers has just escaped from the base hospital. Major Brothers is dangerous. I repeat—*dangerous*!"

Breathing hard, Brothers-H crouched against the wall in an isolated underground corridor, listening to the freezing wind outside the shelter. He had never thought he'd be on the run in this base, never thought teams of security men would be chasing after him. He had lived such a quiet, studious life in the Human Factors Section.

The public address speakers carried a continuation of Campbell's announcement. "Anyone seeing this man, notify security at once. Dr. Hamilton, please return to your office immediately."

Brothers-H took a quick look around and ran to a ladder leading up a shaft to an emergency escape hatch. Scrambling up the rungs, he popped the lid and peered out into the blinding snow and blowing wind. It was always night here. Brilliant lights poured over the compound.

He shuddered, but knew he had to get across the base to the psychology laboratory. That's where his enemy would be. Just as he made to climb out, though, a pair of armed guards crunched by, keeping an eye out for the escaped prisoner. He ducked back down, hiding under the partially closed hatch until the MPs passed.

Brothers-H tumbled down from the hatch onto the loose snow, rolled, then looked around to get his bearings. The Arctic was vast, disorienting. Howling gusts and hard snow felt like sandpaper against his cheeks and eyes.

Finally, spotting the building he needed, he bent low and ran across the uncertain ground.

Inside the atomic storeroom, the four men looked up, alarmed at the announcement. Hamilton-B whirled back to Giles. "The key! Put it back, Major! You were showing me how the dial works."

"Didn't you hear Colonel Campbell? You're wanted in your office at once. We can do this some other time."

"Put it back! I may not have another chance!" Hamilton-B thrust his hand inside his coat where he had hidden the loaded revolver and stepped closer to the weapons officer, but the sentries also moved in on him.

No one said anything for a frozen moment, as Hamilton-B looked at the other three, his hand still inside his coat, then he turned on his heel and marched from the storeroom.

Ingrid sat alone and tense inside the reception room to the Human Factors laboratory. She worked hard to sound nonchalant into the telephone. "No, he hasn't returned yet...No, he didn't tell me where he was going. All I can do is let you know when he comes in." Part of her wondered if the orderly had managed to get himself out of the locked closet yet.

She hung up, then stiffened as the door from the corridor flew open and Hamilton-B charged in, his familiar-looking face in an out-of-character storm of rage. He stared at her with hard eyes, alien eyes, as he flung off his overcoat and dropped it on a chair.

Ingrid quailed as he advanced toward her desk. "Where is he?" She searched his face. Did the impostor know she understood what had happened? Then he dismissed her, as if she were completely irrelevant.

His gaze swept the room, and suddenly he noticed wet, slushy footprints on the floor mixed with clots of melting snow. Ingrid rose, trying to think of some way to stop him, but he followed the footprints to the closed laboratory door. Hamilton-B yanked the revolver out of his pocket.

Ingrid yelled, "Watch out!"

As the impostor psychologist burst into the laboratory room, Brothers-H leaped aside. The other man didn't hesitate. He pointed the revolver and opened fire, but the bullet spanged off the metal equipment racks.

The wild shot disoriented the paranoid Hamilton-B, and Brothers-H leaped upon him—a psychologist, not a fighter, but desperate nevertheless. He knocked the gun from his double's hand and sent it skidding across the floor toward the experimental apparatus.

Without a word, without accusations or demands, the two men fell upon each other, knowing the ultimate stakes of their conflict. Seeing his chances slipping away, the paranoid Hamilton-B fought with the fury of a madman. He knew techniques to overcome an adversary and he had no reservations whatsoever, but Brothers-H now had a younger, stronger body that was conditioned to military combat.

With a surge of energy, Brothers-H pinned the outraged and deluded man on his back against the cluttered desk. Hamilton-B rolled his eyes, terrified, as he cried out, "Go on, kill me! That's what everyone wants to do. Kill me!"

"I'm not trying to kill you," the voice was firm, but gentle and non-threatening. "I'm trying to save you."

Brothers-H tried to drag Hamilton-B to the mind-scanning apparatus, but the other man feigned a moment of helplessness and then broke free of his grasp.

Hamilton-B rushed for the door, ready to shout for the guards, but Ingrid blocked his way, also ready to fight.

Hamilton-B whirled in an instant of confusion, and Brothers-H knocked him to the floor with a hard right punch. The paranoid Major toppled like a tree.

Grasping the unconscious man by the arms, Brothers-H dragged him to the electroencephalograph. "Ingrid—the electrodes! Hurry!"

Knowing exactly what he intended to do, Ingrid rushed to the equipment racks and gathered up the two headsets, checking the cable connections to the apparatus. She handed them to Brothers-H, where he knelt beside his fallen opponent. He adjusted the flexible mesh against the wrinkled brow of the man whom everyone else thought was a placid and dedicated psychologist.

Brothers-H yelled, "Turn on the machine! Do you remember the steps?"

Ingrid toggled on the power switches, spun up the magnetic tape reels, and tuned the oscilloscope screen. Clicking sounds and blinking lights filled the shadowy laboratory. Several of the circuits had gone dead during the earthquake accident only the day before, but the readings were sufficient. They didn't have time for finesse.

Brothers-H worked so intently on adjusting the electrode headset in place around his own skull that he did not realize the other man had begun to regain consciousness, but furtively, without a sound, without a stir.

Ingrid double-checked all the outputs. The strip chart began rolling. "Almost ready," she said, then turned back to look at the two men.

As Brothers-H pressed the last electrode in place on his own temple, Hamilton-B's hand reached out like a cobra strike and grasped the revolver that had fallen on the cold floor beside him.

"The gun!" Ingrid screamed.

This time her warning came too late. Hamilton-B rolled away, rose to his knees, and with the precision of a trained soldier, fired off two rapid shots as Brothers-H charged him. Even disoriented from the recent blow, at such a distance the Major couldn't possibly miss.

The bullets slammed into the other man's chest, and Brothers-H gasped and toppled on top of Hamilton-B. With his last strength he tore the gun from his enemy's hand and crashed it down on the back of the Major's head, knocking him out again.

Terribly wounded, Brothers-H struggled to his feet and gripped Ingrid's arm. "Help me... chair... electrodes.. ."

Ingrid held him, positioned him, helped him up to the chair at the controls. Blood soaked crimson into the fatigues. "I know there's not much time," she said, caressing his mussed hair. "I hope this works."

With his own headset connected in place, Brothers-H reached over with blood-smeared fingers for the controls—but his hand faltered and dropped back to the desktop.

Ingrid rushed behind him. "Tell me what to do!"

With a deep-throated groan, the stunned Hamilton-B rolled over on the floor, already regaining consciousness again and ready to fight. Thankfully, the blow with the gun had not knocked the electrodes from his scalp.

"Selector switch... on Unity Transfer... Final amplifier...full power. Ballast coil... cut-off. Turn transfer gain... up... up... up..."

With dying energy, Brothers-H could only watch as Ingrid carried out his instructions. As she boosted the amperage, the clicking sounds and resonant hum grew louder. Two patterns of waves appeared on the oscilloscope, accompanied by a pair of shadowy cerebral images on the brain screen.

"More..." Brothers-H gasped.

Gradually, as if struggling against the reunification, the separate sets of waves and brain patterns merged closer to one single image.

On the floor, unnoticed, Hamilton-B clawed his way back to consciousness, blinked, and sat up. He looked at the wall, the shadows in the corner but instead of reacting to Ingrid or his look-alike beside the apparatus, he saw a much more terrifying enemy, a deadlier apparition.

The Ice Creature, come to get him at last!

Unfolding itself out of his imagination, emerging from the burden of guilt he had carried within him since the fatal accident on the Hecla Isthmus, the snow-encrusted demon floated toward him, coming closer, menacing. The apparition of dead Private Gordon raised an ice-battered glove and extended it toward him, toward the body of Dr. Hamilton.

Hamilton-B squirmed back against the desk in fear. The spectre came closer, unstoppable, bearing all the weight of damnation with him. His eyes blazed brighter, hotter, *colder*.

But then the psychologist's face softened, fell slack and suddenly calm.

The electroencephalograph rose in tone, into a sharp wail. On the oscilloscope and brain screen, the merged wave patterns separated again, drifting apart into two distinct entities.

The blood-soaked body of Major Brothers gasped and shuddered. With these eyes, now, he saw the Ice Creature coming toward him. Wearing a frenzied expression, he reached forward across the console, then finally fell still with only a faint death rattle from red-stained lips.

The ghost in the air vanished, gone back into imagination and nightmares.

On the screen, one set of patterns—the wildly jumping and chaotic signals—faded, leaving only a single bright brain image inside the apparatus. With the dual mental circuit broken, the machine fell silent.

Ingrid stepped forward, filled with apprehension. Biting back tears and despair, she pressed a hand against the dead Major's shoulder, looking down at his crimson-soaked fatigues. "Too late...ah, too late!"

Hamilton's voice called from the other side of the desk. "No, no, Ingrid. I'm here. Over here...where I belong."

She spun around, unable to contain her relieved smile. The real Dr. Hamilton, his mind and body restored, yanked the last electrode from his scalp. He scrambled to his feet and caught Ingrid in his arms as she rushed over to him. They clung together for a moment.

Hamilton kept his voice low, his lips against her ear. "Yesterday, when I found out that you loved me, I didn't place much value on it." He took a deep breath. "I'm sorry. I guess I simply never needed it."

Ingrid found her smile, used it to change the apologetic air of the man she loved. "Too many people *need* it. What this world needs is more people who *want* it."

Hamilton paused and gave her a puzzled, but satisfied expression. "I owe you so much, Ingrid. How did you really know it was my mind in Brothers' body? What convinced you?"

"I thought you knew." She raised her eyebrows, then fell tighter into his embrace. "It's your mind that attracts me most."

After a moment of closeness, they began to realize the consequences of their situation. There would be many questions, many explanations—and, still, many secrets. Together, they looked down at the body of Major Brothers sprawled on the floor. Ingrid looked at Dr. Hamilton as a compassionate sadness filled his eyes.

"I felt him die," Hamilton said.

"So...did you find out what death is?"

"No. But for Major Brothers I'm sure it's more pleasant than life. He's free now of the ghost of Private Gordon."

"A ghost?"

"An hallucination, a creation of his own guilt-ridden mind. That's what drove him over the edge into his paranoid delusions."

She could hear his reticence, his awe, and knew he wasn't likely to tell these things to anyone else. Ever. She doubted he would use his apparatus again, or even tell another person about it.

A mind-reading machine, a personality-exchange apparatus—perhaps it could be a tool, a miracle diagnosis machine, or it could also be a weapon. Like so many inventions, it could be used either to save lives or destroy them, to make men sane or to drive them mad, to increase human understanding or to betray it. The machine was only an instrument, neither good nor evil—until someone put it to use.

Knowing Dr. Hamilton so well, as well as any human being could know another, Ingrid felt that he wouldn't take the risk.

After a moment's silence, Ingrid looked at him with a new concern. They would have to get their stories straight, since Colonel Campbell was sure to launch a detailed investigation. "When they ask you how he died, what will you tell them?"

Hamilton glanced down at her with a forced wry expression. "Only the truth—that Major Brothers *shot himself.*"

Introduction to
The Man Who
Was Never Born

I DON'T REMEMBER AT WHAT AGE I FIRST READ RAY BRADBURY'S short story "A Sound of Thunder." In it, time-traveling big-game hunters go back to the age of dinosaurs to shoot a Tyrannosaurus Rex, but in a mishap one character accidentally kills a butterfly...an insignificant event, perhaps, but it sets up ripples that change all of history in unpredictable ways.

That story made such an impact on me, my mind, and my imagination...and of course it also ruined most of the off-the-cuff time-travel stories being published in the science fiction genre. Bradbury raised an utterly compelling case for a disastrous avalanche of consequences from even minor meddlings in the past, and I could no longer believe heroes traveling into previous centuries for full-blown adventures and then returning to their home time without the slightest visible difference.

This episode of the OUTER LIMITS was one of those time travel stories that still *convinced* me, and it was also the first in my experience to deal head-on with the ubiquitous paradox problem. "The Man Who Was Never Born" is a variation on the old go-back-and-remove-a-key-figure-from-history idea that has enjoyed such recent Hollywood popularity in *Terminator* and *Star Trek: First Contact*...but with an additional twist.

What do you do if you show up at the wrong time?

In the broadcast episode, a young Martin Landau brilliantly portrayed the poignant and anguished Andro, scar-ravaged and monstrous, but with a heart and mind more noble than any of the mere humans around him. He is faced with a decision and an opportunity that will put his own humanity to the test.

The Man Who Was Never Born

From a screenplay by Anthony Lawrence

I*T IS SAID THAT IF YOU MOVE A SINGLE PEBBLE ON THE BEACH, you set up a different pattern, and everything in the world is changed.*

It's also said that love can change the future. If love is deep enough, true enough, and selfless enough, it can prevent a war, prohibit a plague, and keep the whole world whole.

No matter what the cost.

Out in the bright wilderness of space and time, a ship drifted alone, approaching home. Earth. In the emptiness filled with a billion, billion stars, Joseph Reardon, captain of the one-person explorer craft *Balboa*, had found that such cosmic loneliness could be an exciting, voluntary thing—unlike the loneliness he had suffered among the indifferent population of cities and lip-service friends.

As a private scout, he'd had eight months by himself to cope with that fact. Plenty of breathing space, time for contemplation, he had performed a service for the world while he recharged his mental batteries. When he'd left Earth, Reardon needed to heal from a bad relationship, escape from the professed sympathy of acquaintances, and just revel in the quiet of space exploration. He was a commissioned and independent explorer, doing a job few people volunteered to do.

He reveled in it. He had made himself a better man through study, and meditation, and just plain daydreaming. He had read the classics of literature, learned the philosophies of history's great thinkers...and he had also used the time to assess his priorities.

Eight months had been more than enough for what Reardon needed, nearly the limit of what he could endure. The silence of the cockpit had grown too loud, the loneliness too close a companion, the *good* memories of Earth too bright and tempting.

The supposedly comfortable walls of the spaceship had been the boundaries of his personal world for too long now. The monotony had been punctuated by only a few dangerous but exhilarating excursions onto wild extraterrestrial terrain, asteroids, moons, and even the gas jets in the tail of an outbound comet. Reardon flew and coasted, with no sensation of movement, with the universe crowding around the windows of his craft.

And Earth came closer every day.

Reardon went about the daily routine at the *Balboa's* controls, but with a rising sense of excitement. After cruising the vacuum desert between planets and the fringes of the dark Oort cloud, he saw the marvelous blue-white sphere of Earth ahead. The planet grew larger, filling his view as well as his mind, welcoming him back with open arms. He had already begun to pick up the buzz and chatter of communications from the orbital space stations, the fledgling moon base, a few cargo craft venturing to nearby asteroids.

When he'd left Earth less than a year before, Joseph Reardon had been young and fresh-faced, with strawberry-blond hair, bright blue eyes, and a face that demanded a smattering of freckles. Here alone in the cockpit, he didn't know how the time and journey had changed him. Reardon hadn't thought to look at his reflection in a long, long time.

The *Balboa* was one of many solo scout ships sent out by Space Command, like note-filled bottles cast out to sea. He had lived in the craft, seen many things, gone many places, and recorded them all.

Despite all the images from telescopes, satellites, and robotic probes, humanity refused to consider a wilderness conquered until a real person's footprint stepped on virgin territory. Reardon had been the one to go to those places and plant the flag.

The most important thing in his life now was to go back to the cradle, his home. He would forget the exotic mysteries of alien landscapes and just content himself with the sprawling wonder of one familiar planet. He needed to reacquaint himself with friends and loves left behind.

Earth...its cities, its people, its majesty. In all the universe he had seen nothing close to matching it.

Impatient, as if even the incredible speed of his spacecraft was not enough for him, Reardon adjusted his vector, bringing the *Balboa* in straighter and faster, charting his own course.

But as the Earth swelled, filling his entire front window-port like a blue-white bulls-eye, the alarm signals began to ring. His control panel went wild; readings warbled off the scale, flipping back and forth as if the instruments didn't know how to interpret what they had encountered. Reardon frantically checked the controls, seeking to identify a malfunction. Then he looked up, staring out the window-port.

The Earth became blurry, as if seen through a milky white cataract. A patch of space began to ripple and roil in front of him, like stormy weather.

Reardon worked feverishly to stabilize the controls. He had handled his own emergencies for a long time, taking the necessary actions—and he had seen many inexplicable things. Thus, he was a long way from panic. *So far*.

Then the field of view in front of the window-port began to glow, shimmering in the ship's interior. Reardon fired the *Balboa's* emergency thrusters...but the roiling doorway in front of him engulfed the ship.

The dials spun and squealed, and disoriented readings flew off the scale. Grasped by an unknown force, Reardon twisted and turned, convulsing in his seat. His long-silent vocal cords let out a tiny, choked cry. The crash straps strained against his suit. As the eerie light intensified, swallowed him, Reardon slumped, inwardly collapsing. . . .

The bizarre light died away, like a half-seen billboard flashing by on a desert highway. He blinked.

Earth still hung in front of the ship, blue and white and peaceful. Reardon shook himself, took a deep breath of the cabin's stale air, then studied his control panel. He saw nothing wrong, though a few of the instruments had burned out and overloaded. Oh, well, he could handle the landing without them. He'd gotten used to doing things by the seat of his pants. Earth Control would take him from here.

"This is Starship *Balboa*," he said into the transmitter microphone, a bit shaken. "Earth Control, please establish re-entry pattern." He waited, waited a moment longer than he should have, then turned up the volume on his receiver. He heard only static. "Repeat, this is Starship *Balboa*, Reardon reporting. Please come in, Earth Control. Hey, I've been out a long time and want to get home."

When he continued to hear nothing, he chose not to wait any longer. Reardon fired his own jets, plotted his own course, and followed the descent path through the atmosphere to the calm and peaceful silence of his world. He just wanted to be home.

Something was terribly changed, terribly wrong, as he approached the ruins of what had been the landing field in total radio silence. The ship touched down, stabilized, then sighed with cooling engines. He'd been gone less than a year, but Reardon thought he saw a century's worth of devastation and rubble.

Unstrapping himself, Reardon placed his hands against the porthole in horror and confusion as he looked out onto the face of a strange planet.

The Earth was emaciated and burned, defiled and desolate. The entire landscape looked like one awful scar.

Too full of awe and dismay to take precautions, Reardon wrenched open the ship's hatch and scrambled down the ladder. The gravity felt right for Earth, but the air smelled like sour, old ash. He stood on the broken ground without speaking. He listened to the aching silence of empty air and sun-warmed rocks. The once-magnificent city and spaceport complex had crumbled into nonviolent decay—not incinerated, not exploded...simply *slumped*. The whole world hung quiet in his ears, except for a painful whine of wind.

Reardon staggered away from the ship, his eyes narrowed against the blinding white sun that shone through a prismatic miasma of haze. He stumbled across the rubble, but didn't notice. He couldn't comprehend what he was seeing. Impossible!

In just a few months, Earth had fallen apart, like a flash-burned tree branch that held onto an ash-shadow of its form. Time and weather and neglect had made all of civilization fade into nothing more than an afterimage. In only eight months!

Breathing the dry air, Reardon paused, shaded his eyes and stared into the rubbled distance. Not far away, an obelisk-like object rose out of the scorched and naked earth. It vaguely resembled the steeple spire of a church, or a tombstone for humanity.

Reardon approached the spire, hoping to find some answers, the punch line to this cosmic joke. *What happened, what happened, where is everybody?* He stood below the obelisk, running his fingers across the warm pitted stone, trying to understand the bizarre and desperate hieroglyphics.

In a shallow observation notch atop the monolith, a shadow moved like a spider, rising up into the harsh daylight. Though he had long since stopped contemplating his mutations, the grotesque humanoid figure looked like a man made of melting wax, with lumps and growths and hairs sprouting in unnatural places. One eye was larger than the other, whitish with biological scar tissue that half-obscured sharp pupils displaying a keen intellect. He had watched the glinting spaceship as it landed in the rubble, trying to contain his hope and awe. He leaned forward to watch the intruder.

The grotesque figure slid down the back of the obelisk, dropping with spread feet on the ground. He crept around the base of the obelisk, shuffling, approaching Reardon from behind. He caught his breath.

Could this man bring salvation...or just the final end of mankind?

Skittish to find himself alone on the blasted corpse of the planet he had called home, Reardon heard the sound of approaching footsteps. He whirled, then gasped at the appearance of the monster. The creature before him wore a tattered robe and extended gnarled hands. His fingers were swollen and discolored, like rotted meat.

Reardon snatched out the projectile weapon he carried at his hip. He gripped the gun, brandishing it toward the approaching manlike creature. After so long alone, though, he had forgotten how to talk face-to-face.

"Wait. I am no threat to you." Despite the hideous thing's twisted lips, he spoke in a soft, whispery voice—in perfect English.

"What are you?" Reardon took another step forward, refusing to lower his weapon.

"I am...a man," said the creature. "My name is Andro."

"A man," Reardon said in disbelief. "Where am I? How did I get here? What planet is this?" He used the projectile gun to indicate the unpopulated city fallen in on itself.

"This world is called...*Earth*." Andro nodded emphatically, as if dealing with a stranger from an alien world.

Reardon could barely contain his shock. "No, that's impossible! I left Earth only eight months ago." His voice trailed off as he continued to look around, seeing the subtle details and knowing the truth. "All this couldn't have happened in less than a century."

"Eight months ago? No." Andro said, stepping around the obelisk and coming closer, curious to inspect this healthy, normal-looking visitor. "Impossible. No one has left or returned to Earth in well over a hundred years. We—a few scattered survivors like me—have been here, a handful of non-viable remnants, as the century clock ticks away the doom of the human race. No one has come or gone in all that time."

"Well, I did." Reardon gestured toward his solitary spaceship. "Eight months ago. February 3, 2015. I can show you my logs."

Andro drew a deep breath, then sighed. "We no longer speak of months and days, since nothing changes on so short a timescale...but the year—this year—is 2148."

Andro stood back and watched with deep pity as the starship captain looked about himself in horror and in shock.

"It can't be! It's got to be...2015! It must be!" Finally, Reardon looked at Andro's wide yet compassionate eyes, unable to deny the evidence. "What could have brought me here?"

Andro folded his twisted fingers together like braids. His mismatched eyes misted over, and his voice had an ethereal, speculative quality, as if he were accustomed to random philosophizing. "Time and Space are indivisible. They are as lovers clinging together among the infinite imponderables. Somehow, in your travels, perhaps...perhaps you have moved from one to the other."

To Reardon, it seemed no more impossible than what he already saw all around him. "From space...into time?"

"Through a dimensional warp, perhaps? Across a bridge . . . who can understand the tapestry of the universe?" The hideously disfigured Andro paused, letting Reardon consider.

The mutated creature tossed out ideas like a flower girl strewing petals at a wedding. The space pilot drew a quick, sharp breath. "Yes...something did happen...a brightness, a chill. I seemed to collapse inside, as if I were going into a convulsion. But it wasn't me, or the ship—everything else was convulsing."

Andro replied with a soft smile that crinkled the patchwork skin of his face. "Ah, perhaps a...*time convulsion*, which brought you a hundred and thirty years into the future."

Reardon stood stunned, looking at his ship—the only new and bright thing visible all the way to the horizon. He grew less concerned with what had happened to *him*, and asked what had happened to his world.

"The future, but what could have happened? A nuclear holocaust? Did the old Cold War nightmares finally come true after so much time?" Stricken, Reardon looked around the bleakness.

Andro shook his hideous head. "There was no war. No attacks, no hydrogen bombs."

"Then there must still be cities someplace!" All Reardon could think of, though, was the incredible silence over the comm system when he had tried to contact Earth Control. He already knew his answer.

"No. There are no cities." Andro seemed as embarrassed at humankind's failure as he was saddened by the fate of the world.

"I don't believe it!" Reardon brandished his weapon, though he had no target except his own despair.

Andro took another shambling step forward, his tattered and dust-covered robes swaying around him. "We are the remainders of the human race. We are your descendants. People like me, only a few of us."

"You can't be! If you're human, you're a mutation of some kind!"

"This body, the soma, is indeed a mutation, twisted and distorted far from the original master plan of Nature and Evolution. But despite the failings of the physical form, the psyche has progressed considerably."

Looking at the pestilent disfigured shape of the sole inhabitant he had seen on this dead world, Reardon backed away. "It couldn't have happened in only two hundred years! Not a normal evolution!"

"Oh, it was not normal." Andro swallowed hard. The harsh white sun cast a shadow of the obelisk onto the blistered ground; the shadow looked like a guillotine blade. "It was caused by man, by misguided ambition and hubris."

Reardon realized he was still clutching his projectile weapon. He lowered it, self-consciously. "But you said there was no war."

Solemnly, Andro turned his back on the pilot and stared at the obelisk's weathered hieroglyphics. "When man's concern is only to prepare for defense against himself, he does not prepare for the unforeseen. Early in the last century—not long after you departed your green Earth, in fact—an extraterrestrial microbe was discovered and corrupted by a renowned biologist for his own ambitious reasons."

Andro traced lines and designs on the obelisk, as if following the story told there. "He meant to find cures for cancer and other genetic diseases, but instead he unleashed a chimera, a germ that was like gunpowder to human DNA. Most of us—the vast majority of humanity—did not survive."

Reardon gaped at him, appalled. "One man caused...all this?"

Andro turned his sad eye to the space pilot. "We recall his name—Bertram Cabot, Junior." The creature's voice took on a dark bitterness. "We—myself and scattered others like me—have memorized every detail of his life, his various addresses, his cares, his joys, his friends, his family." His expression took on a far-off look as he recited. "Noelle, they called his mother...Noelle, a woman who issued destruction for all future Christmases."

Reardon kicked out with his boot, knocking rubble aside to discover a few old yellowed bones that looked like kindling. "So, a *microbe* destroyed humanity—?"

Andro continued to study the obelisk, though he plainly knew the story by heart. "There were side effects to the symbiote that Cabot isolated and developed, side effects he did not foresee, which produced genetic changes and inhibited our ability to reproduce. The precious few offspring that did appear were hopelessly damaged." Andro rested his splayed hands on the rough robe on his chest. "Now, only our old ones remember the tall cities and the green forests, only the very old and weary."

Andro shuffled away from the obelisk. He motioned for the pilot to follow him. "Come, I will show you all that is left of moments, men, and places."

Reardon hesitated, afraid to see what the mutated creature would show him, but then he gathered his courage and followed.

Patterns upon patterns of books and records snared his gaze. The archives spread their treasures like precious gems on display in a museum. With his uneven gait, Andro led Reardon into a high, wide room without windows that had been hollowed out underground and reinforced.

The archives looked backward to humanity's marveled past, rather than reminding the survivors of grim reality. Reardon saw alcoves and doors with fretted lids like ears and eyes. On the labyrinthine shelves, millions of ancient bound books rippled like the colored scales of a fish.

He inhaled deeply of the musty smells. He saw the look of gentle awe and reverence on Andro's face, the way he worshipped humanity's lost Golden Age. For the survivors, this library was a place of holy communion, of contemplation, where the world's only remaining faithful souls flocked together without hope. Reardon was struck by the vast loneliness, by a hum of silent energy that reminded him of the dynamo rooms he had seen in great hydroelectric dams.

Andro stood in proud silence, then could no longer keep the words inside of him. "Here lies the protected history of humanity, the cherished words and pictures of all we have known and loved." He raised both hands, indicating the spectrum of bound volumes. "In these pages live the noble Hamlet, and Anna Karenina pulling on her gloves of a snowy evening...Gatsby in white flannels, Moby Dick and Ahab's obsession. Even Mark Twain's whole meandering Mississippi."

Reardon moved to a nearby shelf and scanned the titles on the spines. During his eight-month sojourn, the computer library on board the *Balboa* had provided countless hours for studying the classics of literature, the works of great philosophers. He recognized much of what he saw. But here, everything remained in its original printed form. He ran his fingers over the worn but lovingly cared-for leather spines. He found a familiar title and slid a volume from its shelf. He touched its cover, then cracked it open to look at the yellowed pages.

"Melville." Reardon scanned the words, spoke softly, but then choked. "Hope proves a man deathless . . ."

"There is no hope here," Andro said with finality.

"There has to be!" Reardon responded in a sharp and desperate tone. He slammed the book shut.

"There is no future. Only the safe and dear upholstered memories." The mutated man stood back, as if delivering a dirge.

"But this microbe...this extraterrestrial symbiote—you said your psyches, your *minds* were so advanced. Why couldn't you find some cure or some way out? There must have been a way."

"By then it was too late." Andro shook his misshapen head. "The alien microbe spread like wildfire in a tinder-dry field. Our ancestors had no resistance, no experience, no immunities. The only positive cure was in *preventive* medicine. But humankind was too busy going to the moon, too busy clubbing his brothers over the head with his newfound toy, the atom, to anticipate and resist the parasite that would suck out his right to immortality." Andro indicated his own disfigured and pathetic form. "As you can see, even preventive treatments weren't entirely successful."

"I can't believe there's nothing left for us but this—I won't!" Blinking tears from his eyes, Reardon looked down the dizzyingly long shelves of books, of knowledge: a wealth of knowledge, but with no one to learn it. "I think of my family, my friends, their children, their hope for children. And I can't believe it's going to come to this end!"

Suddenly, the starship pilot grew quiet, then more excited. "Wait! If I can find that time warp again...go back through it . . ."

Andro reacted, as if in all his contemplation and philosophical musings he had never considered the possibility. "Back through time?"

Reardon sniffed, then moved back and forth among the books, agitated. "I came here, didn't I? Nobody's proved it's a one-way street. I'll go back, and I'll tell them how they've got to prepare themselves!"

Skeptically, Andro said, "Even if you made it, they would hardly believe you." His uneven eyes were filled with deep storms of emotion. "You barely believe it yourself when you are here seeing and breathing the reality."

"I'll make them believe me." Reardon had gone alone on a dangerous exploration trip for eight months. He was used to accomplishing the impossible, and he wasn't used to saying number

"They'd take you for a fool or a psychotic. They'd say you were hallucinating after your long isolation." Andro's demeanor changed, though, as he saw the sincerity and determination on the pilot's face, and then his ugly visage brightened as he saw another option. "Ah, there is a way—you could take me with you."

Reardon stared at the mutant, realizing the possibility...but he scowled warningly. "Andro, that...time convulsion...we don't know anything about it, how it works, what created it. There's the possibility we won't make it back."

Now their roles had reversed, with Reardon hesitant and Andro eager but with a trace of resignation. "What would it matter? It would be better to die myself than to sit and watch the world die around me."

The distorted man shuffled forward, beseeching, and then became disturbed and self-conscious. "You need not be afraid that I'll frighten your people unnecessarily. I have the ability to change my appearance through hypnotic suggestion, with my mind. It won't be real, but I can *look* perfectly normal. Pleasant, in fact."

Reardon shook his head emphatically. "No, if you're going with me, they must see you as you are." He took a deep breath and grasped Andro's arm. "That's the one thing that will make everyone believe us."

Again, the Starship *Balboa* approached the pulsing convex mirror on the brink of space and time, although now Reardon set his course intentionally. The *Balboa* searched for a vacuum stream toward a milky white vortex that would whirl it like a matchstick toward a gutter drain.

Inside the cockpit, Andro sat motionless and tense, trying to stay out of the way. He did not know how to be of assistance as Reardon hovered over the myriad instruments. The pilot's face was intense, accustomed to doing everything himself.

Andro had nothing to do but ponder and worry. He had spent years immersed in the literature of humankind, inhaling the thoughts and poetry of a lost age. But Andro had learned very little that he could put into practice. While waiting for the last embers of humanity to fade into ash, he had never entertained a hope that he might actually *do* something or *change* things. Now he was afraid, and he felt helpless. He had to put all his trust in Reardon.

Grim-faced, the pilot maneuvered the ship, retracing his original course. Andro could see perspiration form on the young man's brow as he worked in silence, checking and plotting with the delicate instruments.

Reardon spoke out of the corner of his mouth, his teeth gritted. "I'm positive it happened here." He drew a deep breath. "The passage could be a little rough, if we manage to find it at all. I'll set the ship on automatic pilot...in case I'm right." Reardon locked the dials and scowled, leaning back against his crash restraints.

From the pilot's expression, Andro knew that Reardon had begun to doubt his own beliefs, to feel out of his depth. Andro gulped the confined air inside the craft, trying to sound reassuring. "Now we hope."

Focused on the controls, on the search for the time distortion, Reardon finally risked a glance at his mutant companion. "When...when exactly did Cabot discover the microbe? What year? When was the plague unleashed?"

At last, Andro had a problem he knew how to handle. "According to the Archivum records, the crucial experiments occurred some time after 2015. Cabot was a man of about fifty by then, an esteemed researcher whose opinions were trusted. No one thought to question what he was doing. Bertram Cabot, Junior killed the human race when nobody was looking."

Reardon continued to stare directly ahead. "I left home in 2015."

Andro nodded. "So, in your sphere of time, he is probably a middle-aged man with a well-established career already. I hope we arrive soon enough."

"Nobody knows what that man is about to unleash...but we do." Reardon stared out at the starscape thoughtfully, then let out a long sigh. "Think of it, Andro. What course might history have taken if Alexander, Napoleon, or Hitler had never existed?" His gaze was like a pointed gun as he directed it at the mutant passenger. "What if *Bertram Cabot, Junior* had never been born?"

Andro answered with a thin smile, retaining his grim uneasiness. "I will be satisfied if the rest of the world just listens, believes...and prepares. Then maybe all will not be lost."

Without warning, with the ship flying on autopilot, they encountered the rippling wave-front in space, entering from the opposite side on a slightly different course. "It's here!" Reardon gasped.

Andro held onto the arms of his seat. The *Balboa* shivered, passing through the same shining moment that had first sent Reardon far into the blistered future. Andro experienced amazement and terror—but beside him Reardon began to spasm, twisting in the midst of a bodily scream.

"What is it? Reardon, what's wrong?" Andro tried to lean over, but the restraints held him. The universe seemed to resonate, ripping them through the facets of the time stream.

Reardon writhed, his face wracked with horror and disbelief. His lips pulled back from his teeth. "The warp..."

"Reardon, can I help you? How?"

"I'm not...going to make it through!" The young man's eyes rolled with sick fear. "I can't."

Andro reacted with greater fear for the future of humanity than for the pain of a single man. "You must! Oh, please, you must!"

Growing weak, Reardon sank into himself, his skin and bones glowing, changing. "I'm—*dying!*"

"No! The world! What will happen to the world? What will I do?"

The pilot turned to him, and his eyes opened up. The wide pupils seemed to hold a bowl of stars and swirling nebulae. The universe was eating him up from inside. "Go...on... if you can...—"

Andro finally freed his arm from the crash straps and reached over. "You've got to be there with me. They won't believe it if I'm the only one telling them!" When he touched Reardon's sleeve, his fingers passed right through.

The pilot responded in an anguished, desperate whisper. "Then find Cabot...find Cabot...and *kill him if you have to.*"

Andro's eyes widened with horror at the mere suggestion of violence. He had studied the great thoughts of mankind, worshiped the heights of civilization, and abhorred barbarism. He could never commit cold-blooded murder.

Before he could speak, though, Reardon's face froze, then grew luminescent and transparent, and finally shimmered into a dazzling flare of light, like a distant supernova erasing the starship pilot from existence. Reardon disappeared in a residue of white smoke and whispers.

Abandoned in the ship and given an impossible mission, Andro stared in shock. His twisted and scarred head slumped back in grief until the darkness enveloped him. The time-warp shattered his consciousness, and the ship sailed on without his awareness.

In an isolated meadow surrounded by forests, the metal hull of the Starship *Balboa* gleamed in the sun. Grass and shrubs had been scorched from the autopilot's landing, but the birds and the wind restored the area to a semblance of normality.

Andro couldn't believe what he saw from the cockpit. The lushness of the meadow and the fullness of life dampened the lingering shadows of Earth's scarred future.

After staring out the porthole in amazement, Andro opened the airlock door. He leaped onto the grassy ground, breathing the heady perfumes of flowers and evergreens. Even if he'd had a companion with whom to share his impressions, all the words were gone from his mouth. He had never seen such incredible beauty; even the fantasies he had concocted after reading the poetry of past masters could not match this reality. The photographic and holographic records stored on the Archivum shelves did not do justice to the way life had really been in this Golden Age of mankind.

"Ah, how much we have lost." He reeled, trying to orient himself.

Lurching along on bent legs and a twisted back, Andro moved away from the shining hull of the ship. His head pounded and his eyes filled with tears from the sheer colors and freshness around him. He paused again and gazed upward in fascination. Sunlight streamed like molten silver through the knitted canopy of leaves overhead. He reached out with knobby fingers to brush against a few marvelous blades of grass.

He touched the bumpy gray bark of a poplar tree, then bent to the ground and scooped up a handful of fallen leaves. He let the crumbling forms drift through his fingers and flutter to the ground.

In the distance he saw a serene lake through the slatted tree trunks, like an image viewed through an ancient zoetrope projector. A puttering sound came from a motor boat that glided to the marshy shore. Andro followed the sound with his eyes.

Creeping toward the lakeshore and the visitor's boat, Andro paused to stare for a moment at wild narcissus blooms that thrust like fireworks of color through the tall grass. Plucking one, he brought the flower to his smashed and twisted nose, clumsily yet reverently sniffing its sweet fragrance.

Then his face contorted in anguish as his own memories slammed back down around him. All of this would be gone, if Bertram Cabot, Jr. were not stopped. Reardon had died on the flight back, and now Andro was all alone here. His gnarled hand closed on the purple flower, crushing it with pain and love.

He went closer to the edge of the forest by the lake, saw the small boat dragged up against a sandy clearing. Not far inland, he spied the white form of an angel, a blonde-haired woman in a summer dress, carefree in stunning loveliness. She strolled through the thick grass of the arboretum, her eyes intent on the ground. She had a basket and a net, collection jars, and field guides.

Andro watched her, speechless.

The young woman bent down and snatched something from the ground. She knelt, careful to keep her dress clean as she cradled a tiny frog in her hands. As she studied the specimen, her expression became even more beautiful with questions and curiosity; her sense of gentleness and wonder seemed to match Andro's. His chest clenched so tightly he could barely breathe.

She sat down on a rock, still cradling the frog, and then pawed through one of her naturalist books, which she balanced on her knee.

Spellbound, Andro crept through the undergrowth, peering between spindly trunks of small poplars. The shadows formed a camouflage around him. He couldn't stop himself from creeping closer.

As the young woman regarded her specimen, she frowned clinically as she inspected the frog's belly for spot patterns and compared it to diagrams on the pages of the open book.

The calm frog reacted to his presence, though. It squirmed and sprang free of the young woman's gentle grasp. In dismay, she stood up, trying to catch it again—then she spotted Andro's shadowed silhouette among the trees.

With one hesitant step backward, the young woman stared at him transfixed, though she certainly couldn't see his malformed features. Still hiding in the shadows, Andro extended a hand beseechingly toward her, but knew how hideous he must look. He ducked deeper into the gloom.

He was reminded of Mary Shelley's poignant story of the Frankenstein monster, with its great compassion and sensitive intellect, yet still reviled because of its ugliness. "Please don't run," he said in barely a whisper. Regret shattered his heart, but he did not dare speak louder to her.

The frog forgotten, the young woman snatched up her books and raced back toward the boat. She hadn't really seen him, had merely sensed his presence, and had panicked.

Andro waited until he heard the puttering of the boat motor and the rippling splashes of the departing craft. The young woman left the peaceful forests behind. He wondered if he would ever see her again.

Andro emerged from the trees, finding the place where she had sat, studied the impressions her shoes had made in the damp ground. Upon hearing a small croaking sound, he bent over to find the frog she had held, and he caught it. The frog sat in the blistered palm of his hand, puffing its expandable throat.

He cradled it, studying the wonder of another living creature. He thought of Lenny in Steinbeck's great *Of Mice and Men*, lovingly holding his doomed pet mouse and smothering it with affection.

Then Andro noticed the gnarled and taloned fingers of his hand, and the realization of his own abnormality crashed around him like an avalanche. Sadly, he freed the frog. Shuffling forward, Andro came to the still surface of the lake water and bent down. He held his face close to the water and looked at his reflection for a long, long time.

Andro approached the boarding house at the edge of the arboretum like a panther stalking its prey. White siding, black roof, even a porch swing—it reminded him of nostalgia pictures in some of the Archivum books.

He didn't want anyone to see him or hear him, though he had already decided to don his hypnotic disguise. Andro wanted to learn, to see, to discover...and he deeply wanted to fit in with the people here.

The desperate nature of his mission tugged at him, but for the first time in his life Andro felt a serenity and a delight just to experience the moment. He was alive on a healthy Earth, full of living creatures and a vibrant environment. Surely he had earned the right to savor it, just for a moment.

Could this be the innocent world of 2015, the time when young Reardon had departed on his sojourn of exploration? In all of Andro's studies, Earth before the microbe's conquest had been an idyllic place, but this reality outshone even his dreams.

He approached the raised porch, setting a club foot on the weathered boards in front of the Victorian house. Everything about the place screamed *Home*. From the gables, the roof, the windows, he could see that this place had many rooms, perhaps for college students. Apparently the pond and the forest were part of a sprawling university grounds. The door hung open, letting a fresh breeze into the parlor.

Standing on the threshold, Andro peered inside, surprised to see the beautiful golden-haired woman from the lake. She sat alone at a large table, surrounded by her books and diagrams. The rest of the furniture looked ornate, but old, clinging to a modest style from a previous century. Frilly drapes hung in decorative arches over the windows.

The young woman had her back to the door, intent on her studies, though she appeared to be disturbed. Andro wondered if she remained frightened from her glimpse of him through the slatted trees in the forest.

Did he dare let her see him now? She sipped from a china cup of coffee on a saucer.

Andro took a step into the foyer, but the woman still did not notice his presence. He breathed deeply, concentrated, and used the mental powers he possessed. He and the other survivors in the Archivum of records had few advantages or benefits, but they had at least developed the power of manipulating minds.

Projecting a hypnotic suggestion, he came closer. With a gasp the young woman turned around to see him.

But in her eyes, Andro knew she saw only a normal man, a handsome man, cloaked in a disguise of his own mental image. He thought of how he would have liked to appear, if the world had not ended many years before he was born. In her perception, he stood straight instead of with a hunched back; his skin was smooth instead of lumped and bubbled with tumors; he had neat dark hair instead of bushy clumps. And he wore a nice, dark suit rather than a ragged and shapeless robe. Andro retained an otherworldly presence, mantled with a sad, vibrant glory, but he was calm and self-confident now.

The two regarded each other for a brief, awkward moment before the young woman recovered from being startled. Andro smiled warmly at her, the first to speak. "I'm sorry, Miss. I didn't mean to frighten you."

"I just didn't hear you come in," she said clumsily, then extended her slender hand. "My name is Miss Andresson." Her brow furrowed. "I've seen you...somewhere, haven't I?"

Andro covered his reaction with a gentle smile. "Yes. But not the way I wanted you to see me." When she frowned, he changed the subject. "This is a boarding house, isn't it?"

Miss Andresson pushed herself away from the table, leaving her biology books unattended. "Oh, yes. If you're looking for a room, I think there are a couple of vacancies. Mrs. McCluskey, the landlady, will be here in a minute."

"Do you live here yourself?" asked Andro. "I...I suppose that would be a recommendation."

"Yes. A lot of students from the university live here."

Andro admired the furnishings and the paintings, the framed photographs on the mantel, the ticking clock on the wall. "It's quite beautiful, and peaceful."

"I like it. It's old-fashioned."

Thinking of all the books and treasures and keepsakes so lovingly tended in the Archivum of the blasted future, Andro took a deep breath to drive the sadness from his voice. "I think it's good to cherish fine old things. Beauty is always on the edge of being lost."

"Did I hear someone talking about me?" An older woman stepped into the parlor with an impish smile on her statuesque face. "I'm sure I heard the expression 'fine old thing.'" She beamed a welcome at Andro, whom she also viewed as a handsome, cultured man.

Miss Andresson smiled at the landlady. "I think he meant the furniture, Mrs. McCluskey."

Andro stepped forward with a polite nod. "I'm looking for lodging."

"Now don't tell me a respectable-looking gentleman like you wants to plunk himself down in the middle of a day nursery like this?"

With a shy smile at the lovely young lady, Andro said, "I'm sure it isn't as bad as that."

Mrs. McCluskey took his arm, leading him deeper into the parlor. "Not if you don't mind telephone jabberers and the patter of little feet all night long. They think they're big-shot students at the university, but I still consider them children."

"Ah, but I find a great deal of comfort in the sounds of youth."

"Then you'll enjoy it in stereo if you take up residence here! Come along and I'll show you the room I have available." Still hanging on his arm, she moved briskly toward the hallway and a set of steep wooden stairs that led to the second floor. With a glance over his shoulder, Andro smiled at Miss Andresson, then followed the landlady.

Mrs. McCluskey opened a dark wooden door to a small bedroom, gesturing for Andro to enter. "Don't you have any baggage?"

Andro thought fast. "It will come later."

The older woman raised her eyebrows. "You sound like an Englishman."

"Yes. I'm from..." He tried to remember the name of a city he had read about. "... from London."

Mrs. McCluskey's face filled with delight. "Are you going to be a professor at the school?"

"Possibly. I'm an...archaeologist."

The older woman crossed her arms over her chest and laughed out loud. "Well, no wonder you're interested in old things." She paused to let Andro inspect the room.

"This is very nice." In truth, the smell of the sunshine on the bedspread, the furniture polish on the small oak desk, and the fresh-cut flowers in a little vase on the vanity made the tiny chamber into an Eden.

All business, Mrs. McCluskey brushed her hands together. "It's ten dollars a week, Professor—uh, what was your name again?"

"Andro. Professor Andro." Concentrating again on his mental-blurring powers, he put his hand into his pocket and took it out empty. Like a mime, he enacted the opening of a wallet, reached inside, and counted out imaginary bills to Mrs. McCluskey. She took them, convinced that the invisible dollars were real, and folded them in her palm.

"You'll find the house rules on the closet door, Professor. Bathroom's right down the hall."

Andro tensed. He knew the address, knew the place and its history. And he had a mission now. He turned his dark, intent gaze to the landlady. He said carefully, "I was told a young man lives here...a student by the name of Cabot—Bertram Cabot, Junior?"

Mrs. McCluskey brightened. "Oh, yes! Bert *did* live here, but that was about a year ago. He's been in the army since last November."

Shaken by the information, Andro scowled. "In...the army?" His mind raced through all the details he knew of the hated scientist's life, all the dates and places, all the events recorded before the fall of humanity. "He isn't supposed to be in the army."

"Oh, yes. He's at some big base up north. You should have asked Miss Andresson about him. Bert's her boyfriend, fiancé, actually. They're getting married when he gets in on leave this weekend." The landlady bustled with good cheer. "I've always wanted to hold a wedding in this house. Are you an old teacher of his?"

Andro turned away from her, unable to hide his turmoil. "No, but I do want to talk to him about...his future."

Mrs. McCluskey clucked. "Well, from what I understand, Uncle Sam's got him for another year, then he's coming back here to do some post-graduate work. In biology, or something."

Andro narrowed his eyes. "I see. And he'll be here this weekend?"

She tucked the imaginary bills into a pocket in her apron and turned to go. "With bells on."

"I'll talk to him then. Thank you for your kindness."

"Remember, just yell if you need anything. Heaven knows there's enough noise around here already." Mrs. McCluskey retreated from the room, closing the door after her to give him his privacy.

Dropping the hypnotic disguise now that he was alone in the Spartan room, Andro shuffled toward a mirror on the opposite wall. The wallpaper had a pattern of rosebuds and stripes, and the dresser was a dark wood that did not match the oak desk.

Andro's mutant reflection stared back at him, eyes sad, expression complex and inhuman. Breathing hard, he studied his appearance, repulsed by its corrupt features now that he had seen how beautiful a human being—particularly Miss Andresson—could be.

He reached into the tattered folds of his robe and withdrew a weapon, the projectile pistol he had taken from the *Balboa*, the same weapon Reardon had first drawn on him. He held the projectile pistol in his taloned fingers, remembering what he had promised to do, what he owed to the future, and then placed the weapon inside one of the dressing table drawers.

He had to find Bertram Cabot, Jr.

He had no other choice, despite his revulsion toward violence. He had to think of the broad picture, how many of the unborn would be saved by his action. No one could argue with the ethics of the situation. But was murder ever justifiable?

Mrs. McCluskey returned suddenly and unexpectedly. She shoved open the door, bearing a set of clean towels and wash cloths. Before Andro could reassemble his mental disguise, the landlady saw his monstrous reflection in the mirror, the tumescent and discolored horror of his face. She shrieked in terror and stumbled backward into the door jamb, then fainted dead away.

Distraught, Andro lumbered forward, desperate to apologize, to do something to help. He heard footsteps bounding up the stairs, Miss Andresson's voice calling. "Mrs. McCluskey!"

Especially fearful of what the young woman might think, he reassembled his poet-beautiful face, his clothes, his demeanor, then looked up as she ran down the hall, her face anxious and frightened. Andro knelt next to the moaning and groggy form of the landlady. He cradled the old woman's head, lifting her shoulders from the floor.

"What happened?" Miss Andresson knelt beside him.

"She opened the door and then stumbled back against the jamb. She might have hit her head, or maybe she just fainted." He bent down to Mrs. McCluskey, brushing her face. The landlady opened her eyes in terror. As she drew a quick breath to scream again, she saw the normal face of Andro.

"I'd better call her doctor." Miss Andresson turned and made for the telephone at the landing of the stairs.

"What?" Mrs. McCluskey sat up, shaking her head to clear it. "No. No, dear. I'm all right."

"What made you scream?" The young woman turned, still hesitant.

Andro helped Mrs. McCluskey get to her feet. "I thought. . ." The landlady glanced toward him, then patted his arm. "Forgive me, Professor, I feel very foolish."

"Please, don't." He released her, then stood back, ready to dart into the safety of his new room.

Mrs. McCluskey gave a shrill, nervous laugh. "What I saw...it must have been a shadow on the mirror." She stopped smiling as a flicker of fear crossed her expression. "It must have been. Unless you're...not what you seem to be, Professor Andro."

"Few of us are, Mrs. McCluskey."

The landlady recovered her gruff composure and brushed off her house dress. She picked up the fluffy towels that had tumbled onto the floor. "Well, you couldn't be what I thought I saw." She shook her head. "Nobody could."

Night on this new, vibrant Earth was filled with stars. The insects sang their hymns to the darkness. Andro stepped outside on the boarding-house verandah, moving carefully and afraid that everything would crumble into a cruel dream around him. He smelled the dew and the coolness, the scent of pines from the arboretum and water from the lake and polished wood from Mrs. McCluskey's furniture.

After eating, the other boarders had gone back to their rooms, but Andro saw that Miss Andresson had come out here alone to enjoy the evening. She rested one hand on the porch railing, looking up into the deep universe and counting constellations. She ran a brush through her golden hair, stroking with mechanical motions.

Andro could hear young laughter and bright radio music wafting out of the half-open windows above. Nothing, though, could match the wondrous symphonies of crickets and grasshoppers out in the lawn. As he looked at Miss Andresson's profile, how she turned her high-cheekboned face up to the stars, he was amazed to see the same wonder reflected in her expression, as if she too understood the same marvelous things he did.

Handsome again in his hypnotic disguise, Andro moved up beside her and regarded her with admiration. He nodded toward the gliding brush. "When a woman combs her hair, she imitates the motion of the stars."

Miss Andresson smiled self-consciously. "It's just a nervous habit. I was lost in my thoughts."

"Are you disturbed about something, Miss?" He moved a fraction of an inch away, worried that his presence might have made her somehow uneasy.

"I had a hallucination in the woods this afternoon. Horrible. I love to go into the arboretum alone, to do my nature studies and to think. But this time I let my imagination run away from me."

"Yes, it must have been horrible." Andro turned away from her and swallowed hard.

She laughed at his serious expression. "My psych professor would consider it part of the secret nature of my dreams, a premonition of some great trial I'm about to face." After a pause, she raised her eyebrows. "Like getting married, for instance."

Andro felt suddenly on guard and fought to keep the bitterness out of his voice. "Mrs. McCluskey told me. His name is...Bertram Cabot, Junior."

The young lady took a deep breath and continued brushing her hair. Her knuckles turned white as she gripped the rail. "Yes, and he's all the things I ever wanted in a man. Bert doesn't play at life or dream it—he lives it in all its seriousness and pleasure. . . ." With an unexpected frown, she turned to look him in the eye. "Why did you call him Junior?"

"I understand he has been given his father's name."

Curiously, Miss Andresson regarded him. "No, Bert's father's name is Arnold."

Andro scowled, disturbed and confused. Could all of the Archivum's references and materials be so wrong? How could he believe anything if he couldn't even rely on such simple, basic facts as the destroyer's own name? "No, that can't be..."

Her chuckle sounded like running water. "I should certainly know! I've met my fiancé's family plenty of times."

A storm of uneasiness cast shadows across Andro's illusory handsome face. He turned away from her, stared out into the night. His face was drawn and distressed.

She was perplexed by his insistence. "Why does it matter so much, Professor?"

"Bertram Cabot *Senior*, not Junior," Andro said in a whisper, clenching his hands. "I'm too early! A generation too early! This must be...1965?"

"It's 1964, of course." The young woman regarded him, very confused now. "Is something wrong?"

He continued to mumble without hearing her, caught up in despair. "He isn't born. He isn't even born yet!"

Miss Andresson asked in a confused tone as Andro backed away across the porch, "Isn't born? *Who* isn't born yet?"

Andro shook his head and replied softly and deliberately, "Bertram Cabot, Junior."

"Of course, he isn't born. Bert and I won't be married until next week." She let out a quick, nervous giggle. "You'll have to give us a little time!"

With even greater dread, Andro turned back to stare at the young woman as if she had transformed into a poisonous insect. "Miss Andresson, what is your name? Your first name."

"Why...it's Noelle. I thought I'd already told you." She looked at him, the innocent, unknowing, predestined Madonna of life and death—and only Andro knew it.

"Noelle. You will be his mother." He groaned at her. "You...you will be the mother of Bertram Cabot, Junior."

Two days of anguish and indecision. As the wedding approached, Andro knew he had to find some way to stop the inevitable landslide into the future. He stood at the window of his upper bedroom, parted the lacy curtain with his disfigured hand, and stared down to where he could see his enemy on the porch below.

Outside, impatient on the boarding house verandah, the man named Bertram Cabot stood alone in his military uniform. He looked a bright young man, with dark hair, eyes, and eyebrows. His manner conveyed an impression of impulsiveness, perhaps as a mask of insecurity. He would be very possessive toward Noelle—but then, who wouldn't be?

Watching Cabot pace in front of the house, creasing and uncreasing his army cap in his hands, Andro felt a moment of sympathy for him, but that evaporated as soon as he realized what devastation the young man would unwittingly spawn, the Armageddon his son would create. Young Cabot glanced at his watch and heaved a visible sigh, then sat down on the verandah swing.

Andro decided to make his move.

Composing his illusionary appearance again, the mutant refugee hurried down the creaking staircase, hoping Noelle would take just a few minutes longer. Disguised as a dashing, distinguished professor, he stepped out onto the porch. The uniformed young man rocked back and forth on the swing, squinting into the afternoon sunlight.

Hearing the door open, Cabot turned, his face full of impatient hope, which faded as soon as he saw Andro instead of his fiancée. His shoulders slumped, and he turned back, continuing to rock. He gave only a nod of greeting, preoccupied and impatient.

"You are Bertram Cabot?"

The soldier regarded him curiously. "Yes."

"And you're waiting for Noelle?"

Cabot managed a thin smile. "She said she'd be down in a minute.

"Andro stood beside the innocent suitor, observing the neat uniform, the low-rank insignia. "I've often wondered about that quality of mind that enables a soldier to encounter death with firmness, valor, and boldness."

Cabot shrugged, but sat up straighter, looking more soldierly. "It's like stepping on a rattlesnake. You learn to bite first so you don't get bitten."

Andro paused, gathering his nerve. "May I ask you a question?"

Cabot obviously didn't care, though he had no idea who this stranger was. "Of course."

"To save your own child from destruction, would you press a button knowing it would destroy all the children of another land?"

"An enemy land?" Cabot pursed his lips, then grinned in an effort to lighten the conversation. "Are you asking me that as a future father, sir, or as a prospective scientist with a duty toward humanity?"

"I wasn't aware there was a distinction. Don't they have the same ultimate goal?" Andro's voice turned surprisingly cold. "I can see you have an objective and practical mind. Like father, like son."

Cabot looked at him with a puzzled expression. "Did you know my father, sir?"

"No. I didn't...know your father." Andro shuddered, closed his eyes, then opened them again. "You're marrying a very lovely young woman, Mr. Cabot."

"I think so."

"Do you love her?" Andro pressed closer to the porch swing, now animated and intense.

Cabot scowled, on his guard. "Who are you?"

"What does it matter? Will you answer my question?"

"Do I love Noelle?" Defensive. Indignant. "Yes, of course I do."

"Then you must *not* marry her!" Andro raised his voice and grabbed the young man's shoulder. "Please! You must not."

Cabot jerked away and stood. The swing rocked in a chaotic oscillation. "Not marry her? What are you talking about, Mister?"

"You'll destroy her. You haven't seen what I've seen."

Cabot bristled, brushing imaginary lint from his uniform. "Look, maybe who you are doesn't matter, but my private life is none of your business."

Andro trembled, full of desperation. The porch swing hung as a barrier between them. "Oh, but it is my business. To save all the future children of the world, I must somehow prevent one child from being born. It's my only chance."

Cabot had heard quite enough. "I'm not sure I even want to know what you're talking about."

"You must not marry Noelle! Please, everything depends on it. You must believe that."

Cabot came to his own conclusion. "Just how long have you known Noelle?"

"Long enough that I don't want her...harmed." Andro's mind spun, but he could already see he had lost his chance.

"Say, you're that Professor Andro she mentioned on the telephone." Cabot's dark eyes glittered with triumph, as if he had uncovered a conspiracy.

"Yes, yes! You must understand..."

"Oh, I understand enough." Cabot pointed a finger at Andro. "You stay away from her."

"But I'm trying to help her *and* you. And everyone. You must believe that."

Cabot's fists clenched, and he kept his anger and violence under control with only the greatest effort. "Who do you think you're kidding?"

Andro clutched his hands, aching and pleading. "If I could only make you understand that your innocence is your only crime, that knowing no evil, you can suspect none."

Cabot became livid. "I might wear this military uniform, Professor Andro, but I'm not stupid and I'm not uneducated. I can do without the philosophical snow-job."

Filled with anguish at the almost certain need for eventual violence, Andro could not keep the threat inside of him. "If you try to marry her, I'll have no choice."

Cabot stepped forward, his shoulders squared, his face ruddy with a threat of his own. "You keep away from her, or *I* won't have any choice!"

Just then, Noelle emerged from the house in a clean white dress, smiling. She saw the two men glaring at each other and hesitated for a heartbeat, the happy expression frozen on her face.

Cabot moved quickly to Noelle's side, taking her arm. "Come on, let's go." He hurried her down the porch stairs and to the gravel driveway where his car waited. Noelle glanced over her shoulder in confusion back at Andro. He could tell by her reaction that he mystified, compelled, and distressed her...as if she'd never had another man look at her the way Andro did.

After they had gone away, roaring off with a spray of gravel from Cabot's whitewall tires, Andro allowed the illusion to vanish, and he turned into a monster again.

During their courtship, Noelle had loved to walk with Bert along the paths in the arboretum, smelling the evergreens and listening to the birds. They had both taken classes in biology and learned from university naturalists on day hikes, but when they were together in the forest, they chided each other whenever they tried to identify specimens or studied with a scientific rather than a romantic eye. A walk in the woods was their special time, when they could remain absorbed in their relationship.

Now, though, she sensed that Bert was troubled over the strange quarrel he'd had with Professor Andro.

Leaving the boarding house tense and unsettled, the two of them had found their quiet and private spot, and Noelle lay in the cool grass. With a worried frown, she glanced at her fiancé, who sat some distance away in his neat army uniform...but he might as well have been sitting behind a solid wall. He pulled up his knees, and his eyes shone bright with resentment toward Andro.

Noelle offered a tentative smile, trying to break the ice. "So, we've had our first argument." She paused, then finished, "Over an outsider."

Bert said nothing, but rose on stiff legs and looked off into the forest shadows, as if afraid of discovering an eavesdropper. She remembered how they had relaxed together, enjoyed every moment of their companionship, especially here. And now Bert looked as if he wanted to hurry away. She didn't know how she could recapture the lazy, contented feeling. She sat up, adjusting her dress in the grass. "Do you have to leave?"

"I have to go to the school." Cabot looked uncertain, making up excuses. "I, uh, have to arrange my post-grad courses for next year...when I get out of the service. Now's the best time to establish the curriculum I want."

Noelle looked into the sky, watching clouds like finger paintings across the blue background. "Next year. . . Just think, by then we'll have been married a whole year."

Now he tentatively broached the subject that held him in such anxiety. His sharp eyes caught her until she looked away. "I'll be away in the army, Noelle. You still feel...you don't want to wait until I come back? To get married, I mean?"

Noelle smiled with as much reassurance as she could muster. She had expected him to have last-minute doubts, of course...but she hadn't expected them to trouble her so much. "Oh, Bert—Mrs. McCluskey would be devastated. She's had the parlor drapes cleaned and the rug shampooed. She's always wanted a wedding in her house."

He leaned over to give her a peck on the cheek. Bert had delved into the subject as much as he dared. "All right. I'll try to hurry back from the school. You never know how much time it takes to fill out all those forms."

He turned to leave her there alone, not even offering to take her arm and walk her back to the boarding house. Noelle wanted to call after him, but restrained herself. Instead, she watched Bert push boughs out of his way and make his own path through the woods. She continued to watch the silent trees long after he had left.

Then, from the other side of the clearing, Professor Andro came into view. Noelle turned and saw him, her eyes widening, but she said nothing. Andro spoke after a moment of silence, "I followed you."

"I know." When he raised his eyebrows in question, she flushed with embarrassment. "Even with the trees all around us, I could feel you...somewhere near."

Andro looked down at where she sat on the grass, her feet tucked under her. His expression ached for her. "May I sit close to you?"

Uncertain, Noelle looked up at him without smiling, her thoughts scrambled. What was she doing? For days now, her thoughts had been muddled whenever this strange man came near to her. She felt the tangible warmth of his presence, which disturbed her. Noelle looked away from him and said nothing.

Without further invitation, Andro crouched beside her, awkward and uncomfortable. He tried to make his voice work, as if he was bursting with things to say to her, but couldn't force a single one of them out of his mouth.

An aimless butterfly drifted close to them. Noelle tried to grasp it in her palm, but failed. "Did you know that butterflies sleep?"

Andro said with far too much interest. "Do they?"

"Like a baby." Noelle laughed as she found a safe topic of conversation. " When there's an eclipse, almost the whole insect population goes to sleep."

Andro's face held a dreamy smile. "The insects I've seen, since I came to this place...they all seem so sure of themselves." He looked at the ground, as if the blades of grass held an entire universe.

"I was thinking about you, Professor. Bert was with me earlier, and I know that you two exchanged words...about me." Noelle touched Andro's arm. "I don't understand you. You don't seem like a professor.

You're more like a prince...a cheated nobleman who's been imprisoned for a long time on a desolate island. Sad, but still gallant."

Andro moved even closer toward Noelle. "I'm glad you think of me that way."

Noelle admired his face. "You must be very noble." Then, embarrassed at the intensity of his piercing eyes, she plucked a delicate meadow flower from the ground. "When I finish with college, I'm going to be a naturalist, a female Thoreau. That's why I have such a consuming sense of wonder about such things as the sleeping habits of butterflies."

Andro smiled, making it intensely obvious how much he appreciated her warmth and intelligence as well as her beauty. Noelle watched him, fascinated. "Tell me who you are."

Andro looked at her, at her wide eyes, and then down to her lips. He leaned forward and kissed her gently, as if he wanted to fall headfirst into her soul. The kiss lingered a moment, and Noelle's mind reeled—she'd never been kissed that way before, not with such intensity, or such wonderment. Then she pulled away, suddenly tumbling back to her senses. Noelle scrambled to her feet.

Andro got up beside her, held her, and whispered intensely. "Noelle, I don't know how to tell you, to make you understand, but you must love me. It's the only chance."

Shaken, Noelle started to pull away. She shook her head to barricade herself from the temptation, from the choices. "Don't say anymore, Professor Andro, please."

Now his intensity became a different thing entirely. "I can't let you marry him!"

Noelle clutched her chest, where the ache had become physical. She stumbled toward the trees. "I've got to—please let me go."

His eyes wild with desperation as much as sorrow, Andro clasped his hands as he beseeched her. "Listen to me, Noelle. Listen to me. Together you and I can save Eternity."

But she pulled away from him and sprinted through the woods. After she had run out of sight of the meadow, she collided with Bertram Cabot as he dashed back toward where he had left her. He must have heard their raised voices. His face was filled with concern, his eyes narrowed, and his body tense, ready to take action.

"I heard you talking, the shouts ..." He regarded her disturbed face, then flushed as Professor Andro rushed through the trees after her. Bert's voice became hard and angry, without love and allowing no argument. "Go to the house, Noelle. I'll catch up with you."

Noelle saw the two men and hoped for understanding and tolerance. "Bert, please..."

He didn't want to hear it. "Go on. Do as I tell you."

Noelle hesitated, but her fiancé urged her away, not caring about her feelings at all, just his own male pride. Swallowing hard and not knowing what she wanted to happen, she turned and moved obediently off through the woods, but stopped close enough to hear.

Slow and deliberate, his face dark and threatening, Bert moved toward Andro until they stood face to face, as if frozen there. For a moment, her fiancé clearly didn't know what to say.

"Noelle and I are going to be married, sir."

Andro replied quiet and level, "Not if I can help it."

"You can't help it, or stop it."

"I *have* to stop it. I would try anything to stop it." To Andro, the problem seemed to carry a universal importance, not merely the choice of one heart over another. The professor hardened as Noelle watched through the trees, resigned to a disagreeable task. "I must no longer concern myself with your innocence any longer, Bertram Cabot. I can think of only one thing—the children of all the world."

As he spoke Andro became wracked with the torment and frustration of his task, while Bert seemed simply incensed and confused. "You're out of your mind, Professor. You don't make sense, but you'd better leave Noelle alone."

Lurching forward with a surprising manifestation of brute strength, Andro grabbed the coat lapels of Bert's army uniform. He shook the astonished younger man like a leaf in the wind. "I don't want to kill you, but I will. You—or her. I must. I *must!*"

Noelle was about to cry out, but suddenly Andro changed into a different person, all of his violence draining away into shame as he became aware of his brutality. The emotion had consumed him, and he seemed to crumple inside. Stepping backward, Andro let go of the terrified, shocked Bertram Cabot who seemed astounded that the other man had preempted his indignant anger.

From her hidden observation spot, Noelle's heart went out to Andro as he turned away from the man in abject frustration. Bert recovered his indignance, glared at Andro, then stalked swiftly off through the woods, looking for her.

Still shaking in the place where the confrontation had occurred, Andro watched Cabot go, distraught. Then, he sank pathetically down to the soft grass. With his bare hands, he dug into the tender shoots of grass and clutched them. Just before she joined Bert, Noelle thought she saw Andro's hand turn into the lumpy claw of a beast in horrible contrast to the beauty of the ground.

Then the illusion went away, and Noelle decided it must have been her imagination.

In the parlor of the boarding house the organist played the traditional wedding march. Andro could hear the music even through his desperately shut door. Mrs. McCluskey had spent days decorating her big house, arranging flowers, hanging crepe, borrowing chairs for the audience. The guests had been arriving all morning, and Andro had hidden in his room. He huddled on the bed, suffocating in despair. Every joyous noise was a reminder to him. He locked the door.

Trim and impressive in his army uniform, Bertram Cabot had arrived with his military friends, the best man and his groomsmen. The bridesmaids wore dresses that rustled like moths' wings whenever they moved. All of them carried bouquets, all wore pearl necklaces. And Noelle was lovelier than every single one.

Andro had promised himself he would not sob. But now the terrible decision bore down upon him. He was a thinker, a man who loved poetry and philosophy and artwork, and yet all of his plans had failed. He had used logic, or passion, but now violence might be the only way he could possibly save the future.

The strains of organ music drifted up to the second floor, and he heard the talking guests, the witnesses. All those people gathered down in the parlor would likely be dead by the time the ambitious son of Bertram Cabot and Noelle Andresson reached the age where he performed his devil's work with the extraterrestrial microbe, by the time he unleashed extinction upon helpless humanity.

None of those people down there in Mrs. McCluskey's front room could comprehend the sacrifice that had to be made. No matter what the cost.

Andro squeezed his milky eyes shut, and he clenched his twisted body so hard that he trembled. A tear crept out from between his eyelids.

On top of the dressing table lay the projectile weapon he had taken from Captain Reardon. The *Balboa* scout ship still rested in an isolated meadow deep in the arboretum, a perfectly functional craft. Afterward, after the planned assassination and his own damnation, Andro might even manage to get away—if he decided he had anything to live for after all.

As the wedding march continued, Andro's lumpy hand grasped the gun. He stared at his hideous reflection in the bureau mirror, and emotions welled up inside of him. In a blur of motion, he hurled the weapon at his monstrous visage, unable to bear the sight, unable to stand the weight of his responsibility.

The mirror shattered in a fountain of glass. Some of the jagged slivers caught fragments of his reflection. The distant wedding march filtered through from downstairs, falling into silence as the actual ceremony began.

The twisted and mutated Andro crept down the wooden stairs, gripping the rail with one clawed hand to steady himself. He reeled, his eyes seeing red from the fiery determination in his mind, but everything around him turned black with despair. Was even the future of the human race worth all this anguish? How could one man suffer so much?

The air was laden with the perfume of lilies, roses, and honeysuckle. Andro clutched the railing in one hand, the weapon in his other, as he stared out into the parlor tableau in front of him.

Noelle's wedding was simple and full of light, pure and lovely, just the type of ceremony that suited a woman like her. Andro could barely breathe around the lump in his throat.

Noelle stood mantled in sheer lace, achingly white in the sunlight that poured through the garden windows. She looked like a porcelain doll, a vision of loveliness, but she did not appear to be happy or filled with joy, as a woman on her wedding day should have looked. Instead, she stood beside Cabot, fixing her eyes on the thin minister with gray hair. The gaunt man stood straight-backed as he read from a thick, dark volume in his outstretched hand.

Andro knew the words encompassed a solemn ceremony, but the minister mumbled his recital as if he had done it too many times before. As if it meant nothing to him. Andro didn't want to hear the words anyway.

Behind and around Noelle and Cabot stood a preening Mrs. McCluskey and members of the wedding party, companions in formal military dress, as well as two little girls and two boys, each overdressed and uncomfortable in the flower-bedecked room. Apart from the bored minister, the rest of them faced away from the stairway, unaware of his presence—which was a blessing, because at the moment his thoughts were in such turmoil that Andro could not maintain his hypnotic illusion of a dashing, *normal* man.

As the ceremony progressed, Noelle seemed to grow sadder, trapped and hopeless until slowly she became aware of his presence, a flicker of instinct that compelled her to turn and look behind her. Her gaze locked onto Andro's with a jolt of imagined electricity.

He started, ready to run as he realized he had not formed his disguise yet—he must appear hideous to her—but Noelle seemed to see him as normal, handsome and forlorn as he stared at her from the stairway.

When the minister's voice rose, though, a lilting monotone that ended in a question, she forced herself to turn back and attend to the wedding. Before she looked away, Andro saw tears rising in her eyes. Noelle fought back the emotions, though. He could not imagine that she would flee the parlor and run away from the wedding. She didn't know how much was at stake.

Then Andro could finally hear the minister. "And if there be anyone here who maintains that this man and this woman should not be united in holy matrimony, let him speak now or forever hold his peace."

Seeing his opportunity, Andro brought up his leprous, twisted arm with Reardon's projectile weapon clutched in his fingers. He leveled it purposefully at Cabot's back. With a growl deep in the bottom of his throat, he felt an overwhelming anger at this man...and also a despair at what he himself had been driven to do.

Andro had never harmed a living creature in his life.

His arm began to tremble uncontrollably as he tried to force himself to pull the trigger. Seeing the man, the other people, the flowers, the little children, he could not force his muscles to obey his wishes. He *could not kill*.

Mrs. McCluskey turned and glanced into the hallway. She saw him, then shrank back, reacting with alarm. Andro had managed to summon enough strength to raise his mask of illusion, but he could not make the weapon disappear from the old woman's eyes.

"Look out!" she yelled.

While Noelle stood transfixed, two groomsmen in military uniform rushed forward without hesitation. Others in the audience screamed and scrambled for cover, seeing the strange gun. Andro still couldn't fire. The parlor turned into bedlam, with flower vases knocked over; one of the framed paintings fell from the wall.

The groomsmen tackled Andro on the stairs, trying to wrest the weapon from his hand. Andro attempted to pull away from the young men, making wordless sounds.

After checking that she was safe, Cabot left Noelle's side and rushed toward Andro. He knocked the groomsmen away so he could get closer. Andro struggled furiously, and Cabot moved in, wrestling to hold him. He raised his fist and smashed it into Andro's face.

Knocked backward, Andro fell into the wall, disoriented and nearly unconscious. The other men surged forward, but they froze in shock as Andro transformed in front of them. He shed his handsome appearance in favor of his true shape, his scarred and mutated hulk clad in a tattered robe, stained with the despair of a dying race.

The groomsmen staggered back, and Cabot looked down at the pathetic man with a face filled with nausea.

Noelle remained where she was, still clutching her bouquet, veil tossed away from her eyes, as she watched, incapable of stopping anything. Andro struggled to get up, stared at her in despair with one squinting, tumorous eye—but he saw no revulsion or horror or fear in her face. She seemed to see him still in the same way she always had.

Others in the room, however, screamed with great gusto.

Several people ran out of the house. Mrs. McCluskey backed against a wallpapered archway, terrified to revisit the nightmarish vision that had startled her on the day Andro had rented his room.

As the others reacted in horror and confusion, Andro recovered a few shreds of self-composure. He climbed to his feet, taloned hand to his head, in pain. Now he didn't bother with the illusion, but instead he lurched forward, just trying to get away. As he searched the screaming people for a way out of the house, his gaze fell upon Noelle.

He tried to hide his face, to duck away, to keep her from seeing his true shape. But she didn't cry out like all the others.

Like a wounded beast, he lumbered out of the house amid more panic as the wedding guests fled. He dashed toward the cover of the thick forest, knowing of no place else he could go.

Behind him, from the open porch door, a stricken Noelle watched Andro rush out of the house. She seemed unable to comprehend the panic of the others. After a moment of hesitation, she set off in a run after him, gathering up her lacy white wedding dress and dashing through the thick grass and weeds.

From the porch, outraged at the disaster, Cabot shouted at the top of his lungs. "Noelle!"

But she did not stop.

After running what seemed like aimless miles, far from anyone who had seen him at the ruined wedding, Andro slumped beside a tree. He felt the rough bark against his blistered skin as he fought back sobs, head bent forward. He felt as devastated as his world had been.

"Andro!" Noelle's voice cut like birdsong through the trees. "Andro!"

He shrank away, trying to hide his grotesque appearance. He didn't think he had the heart or the energy to maintain the lie. He hoped she wouldn't find him, couldn't understand why she had come this far. He had destroyed everything, accomplished nothing. The future was still doomed. But Noelle seemed to have a connection with him, some instinct that kept bringing them together.

Andro hauled himself to his feet, but huddled against the tree trunk. He ducked to one side, shielding himself, but then he decided he would not hide any more. He had already lost his chance to prevent the disaster, had ruined the fate of mankind as sure as if he had created the extraterrestrial microbe himself.

And he had also lost any chance with Noelle. He turned, lifted his tragic eyes, and stepped out into the open, surrendering just as Noelle broke through the trees. She stopped as she saw him.

Andro did not use his mind powers, made no effort to hide his normal appearance. He felt he owed that much to Noelle at least. He had to let her see his true, misshapen self.

Instead of shrinking back in disgust, though, Noelle looked at Andro as she always had. She stepped forward, holding the hem of her wedding dress up from the tall weeds. Her actions made her tentative and afraid, but not repulsed. "Andro -?"

Andro couldn't bear to have her look at him. He responded in a croak. "Go away, Noelle—please, go away."

"They hurt you. Back there, I'm sorry -"

"I'm all right." He continued, confused and disturbed, "How could you come here, after what I did? After what you saw?"

"I wanted to talk to you. I think...I think we both have a lot to say to each other."

"But you saw me. Weren't you frightened, like the others?"

Noelle shook her head. "All men have their moments of violence, Andro. In some, it's a part of their nature, with them forever. In others, the violence passes. I saw yours pass."

He still couldn't believe it. "But didn't you look at my face? The change? The others saw how ugly I am. I know...I lost control."

Noelle tugged away her veil and held it in her hand. Andro thought she looked even more like an angel. "I didn't see anything, Andro, except that you just couldn't bear to have me marry him. And you tried to stop it."

Andro returned her stare with a blank look of his own, then realized that somehow she did not see his bestial appearance. Even now. Somehow, Noelle envisioned only what she wanted to see. "You haven't looked upon what I really am."

"Then tell me, Andro...tell me what you really are." Her face carried a bit of a bemused smile.

Andro forced out the word, filled with anguish. "Ugly."

Noelle shook her head. "There's no ugliness in you, Andro. I know there isn't."

"Not *inside* me, Noelle—not in my heart or my soul."

She reached out to touch him, running her fingers along his cheek, as if she didn't feel the scars, the leprous discolorations, the twists of flesh. "Not your face, either."

"This face...it's a suggestion, just a hypnotic mask to cover a visage as corrupted as the world in which I was born. I am that horrible hallucination you saw in the woods on my first day. You screamed then. I am the great trial you were about to face." His shoulders shuddered with half-contained sobs. "But it's all over, Noelle. Go back to your wedding. Fix up what you can, live your life, and don't worry about the future."

She put her hands on her hips. "There isn't going to be any wedding, Andro. I don't love him. I don't think I ever really did."

Andro couldn't allow himself to hope, though. "Oh, you'll still marry him, eventually. No matter what you tell yourself today. I know now that you can't change things that are meant to be." After a beat, Andro took a ponderous step away, heading toward the trees again. The starship was back there, somewhere. "I have to leave, Noelle—I'm going back to where I belong."

Disturbed, near panic, Noelle ran after him. "Andro!" She clutched his arm. "Take me with you."

Andro spun around, startled. "No, Noelle. No! It isn't possible."

Sunlight gleamed down on them like a luminous shower, and the thick evergreens rustled together, whispering secrets. Noelle moved to Andro and touched him again. Her face radiated a curious need for him. "Please, it's *you* I love, Andro. I don't know how it happened or why, and I don't care. I only know that I want you, need you. I was fooling myself with Bert."

Andro cringed at her touch, ashamed to see that he had caused such raw emotion. "Oh, Noelle, I didn't mean for you to fall in love with me. That was never my intention."

"Didn't you mean to kiss me, to touch me?" She refused to move away.

"Yes, but I couldn't help myself."

She pressed him, her eyes intense. "It must have meant something to you, Andro. I know it did. I saw you on the stairs during the wedding and I saw you arguing with Bert out in the forest. I know you love me."

Andro turned away, agonized. He had never expected this young woman to feel anything for him. It was more than he had possibly hoped for. "I *can't* love you—and you must not love me. Everything is already lost."

Noelle, disturbed and confused, clutched his sleeve. She didn't seem to feel the ragged, rough fabric from a devastated future. "Why? Why?"

"Because there is no hope for us. Because we can't change destiny. I already know what the future holds...and it is dead. There's no hope left for tomorrow."

Noelle regarded him with sad disbelief, then she started to move off, desolate and rejected. Andro could not stop himself from moving back to her. He held her against him. "Noelle, please try to understand."

"I can't. I don't understand you, what you mean or what you want." Her now-stained wedding dress rustled in the grass.

Andro tilted her head to look into his eyes. "Noelle, look at me. Just *look* at me, and you'll see."

With a glimmer of fear, she did gaze into his eyes, deeper and deeper, and now he used his strange mental powers to show her the images within his mind. Noelle plunged into a cold sea of memory in the dark of Andro's past, a succession of images in time and space. He watched her react with amazement, then fear and disbelief.

Far within his deep eyes, the pupils became the receptacle of swirling impressions—space, infinity, destiny. "There *are* travelers in time," he said with somber intensity. There are people in tomorrow's cities, living, breathing strangers whom you never see, but they are still there just the same."

Andro's bottomless eyes became a kaleidoscope of human activity, cities not so terribly different from these places of 1964: people scurried down similar streets, running from something. Then the buildings and roads became deserted and lonely, hollow and inhuman.

"But instead of the glorious future all men envision, there is only a dark and empty road that leads to misery and mourning."

As Noelle stared, transfixed, she saw an emaciated and burned landscape, a buried church steeple, the weird monolith monument that recorded the last days of humanity.

"This is the world from which I came, Noelle—the world of the future—a world that *you* will help make, you and your son, Bertram Cabot, Junior."

He turned away, breaking the hypnotic connection between them. "I wanted to change it. I tried! Do you realize what I had to do? I had to prevent you from bearing a child, *Cabot's child,* the man who is destined to grow up and be the catalyst for the world's end." Noelle stared at Andro, speechless in disbelief. "The truth is in my eyes, Noelle."

She searched his miserable face, distraught, but then she sank against him. She pressed her face against the tattered robe on his chest. "Is...that all I meant to you, a means to an end? A way to save the future?"

Andro stiffened. "No, Noelle. You can see the answer to that in my eyes, too."

"Then you've served your purpose. I'll never have that child. The future will be different after all."

Andro shook his head, unconvinced but seeing no way out. "No, next year or perhaps later, you'll find Bert again, or he'll find you. You'll marry him, and you'll have that child. It's destiny, unless you die, right now, or..."

"Or unless I go with you!" She pulled away, excited. "You *can* change destiny, Andro. Take me, keep me...don't let me and Bert find each other again."

As Andro stared down at her, his face opened with wonder as a new opportunity appeared before him. "Is it possible? We could create another future, you and I—a better world."

For the first time in days, Andro's hope returned. Finally, with a building surge of release, they kissed.

Still dressed in their wedding suits and formal dress uniforms, the groomsmen armed themselves and marched out through the dense arboretum. Cabot himself held the futuristic projectile weapon Andro had dropped while the other men carried rifles taken from their own trucks and one from a cabinet in Mrs. McCluskey's den.

Grim-faced, Cabot led them. He was blinded with fury toward the insane stranger who had tried to shoot him on his own wedding day, the man who had stolen his fiancée, who had ranted strange delusions and made bizarre threats. Cabot was incensed at what Andro had done to him...and of course he was worried about Noelle, too. Andro had worked some sort of spell over her and Cabot was afraid for his wife-to-be.

How could one man ruin so many people's lives? Cabot's future had been set on a wide and straight path until now. He meant to find Andro and take Noelle back, by force if necessary. The professor had attempted to kill him, after all—everyone had seen it. Cabot convinced himself that whatever happened during the pursuit would be...well, would be self-defense.

Bertram Cabot knew what his future should hold, and he would allow nothing to divert him from that. Holding the projectile weapon, hoping that it would work, he stalked forward with his companions, following the path Noelle had taken.

Such a joyous smile felt strange on his face. Andro took Noelle's hand and led her deeper into the forest, toward where the *Balboa* had landed. He had studied the ship's controls, knew well enough how to operate the automatic pilot. They could get away from here, into a future that would be brand new for both of them.

"I wonder what it'll be like...where we're going?" Noelle strolled beside him, no urgency now, just a contented eagerness. "Even if it's still ugly, I won't care, Andro. I'll be with you."

Andro shook his head, striding along with a new bounce to his step. "No, it won't be ugly. We're changing that. It'll probably be beautiful, fresh and different—even more beautiful than this."

Noelle laughed with a sound brighter than wedding bells. "The future usually is."

Andro looked up, studied the canopy of branches. "It's not far now—just through those trees and into a clearing."

Then, with a crashing sound, Cabot and his groomsmen charged through the bushes, making their own path. Seeing the two of them, Cabot shouted. "Noelle! Get away from him." He extended the projectile weapon, not sure how to work the trigger control, and unexpectedly the gun went off with a loud, whining blast.

Projectiles struck the tree trunk next to Noelle and Andro, splintering great smoking chunks in all directions. The other men reacted, also bringing up their rifles and shotguns.

Biting back an outcry, Andro grabbed Noelle and dragged her to one side, dashing into the thicker trees. One of the keyed-up groomsmen fired another loud, cracking round into the woods.

Noelle and Andro ran together. He held her arm, helping her along. In her wedding gown and formal shoes, she had trouble keeping up on the rough terrain. Branches and brambles clutched at her white lace. The flowing veil drifted out of her hand, snagged on a bush and remained behind.

Not far to the rear, the men shouted. Andro could hear Cabot bellowing for them to stop shooting.

Andro helped her climb a rise, pushing aside weeds and scrub brush. There in front of them they saw the waiting scout ship, still gleaming in the meadow sunlight, as if eager to reach toward the sky. "There! We've got to get inside, Noelle. Hurry!" They sprinted across the clearing, rushing toward the ladder.

Behind them, scrambling and puffing through the underbrush, the four men climbed the hillside, holding their rifles in hot pursuit of their quarry. Cabot didn't want anyone to hurt Noelle but if they should happen to shoot Andro, he wouldn't be too upset.

Like a ghost trapped on a low branch, Noelle's wedding veil fluttered in the faint breeze. Cabot snatched the gauzy white cloth, then squeezed it in his hand. His face was red and streaked with sweat, but he refused to allow any tears to shine in his eye. He ran onward with renewed anger.

In the clearing, Andro helped Noelle climb the access ladder of the Starship *Balboa*. He looked behind him, hearing the loud footsteps of the pursuers. In frustration, Noelle kicked off her shoes and climbed barefoot, reaching the hatch and tumbling inside.

The men burst into the clearing. With a shout, one man pointed his rifle and fired. The shot sang against the hull, leaving a white starburst where it had ricocheted on the metal. Cabot arrived, along with the remaining groomsmen, all of them raising their weapons.

Andro dove inside the ship, and Noelle helped him to swing the hatch shut just as gunfire erupted, battering like a hailstorm against the hull.

Outside, Cabot and his companions raced toward the craft. Their momentum kept them moving despite their amazement and confusion at seeing a spacecraft in the middle of the university arboretum. As he ran, Cabot continued to clutch the bridal veil Noelle had dropped.

Inside, after they had strapped themselves into their seats, Andro worked the controls. He had watched Reardon, knew the basic principles of how the *Balboa* operated. He refused to let doubts paralyze him, now that he had a bright hope at last. Noelle sank back into the seat, exhausted.

Through the ship's front ports, Andro watched Cabot and the groomsmen stumble to a halt, shielding their faces as the rockets fired. A loud roar filled the air, blasting tree branches and grasses.

The pursuers staggered back in awe and fear. Cabot opened and closed his mouth, shouting something. Andro thought it must have been Noelle's name. Then they left the ground behind as the ship leaped into the air, escaping from gravity, and Earth, and the past.

Once again forging a path through the bright wilderness of stars and infinity, the *Balboa* left Earth orbit and headed outward. After tense moments in which Andro tried to reassure Noelle--though he clearly had no such confidence himself--they waited, trusting the ship's autopilot.

And finally they saw in front of their course, poised like a swimming silver fish, the pulsing convex mirror on the brink of space and time. "That is my doorway home," Andro said to her, looking across at the second seat. "Or to a home I've never seen."

"A new home for the two of us," Noelle said. She reached over to lock her hand in his. She had passed beyond fear and regrets now, and simply looked forward to seeing the new future Andro would show her. He returned her grasp with a fervor of his own.

Then the *Balboa* entered the time convulsion for the third time, questing for the right destination, an altered time stream. They would go to a future without the horrible plague, without the end of humanity, without Bertram Cabot, Junior.

Inside, as the walls shimmered and reality changed, the two clutched each other tightly. The air filled with a high-pitched whine of deceleration and distortion. The universe seemed to shudder, convulse. Noelle didn't understand it, and she turned to Andro for reassurance. Something seemed...*wrong*.

The light in the air grew brighter, and Noelle felt Andro's grasp fading, becoming more indistinct. She squeezed, pressing tighter to retain her grip, but Andro was...going away from her.

His face creased with anguish and dismay, transfixed, as if nailed to a particular point in time that no longer existed.

"Andro! What is it—what's wrong?" Noelle strained against the force of increasing gravity, trying to get nearer to Andro.

He became white and drawn, as if in utter agony. "Something...is happening to me...ever since we entered the distortion." He cried out, his body twisting and shuddering. Then his face filled with absolute horror as he came to a realization. "Noelle! I didn't think. Oh, no!"

Panicked now, Noelle detached her crash straps so she could move closer to him. "Andro, what is it? Please tell me! Didn't we change the future?"

Andro was wracked and still growing weaker as the pain stripped away his very soul. "Listen to me, Noelle. We've created a new future...a different future into which... *I was never born!*"

She stared stricken at Andro, her eyes huge with shock and disbelief.

He could barely gasp out the words. "If you'd married him, had his child...my world would have come to pass. But this way...we've changed it all...all of it." His entire body went bright for a moment, as the air blanched white. His last words were like a resonance on the heartstrings of the universe itself. "*And I was never born!*"

Before Noelle could go to him, Andro disappeared, flickering and fading into nothingness...as if he had never existed.

Noelle's face froze in horror. Alone in the spaceship, she turned her eyes away from the empty seat, unable to bear the sight of the unoccupied space. Andro was gone, as if he'd never been there...as if he'd never existed. A scream surged out of her throat, a cry like a wounded animal.

"Andro, Andro, Andro..."

She wept into the emptiness as she drifted into the uncharted future, all by herself.

NOTE: As a matter of historical interest, I have added the last two pages of the shooting script—an epilogue never included in the actual episode. As a coda to the tragedy of Noelle Andresson, it makes the resolution a bit more uplifting, but in my opinion takes away some of the emotional punch.

Introduction to Memories On Ice

Since "The Human Factor" episode was first broadcast on *OUTER LIMITS*—final script, May 1963—a lot has changed in the world.

In those days, families actually spent their vacation money building air-raid shelters instead of going to Yellowstone. We've gone from the Cuban Missile Crisis and Kruschev banging his shoe on the table and the everyday terror of imminent nuclear Armageddon to the total downfall of the Soviet Union and the end of Communism as a global threat to freedom. The scary monster in the closet turned out to be a shadowy clothes draped lopsided on a hanger.

I thought of the people on Point Tabu, the Greenland warning station, and how they had devoted their lives to doing anything and everything to protect the free world. What would have happened to the empty, abandoned base over thirty-five years later? What, exactly, would poor Private Gordon's wife and son have been told about the accident on the Hecla Isthmus?

It's only been a few decades, but the very foundations of reality have changed. How would a 1963 man rooted in the Cold War, a paranoid man, react to the world of today? Would he cope, would he rejoice...or would he disbelieve? Does a constant threat against one's deeply held beliefs make one forget the core of those beliefs?

Is *victory* always the goal of a long conflict?

Memories On Ice

T HE SUN NEVER ROSE HIGH IN THE FROZEN SKY, as if afraid to peek above the Arctic horizon. Gray-locked clouds hammered down with the oppression of utter *cold*.

The titanium-armored prow of the modern ice-breaker *Polaris* crashed toward the coast of northern Greenland. Weather or no weather, the ship had a timetable to keep. Blue-white chunks of ice broke away like plaster as the massive ship forced its way to shore, splitting the crusted skin on an ocean that waited for spring.

Standing on the prow of the frost-covered ship, Andrew Gordon gripped the rail with mittened hands. He squinted into the winter murk. The grinding, squeaking sounds against the hull were like fingernails on a chalkboard. The frigid air wanted to freeze his eyeballs solid, cover the insides of his lungs with a layer of frost.

Pale-faced, an American researcher who had pulled himself up by his own bootstraps to be *here*, *now*, Andrew was not used environments such as this. But his father had lived here when this place had been a military base—and Private Gordon had also died here. Andrew could tolerate the conditions for now.

The white air and fog prevented him from seeing any remnants of buildings on the Greenland shore. Point Tabu. The U.S. Army research and defense station had been abandoned decades before, at a time of incredible world tension and paranoia. Andrew hoped the Arctic deep freeze had preserved everything from that time. *Everything*. He had no other way to find the answers he'd needed for most of his life.

The wind was like razors on Andrew's cheeks, but he pressed his lips together in a grim line: chapped, tasting of camphor and wax from the lip balm the Russian had given him. He still couldn't see much of anything in the gloom. He didn't know exactly what he expected to find.

His ears were so numb that he didn't hear the other man approach until a shadow appeared in his peripheral vision, cowled by a fur-lined parka.

"Satellite reports, my friend," said Gregor Orlov with a thick Russian accent. "We cannot see the aurora because of the thick overcast, but the solar storms are increasing. Our team should have been in for a fine show." He shrugged inside his massive coat. "Someday, the sky will clear."

Distracted, Andrew took a deep breath, exhaled cold steam. "The fog isn't uncommon for this time of year," he said. "The ice sublimes, and the air temperature keeps the mist hanging low, even though it's well below freezing."

The Russian gave a hearty laugh and slapped him on the back, jarring Andrew against the rails just as the ice-breaker crushed its way through another thick sheet. "You don't need to tell me about ice and winter, my friend. In Archangelsk we learned every nuance of the cold. Your worst winter in Indiana would have been a summer vacation for my family."

Orlov had gone to the University of Moscow, but had grown up in the far northern port of Archangelsk, from which the *Polaris* had originated on this expedition. The scientific research vessel investigated, among other things, the northern auroral displays directly below the Van Allen belts during times of solar maximum. After concerns about the increasing ozone hole at the bottom of Antarctica, worldwide scientific groups had allied themselves in order to keep watch on the atmosphere above the northern icecap.

With a crew of Russian, American, and German meteorologists and solar physicists, the *Polaris* had skated the edge of the Arctic Circle, westward from the tip of Russia around the Norwegian coast and across to Greenland, where they would attempt to make a passage up to the north magnetic pole, but so far the weather and the ice pack had not cooperated.

Finally, after moments of silence during which Andrew and Orlov heard only the grinding molars of icebergs, the ship came to a stop. The icicle-encrusted bullhorns on the corners of the bridge housing announced in English, Russian, and then German that the *Polaris* would remain here for the time being.

"Now we must wait for spring," Orlov said. "According to the sunspot activity, the solar maximum should continue to increase the auroras for another month yet. Within a week, the captain hopes to proceed northward. The ice is breaking up, and we should be able to get closer to the pole itself."

Andrew continued to stare toward the shore, which he *knew* hovered in shadows not far away. "My father died here, Gregor," he said, surprising the Russian meteorologist. "At the old military base."

"What?" The hooded form turned toward him. "Explain this to me."

"Years ago, back when Point Tabu was a watch center for the U.S. military, part of the DEW Line, my father was a Private in the core of engineers. His division was trying to blast through the Hecla Isthmus to provide an open-water passage for American nuclear subs."

"Ah, back during the Cold War days," Orlov said with a sage nod. "In my country, we were paranoid too. We had many submarine bases up at these high latitudes."

"According to the telegram, my father died in an avalanche during blasting. I don't know exactly what happened." He faced forward, into the bitter wind. "All I know is that the submarine channel was never completed, and this base was eventually abandoned."

For a moment, the mist cleared and they could see the snow-covered rooftops and a few collapsed Quonset huts, leftovers from a different time. During its peak, Point Tabu had held nearly two hundred men and women, living like kangaroo rats with underground tunnels, bunkers, and weapons storage areas. A few token scientists had been stationed there, but the inhabitants were mostly military.

After the Bay of Pigs and the Cuban Missile Crisis and other crux points of the Cold War, all Tabu personnel had been reassigned and the entire base erased from the map. The U.S. government found it less expensive to erect completely new structures at a different location than to keep repairing and upgrading the old base. In isolated areas like this, the U.S. Army's favorite three words were, "Abandon In Place."

Earlier, Andrew had spoken to the captain of the *Polaris*, a gruff Ukrainian who had absolutely no interest in science, but merely loved to pilot his ship. The bearded man was paid for a mission, and he did his best. Combined with Andrew's own broken Russian and the Ukrainian's broken English, they had managed to discuss the weather and come to a decision earlier that day. They would put up here, next to Point Tabu for a week or so, while spring continued its gradual thaw.

Andrew hadn't told the captain about his personal interest in the base—and the Ukrainian hadn't bothered to ask.

Now, on the icy deck, Orlov tugged on Andrew's thickly covered elbow, drawing him toward the door and into the warmer depths of the ship. They could have some hot soup and tea together before the boats would be dispatched and a handful of crewmembers could go ashore.

"You have several days to investigate," Orlov said. "I don't know what waits in that base for you, my friend, but I hope you find what you are searching for."

Surprised and embarrassed, Andrew followed the Russian into the ship. They shut the heavy metal door with a clang that drowned out the cold wind. Sweat burst out on his face from the heavy warmth. "Did I say I was searching for anything, Gregor?"

The Russian smiled as he wiped clustered frost from the reddish hairs of his beard. "You have that look about you."

As an Army brat, an infant on base housing in the continental U.S., Andrew had never known his father. Walter Gordon had been an unremarkable and unmourned young Private given an unglamorous assignment up at Point Tabu in Greenland. His transfer to the DEW Line came either through the vagaries of Army personnel departments, or as punishment for some never-recorded indiscretion. Despite inquiries and sifting through old records, Andrew had not been able to determine the reason, and his withdrawn mother Blanche had offered no explanations of her own.

He had been two years old when his mother received the telegram informing them of her husband's death, his body never to be recovered under a collapsed ice shelf on the Hecla Isthmus. Since then, the Army had taken care of his mother in their own bureaucratic way, and she'd never had the ambition to do much else with her life.

Instead, young Andrew, fatherless and with few prospects, had been forced to make his own future.

He'd gone to the University of Indiana, interested in astrophysics and meteorology, and had excelled in both subjects. He worked and studied as if possessed. His sullen mother was no doubt proud of him, but she showed it little; she didn't seem to know how. Day after day Blanche sat around smoking with other drab housewives in their kaffeeklatsches or watching soap operas; most evenings she drank a few too many highballs. She was coasting, slumming, dying in slow motion. Andrew Gordon had no one to impress but himself—and his own standards were a tough enough measure to meet.

At the University of Indiana he had taken an elective psychology class, something that hadn't interested him at the time, until he discovered that the professor, a Dr. James Hamilton, had also been stationed at Point Tabu in Greenland during the early 1960s. Intrigued, Andrew signed up for the course and studied the background material, memorizing the c.v. of his professor.

Dr. Hamilton had been at the Arctic base exactly during the time when Private Gordon had died on the Hecla Isthmus. Hamilton had been in charge of the Human Factors section, in the perfect place to study people under extraordinary pressures. Maybe he'd even known Andrew's father.

The good doctor had chosen to be reassigned not long afterward, shortly before the base was closed down for good. Even though their work was disparate, the base was relatively small and the people would have been confined together for many months. Andrew thought it likely that Dr. Hamilton would remember a Private Walter Gordon.

Upon returning from Greenland, the psychologist had made quite a name for himself in ground-breaking analyses of the paranoid mind. Hamilton seemed to understand the pressures and the fears in an intuitive way that most other detached psychologists did not. During his career the doctor had published numerous well-received papers and could have received prestigious appointments, could have landed a Chair at the most respected universities. But instead Hamilton had married his assistant, also a refugee from Point Tabu, and had settled down at the University of Indiana, where he'd lived a quiet life teaching freshman-level courses for the past thirty-odd years.

The opportunity intrigued him, and Andrew could not let his questions remain unasked.

He had waited a month, listening to Professor Hamilton's lectures, and finally he ventured to meet the old man during his office hours. When Andrew knocked and pushed his way in through the mostly closed door, the professor looked at him with tired eyes.

Though cigarette smoking was frowned upon by the dean of the university, Hamilton's office reeked of tobacco smoke, and his ashtray was overloaded. The professor regarded Andrew without much interest, considering him another student with another question. He had a seamed face, huge bushy eyebrows, and patchy gray hair.

"I take it by all the inquiries on your face, young man, that some part of my lectures in this past week have not been crystal clear?"

"Oh, your lectures were just fine, Professor," Andrew answered, then swallowed hard. "It's your past that isn't clear to me."

Surprised, Professor Hamilton reached into a pack on top of his desk and withdrew a cigarette; he lit it in a quick, smooth motion out of long habit. "What part of my past could possibly interest my students? It has nothing to do with getting a good grade."

"The grade doesn't mean so much to me, Professor. What interests me is...Point Tabu."

The psychologist looked as if he had been involuntarily subjected to electric-shock treatment. After letting him reel for a second, Andrew continued. "My father was stationed there, up at that base. He...he died there in an accident. Private Walter Gordon?"

Hamilton raised thick bushy eyebrows. "Gordon? I remember when Major Brothers shot himself, but...oh, *Gordon*. Yes! The one who died in the Isthmus."

"Yes," Andrew said with an involuntary shudder. "I never knew my father. I was only two years old when we got the telegram. Do you think...do you think you might remember him? Tell me something about him?"

Professor Hamilton drew a long, deep drag from his cigarette, keeping his eyes closed. "Oh, I knew him, young man. In fact, I was quite aware of the tragic accident and its effects on other members of the base, especially on Major Frank Brothers, his commanding officer. I was doing psychology research, you know, stationed up in the cold and isolation, buried underground with few other people to see, where it's dark for six months out of the year and cold for all twelve." The professor coughed, but continued talking between his wheezing. "You know, we saw plenty of cabin fever, paranoia, isolation syndrome."

"Is that where you got your background for your earlier papers?" Andrew said, to show that he had done his research on the man. "Is that why you understood the paranoid mind so well?"

"You've read my old papers?" the professor said, raising his thick eyebrows. "Oh, you are an unusual student."

"I was interested in learning more about my father, sir. You're the only connection I've had so far. The only one who might have a story to tell me." He tried to keep he pleading tone out of his voice.

"Well, I did know plenty about deep paranoia from my time on the base—but not just because of researching and observing the other personnel." The scientist shook his head, finished one cigarette and lit another. "No, it has more to do with an unusual research project I was doing on my own. A prototype device I invented." His eyes bore a far-off look and he fell silent for a long time. "But I left it there, at Point Tabu, when we shut down the base. I never published my work on that device, never talked about it. But the experiment did make me...make me understand a great deal about human nature—and about what really happened to your father."

Andrew drew a quick gasp. "Please. I know you just told me you've never reported it or published it, but if you were ever to make an exception, please tell me now. I need to know. It's been more than thirty years since my father died. What harm could it do?"

Hamilton gave him a long smile on his craggy face. "Oh, it can still cause plenty of damage, young Andrew Gordon. But it's about time I got this off my chest, and I can't think of a better person to tell it to." The scientist reached over and grabbed a stack of journal preprints, psychology magazines, and various standardized test scores from the only other chair in the office. "Sit down." He patted the worn gray naugahyde seat.

Andrew did, giving him his full attention as Professor Hamilton explained about his mind-recording device, how memories and personalities could be uploaded from one brain into another...and even, under certain circumstances, *exchanged*.

Andrew had never heard of a man named Major Frank Brothers; Hamilton had changed the subject's name and reported him as a case study in many of his earlier works on the paranoid mind. Hamilton claimed the two of them had switched places when the experiment went awry, and Major Brothers—inside Hamilton's body—had seen demons in every shadow. He'd been desperate to destroy the Hecla Isthmus and annihilate the manifestation of his guilt that lay buried beneath the ice.

"Guilt over the death of your father, Andrew," Hamilton said.

"How?" Andrew asked. "Why? What did this Major Brothers have to do with my father's death? I thought it was an accident."

The old man took a heavy breath again, stubbed out his smoldering cigarette butt, and rested his chin in one gnarled hand. "To a certain extent it was an accident...but even after an accident happens, certain actions can make things better—or worse. Major Brothers made everything worse, and later he almost destroyed our entire base. He left your father to die in the ice without so much as attempting a rescue, and he couldn't live with that."

Andrew was engrossed by the whole story. Professor Hamilton insisted that all the equipment, all the data still remained there, shut down in the abandoned Arctic base where no one would ever find it. He expected his young student to walk away, his ghosts put to rest, the questions about his father answered as much as they would ever be.

But instead, the tale had clung to Andrew for years, haunted him as he continued his studies.

Everything had led up to this point now, when he'd finally gotten himself assigned to the Arctic research vessel *Polaris*. He knew the icebreaker would stop at Point Tabu en route to the magnetic pole.

Which was exactly where Andrew Gordon wanted to be.

The abandoned base was like a haunted house set to deep freeze. Frost covered the walls, the pipes, even the army-surplus furniture still painted a seafoam green. It was as if the early 1960s had been stored in acrylic and placed in a refrigerator, an accidental museum because of the high cost of removal.

Andrew walked alone inside the ruins, exploring the intact buildings while the rest of the *Polaris* team members set about rigging electric heaters and erecting cots, sleeping quarters, finding a place for themselves to stretch out away from the cramped closeness of the icebreaker ship, on solid—if frozen—ground.

In its heyday, this sprawling complex had housed two hundred hapless people, and Andrew had little difficulty losing himself, ducking away from prying eyes. He wanted to be alone here, to do his own explorations. He needed privacy to deal with his questions and with what he intended to do.

Reaching inside the warm depths of his thick parka, he withdrew a folded map, a faded photocopy of an old base plan from which he had identified Dr. Hamilton's lab and offices. *The Human Factors Section*. He had little confidence that anything would remain functional after such a long time, but there was always hope. The Army had shut down the base rather suddenly, pulled all its assigned personnel, and left the remainders to the elements.

For decades, Dr. Hamilton had felt little need to retrieve his apparatus, his notes, anything that would have reminded him of the terrible ordeal he'd undergone at Point Tabu. One couldn't just hop on a bus and show up in the wilderness of northern Greenland, after all.

Enough time had passed, though, thirty-five years. Surely that was long enough for ghosts to be laid to rest, to go to sleep in the cold Arctic night. That left only curiosity and, Andrew hoped, some answers about what had really happened to his father, what had occurred during the final dark days of Point Tabu.

White breath curled out of his mouth and nose like the smoke of a sleeping dragon. Some of the ceiling girders had slumped with the weight of decades of snow. As he shone his flashlight into murky corners, the beam glittered off ice crystals that shimmered like salt pillars. Icicles drooped from the furniture. The air itself seemed to have gone into hibernation, carrying little sound, only an oppressive silence.

Back where the other *Polaris* team members worked in the central maintenance rooms, two of the engineers were tinkering around, trying to get the old generators started again, though they must have known the equipment, the wires, and the water pipes would have long since fallen to pieces. But Andrew knew some of the engineers on the crew, and knew just as well that they wouldn't shirk the challenge.

As if to surprise him, a loud hum growled through the bowels of the base. After several creaking groans, a few of the caged light bulbs flickered. Sparks flew from other fixtures, but the intact bulbs glowed a warm orange, gradually brightening to a yellowish-white.

Andrew blinked and looked up. Many of the bulbs were blackened, the fixtures broken or collapsed, but the base's power did go on. Perhaps everything at Point Tabu remained in better shape than even he had hoped.

Good, he thought. That meant his chances of finding something here were even better.

Andrew switched off his flashlight and cautiously entered. Dr. Hamilton's lab room looked like...like a scientist's office from Cold War days. It had a rounded metal desk, mostly empty bookshelves, and an ugly black telephone in the corner. A bank of apparatus looked as if it had been built from Army surplus parts; the device had metal walls, equipment racks, and—yes, indeed—even an oscilloscope screen. He was sure the device would click and beep and whirr when functioning.

He stepped lightly, feeling as if he were trespassing. He recalled vividly the story the old psychologist had told him. Major Frank Brothers had died here in this room, driven mad with guilt over his negligence in the death of Andrew's father.

Growing bold, Andrew ransacked the desk drawers, pulling out an old, musty-smelling logbook. He flipped through it, using his flashlight to supplement the dim glow from the one functioning bulb in the lab room. He scanned the faded handwritten notes that confirmed what Professor Hamilton had told him in the university office. He found descriptions of the experiment and the "mind-reading" apparatus the psychologist had developed here on his own free time where the rest of the Tabu personnel kept watch for a Soviet nuclear attack.

Pacing the room, Andrew went to a sagging metal file cabinet and yanked it open. He used his teeth to pull off his thick mittens when he saw the paraphernalia on the shelves. His heart fluttered in his chest upon seeing round steel cases that held magnetic tapes, reel-to-reel artifacts eight inches in diameter. If he could figure out how to thread the brittle old tapes through the machine, and if the base generators provided enough power, maybe he could get Hamilton's apparatus working again.

With trembling fingers, not just numb from cold and his own shivers, Andrew threaded the magnetic tape through the old-style reader, missing the mark twice, until finally he got the loop in place and locked down the old mind-reading apparatus.

The lights flickered, then went out, plunging him into darkness lit only by the column of his flashlight lying on the table. He had time enough to blink in disappointment, and then the power came back on again.

Somewhere on the base, the *Polaris* engineers continued to fumble with the generator. To them, Point Tabu had no urgency, no memories. It was just a challenge to be solved, a funhouse, a museum of the Cold War: a northern defense perimeter where scrambling fighter jets could rally to strike back at a long-anticipated Soviet missile assault from over the North Pole.

When the generator power seemed stable enough, Andrew reached forward and snapped the metal toggle that powered up the clunky device. The metal switch clicked like a brisk slap in the face. The machine hummed and vibrated, warming up. The lights blinked and beeped and hummed, just as he'd expected.

Dangling in front of the gadget were two headsets, flexible caps now frozen stiff and hardened with age. Andrew snugged the ring of electrodes over his head, positioning them, pressing them tightly against his skull. God, he hoped he was doing everything right. It made him feel like an extra in a cheesy mad scientist movie.

After he pushed another loud toggle switch, the reel-to-reel tape began to spin, reading data into the machine. The cascade of lights blinked more furiously.

The rest of the team wouldn't find him down here for a long time; the other scientists wouldn't even begin looking for him until tomorrow—longer, if Gregor Orlov kept them busy.

Still, Andrew felt a sense of urgency, an eagerness to be *finished* with this, for better or worse. He had waited a long time to be here. He flipped the last switches. The tape sped up. He hoped the flimsy ribbon wouldn't snap and break with age.

And then thoughts began to come into his head. Static at first, whispers...and then real information.

The recording was working, even after years sealed here, gathering cold dust and forgotten! The memories Dr. Hamilton had read and captured with the device indeed remained stored on the magnetic reel. The tape casing carried no label or no markings, but as thoughts, memories and echoes began to rise in front of his forebrain like images played on a computer screen, he knew he had found the correct tape.

As part of an artificial past, Andrew *remembered* rigid military training, an unwavering sense of right and wrong...a terrible fear of a Communist takeover of the world, Soviet intervention...the predicted horrors of a nuclear holocaust.

Then, after being promoted in rank, the honor "he" felt from being assigned to this important mission at Point Tabu. He, *Major Frank Brothers*, was charged with clearing the Hecla Isthmus to make a new submarine channel. American nuclear subs could have what ancient mariners had dreamed of for centuries—a true Northwest Passage that would allow them to sweep under the ice from Greenland, skirting the actual pole, and then down through the Bering Strait. From there, they could strike the far western coast of the Soviet Union, Siberia, Vladivostok, and the Kamchatka Peninsula.

Dr. Hamilton's ancient apparatus heated up, humming, vibrating and laboring hard and still-deeper memories scrolled out from the ancient magnetic tape. Andrew sat back in the creaking chair, his hands clasping the cracked arms. His jaw clenched, and the tendons in his neck stretched taut.

He *remembered* seeing nuclear tests in the South Seas. He *remembered* reading of the Julius and Ethel Rosenberg trial, the Manhattan Project, the horrors of repression and torture behind the Iron Curtain...and above all, the driving, burning need to stop the Communist insurgence, the fury to do anything and everything to protect his American way of life...even if it meant that some had to be sacrificed.

Like Private Gordon.

The ultimate reward, the triumph of freedom, was worth any price. The Hecla Isthmus had to be cleared so that submarines could pass, so that America could be defended against the greatest threat it had ever faced.

Power surged in the apparatus, the old recorded thoughts of a man long dead became sharp and powerful, insistent. Andrew winced, and reached up at the last moment to clutch the headset. He ripped it away from his brow as sparks showered from the old circuits.

And he became Major Brothers.

Everything felt wrong. Disorientation, changes...nightmares. It was some kind of plot.

Major Brothers instantly knew that the worst must have happened. The last thing he remembered...he had been here under psychiatric observation in the Human Factors Office with that stuffed-shirt humanitarian Dr. Hamilton.

All the personnel on the base, from the engineers all the way up to weak-spined Colonel Campbell, seemed to be dragging their feet. They refused to see the urgency, slowed him down in his vital work even though the necessary atomic cartridges had arrived. He could blast the isthmus to glowing dust!

Everyone with a brain knew the Soviets were pressing onward, completing their projects by fiat rather than through democratic means. Their sick goal was world domination, their perceived destiny—and the Commies did not allow distractions to swerve them from their path.

Major Brothers had been hooked up to the psychologist's strange brain-scan apparatus, staring at the other man's dark eyes and bushy eyebrows. It had been an experiment, but what had Dr. Hamilton really been up to? Was it a trick of some kind? Was the scientist an infiltrator, a double-agent?

Between the two of them...something strange had happened. He remembered thinking *he* was Dr. Hamilton for a while. They'd shared thoughts, the two of them, exchanged places. Brothers had tried to use this to his advantage to complete the destruction of the Hecla Isthmus, to bypass the obstacles so he could use the atomics to blast a channel clear—and destroy the evil Ice Creature's presence!

But then the two of them had switched back...or so he thought. Major Brothers remembered a gunshot, agony.

But he had fired the gun himself, aiming at Dr. Hamilton, the man who wore his body...yet he felt the bullet wound and the shattering pain. One final time, that monstrous vengeful specter from the ice crevasse had appeared in front of his dying eyes.

Then nothing...static...and now he was here, and the Point Tabu base was *wrong*. His surroundings had changed. Frost and ice rimed the furniture. The air had a sluggish, dead quality to it. The rooms were dark, quiet, abandoned.

He prepared to shout for the guards, but caught himself. Somebody else might be watching, listening, and it might not be a presence he wanted to encounter. He didn't even recognize his clothes, his shoes. How much time had passed? His body still felt wrong.

Major Brothers grabbed the desk drawers and yanked them open. He ransacked the file cabinets, but they had been emptied and forgotten long ago. The furniture stood dusty, sagging, old. He couldn't forsake the feeling of ponderous age that pressed down, making Point Tabu into a fossil bed.

This was impossible! All of the equipment had been new, polished, freshly painted standard military gray or seafoam green. Dr. Hamilton had just invented his apparatus, just tested it on him. The padded chairs had been newly installed. This entire section of living modules had been dug and furnished only months before, when the Greenland base was expanded.

Major Brothers pounded a fist against the side of his head to jar his memories loose. His recollection had so many holes. He couldn't understand what had happened. Had he survived some new terrifying weapon the Soviets had unleashed to wipe out American defenses at the DEW Line? Had he lived through the electromagnetic pulse from a nuclear air burst?

Must be degradation in the tape. There are gaps. But I didn't realize the memories would be this clear...I really feel like I am Major Brothers!

Brothers felt an alien presence inside his skull, an invader. Other thoughts. Another mind...maybe some sort of post-hypnotic suggestion that had been brainwashed into him. He gritted his teeth, looked around wildly, but saw only the empty room.

You've got it backwards, Major. You're *the stranger here.* The voice fell silent, then came back with a resurgence of anger. *And you're the man responsible for the death of my father!*

Using his indignant outrage as a crowbar, Andrew Gordon levered himself to the forefront of his own mind, knocking the stunned thoughts of Major Brothers into the background. He felt his hands again, flexed his fingers and his arms. Heavy sweat caused by the Major's unreasoning paranoia poured from his body core into the warm, thick parka, soaking Andrew's sweater.

Major Brothers' thoughts scrambled inside his skull like a caged animal, but Andrew tried to feel his way, to communicate with the stranger in his midst. "Listen, Major. You need to know what's happened."

Andrew summoned clear thoughts about Dr. Hamilton's brain-scanning apparatus and what had happened to Brothers some three-and-a-half decades ago, how he had died, and how Andrew had made his way here years later, found the machine and the records, and brought the ancient recording back to life. "The thoughts in my head now are no more than leftover memories preserved on a decaying magnetic tape. That's all *you* are, Major."

The presence of Brothers raged, disbelieving the incredible story. He remained desperate to finish his task, to destroy the Isthmus and to cauterize the guilt within him, an obsession that had survived even his own death.

Andrew could not understand the driving blind fear and paranoia. "The Cold War is over now," he said out loud, talking to himself. His words echoed in the chill laboratory office. "The Berlin Wall came down in 1989. There is no more Iron Curtain, Major. It's rusted and fallen apart. Communism failed. The Soviet Union fell—it is no more."

He took a deep breath, trying to hammer through the blazing insistence of the dead soldier's mindset. "McCarthyism, fallout shelters, duck-and-cover air raid drills—all of that was just a series of mistakes, overreactions. After Hiroshima and Nagasaki, no other atomic bombs were ever used in war. All the terror of nuclear warfare came to naught. It's been dismantled."

Andrew whispered, calming himself. "We're at peace now, Major Brothers, and you need to be at peace so that I can learn what happened to my father...Private Gordon. Walter Gordon."

Inside him, Andrew felt the other subset of memories recoil in terror. Major Brothers metaphorically reeled backward as he realized whose body he now inhabited. The son of the monstrous ice-ghost that continued to follow him! Together, these two meant to kill him!

In absolute panic, Major Brothers surged back to prominence, hijacking Andrew's body. Controlling the resistant muscles, he staggered forward until he struck the hard edge of the desk with his hip. He spun around, grasping for balance. The Ice Creature was here, still here on Point Tabu! He hadn't escaped it, after all these years. Major Brothers sensed the ghost approaching, felt its cold, clenching hand reach toward him—and as he looked up with wild eyes, once again he saw: the shimmering image was shaped like a man clad in thick, army-issue arctic gear, but encrusted with ice chips and snow. The once-human face had been crushed, battered, buried under a thousand tons of glacier. The skin was bruised and blue-red, the color of flash-frozen rotted meat.

The only thing that burned through the cluttered mass of frost and preserved skin were the *eyes*, blinding bright and sharp as ice picks.

Private Walter Gordon—the poor man who had fallen into the crevasse, a mediocre worker but a good-natured soldier—just an expendable part of the demolition and engineering team. Gordon, who had cried out for help as the ice walls shifted and the rest of the company fled for stable ground. Everyone else had heard the young man's screams—he had a wife, a new baby back in the States, but Major Brothers had put the mission first. His assignment, his duty.

He'd left Private Gordon there to die, to be ground into frozen dust between giant teeth of ice. And now the horrible ghost stood there, furious and vengeful, extending an accusatory finger that could rip Brothers' heart out.

That...that's my father!

As soon as Andrew's voice echoed in the Major's head, the apparition vanished, and he stood all alone in the lab, disoriented. But Brothers refused to relinquish bodily control to Andrew. He knew the demon was not gone. It was simply driven back like a vampire from a crucifix. For the moment.

Inside a single skull, two minds struggled for dominance and finally found common ground. There was one thing that both of them desperately wanted, and by cooperating they could achieve it together, despite their animosity toward each other.

Both men needed to go to the Hecla Isthmus.

While the other crew members from the *Polaris* bedded down for a sleep period—the sun never went below the horizon at this time of year—Andrew felt his driving energy increase. He could not sleep or even pause, especially not now that he had Major Brothers to guide him. Both of them needed to journey across the ice, each propelled by his own need. They would trudge across the ice pack and permafrost to the site where the corps of engineers had attempted to blast through nature's toll gate.

Major Brothers knew the way—it had only been months to his abridged memory. Andrew wanted to see with his own eyes the spot where his father had died, where poor Private Gordon had tumbled into a crevasse. Brothers' guilt, mixed with Cold War paranoia, had unleashed the vengeful ghost of his victim.

Bundled in his thick parka, Andrew grabbed a GPS portable locator, hand-heaters, and supplies from the small cutter that had left the *Polaris*. No one saw him go. Not wanting to face any living being from the present or from the 1960s, Andrew/Brothers ducked around corners or hid in darkened rooms whenever he heard one of the other inhabitants coming close.

It would take him a day of hard trudging, even in good weather, to reach the place where the demolition team had erected their base camp so long ago. But Andrew knew it would be a week before *Polaris* attempted to head north again up the Greenland coast.

In that time, Andrew would have done what he needed to do, or else he would be stranded here in the abandoned Arctic base.

Tugging the fur-lined hood of his parka forward to hide his face, he adjusted his mittens and then pushed open the heavy door. Outside. He bent over against the wind and let the door slam behind him. His thick boots crunched out onto the ice and snow. The ever-twilight Arctic sun showed him the way. A compass would do little good here, so close to the magnetic pole, but Major Brothers had a primal instinct. And the Isthmus called to him like a physical thing.

Low sunshine glinted across the broken glacier fields. Andrew's goal was a distant line of crags covered with a frosting of snow. His feet and hands and body were numb, not just from the cold or from weariness, but from detachment. His body moved like a machine that took him across the white field. The thin winter fog hung like tangible gloom in the air. At times the sun shone like an cataract-smeared eye, and at other moments it was just a milky-white spot fighting through the frozen mist.

Inside his head a debate raged. Andrew tried to tell the packet of memories that had been Major Brothers all the events that had happened since 1963, how much the world had changed. Tensions had gotten worse for a while, of course, beyond the climax of the Cuban Missile Crisis and the Bay of Pigs, continuing with a low-level simmering anger for decades until it all fell apart for the Soviet Union. Not with a bang, but a whimper.

Andrew said to the voice inside his head, "Some might call this a demonic possession. You're another presence, something many people would consider evil, haunting me."

But Major Brothers echoed back with supreme confidence. "On the other hand, I might believe that through supernatural means I've been given a second chance to do what must be done."

Andrew could feel the Major's anxiety like a tangible thing: his grim orders and nightmarish fears of nuclear holocaust, his mixed feelings about being stationed here where he could defend his world against the Evil Empire. Andrew actually thought the memories of Major Brothers would have felt at peace upon learning the news: his Communist enemy had fallen, vanquished through the efforts of freedom and democracy, exactly as he and his generation had always been taught would happen...though the end had been far less dramatic than many had feared.

But Brothers screamed within him, denying the information, shouting that he couldn't believe what Andrew was telling him. It must be a trick, a cruel joke.

Some men are not complete without their enemies, Andrew thought, and he had one such man trapped inside his mind.

After an unknown time of marching, plodding, staggering across the trackless wasteland, Major Brothers led him like an iron filing drawn by a magnet. The two conjoined men stood before the bastions of the sheer glacial mountains that formed the Hecla Isthmus—a wall of rock and ice that blocked northern Greenland from the open Arctic Sea.

Andrew stood before the barrier, a towering cathedral of ice with cracked spires and parapets, enormous blocks of translucent blue-white like stained glass windows that had crumbled to the ground. Feathers of snow blew around, spraying like frozen fountains as frigid air caught around the wall and retreated with the backflow.

Behind him, the plain of ice and snow spread toward the distant and unseen Point Tabu base. The flat ground was punctuated with protruding boulders and yawning fissures. He looked up and began to follow the line of the ridge. *Here...here.*

He saw in his mind's eye what Major Brothers remembered, what had haunted his nightmares ever since the fateful accident. The crew of engineers with their explosives and drills had planted dynamite and heavier bombs deep in the fracture points and fissures. They would prepare for the insertion of nuclear cartridges that would erase this barrier forever.

The Isthmus was already seismically unstable. Huge icebergs shifted and ground together in the choked, confined waterway. Glaciers tumbled like asteroid-sized boulders hurled from invisible catapults.

Brothers remembered the face of Private Walter Gordon, just one of the other workers on his crew, a man bundled up in scarves and parka. The engineers all wore snow goggles because it was heavy summer and the sunlight was bright, reflecting off the prismatic angles of sheared ice. Gordon had gone into the tunnels, preparing for the next stage.

An earthquake had struck just then. The ground rumbled, the cliffs shivered. The ice barrier cracked. Snow fell, and great blocks from the glacier broke free. Private Gordon had been stranded in the opening where he'd been ordered to plant his blasting caps and dynamite.

The rest of the crew fled the unstable ground. Major Brothers had shouted for Gordon to retreat, but then a crack had opened up. The young private—a man who had a wife and infant son back in Indiana—had fallen into the fissure, dropping beyond any possible rescue.

The remaining men rushed to the safety of the plain, but the explosives had already been planted. As Private Gordon tumbled down, he caught himself on a knob of ice, a broken ledge, and his leg shattered. More snow fell loose, blanketing him, battering his body.

As Major Brothers ran, ordering a retreat, the last thing he heard was the plaintive cry from his lost man. But the ground was too unstable, the ice still trembling, crumbling. If the commanding officer had gone in, sent rescuers back, he might have lost more men, and that would have delayed the explosions. It would have ruined his timetable, complicated the mission, the objective.

Besides, there was no chance. Private Gordon had to be dead.

There was a chance! If you heard him calling, there was still a chance.

"No, there was no chance!" Major Brothers shouted out loud, his words echoing like blasts from a warship striking a fortress wall.

Major Brothers had ordered all the explosives detonated anyway. He had done what he thought would prepare the Isthmus for the atomic cartridges, but the barrier had proven too strong. During several avalanches, the preparatory work had tumbled down, burying Private Gordon forever.

Or at least it should have.

Private Gordon was dead, a casualty of undeclared war. The Major had left Andrew's father behind—but for the rest of his life, Brothers had never been free of Gordon's memory, his guilt, or his ghost.

Now, as he stood before the barrier, Major Brothers claimed full possession of Andrew's mind and he raised his hands, fists clenched within thick mittens. He shouted into the wilderness, "Leave me alone, damn you! I was just doing my duty!"

With a flicker of reality, something changed deep inside the wall of ice. Something indefinable, a shifting in the color of white, a play of shadows across the rippled translucent surface.

Major Brothers backed away, while Andrew tried to peer closer, curious and hopeful.

Andrew saw nothing in the bleak wall, but Major Brothers knew exactly what it was. "The creature's coming! We've awakened him again. I can't destroy him."

He stumbled away from the frozen tomb, but Andrew exerted control again, forcing himself to look back at the shimmering ice. He thought of how much his life had changed in just a day. He had planned to be no more than a meteorologist on an expedition to look at increased auroral activity. He had hoped for a chance to see where his father had died.

Instead, now Andrew stood with another man inside of him, isolated and alone in the Arctic wilderness, staring at a mute layer of ice...where his father's ghost had been imprisoned.

From inside the nearly opaque cliffs of the Isthmus, he saw a flicker of shadow, but the eyes in his head were guided by Major Brothers. The shadow figure became more distinct, darker, ominous. Padded chest and legs, moving slowly, swinging arms as if walking through thick syrup, a terrifying spectral form that he knew in his heart would have the face of Private Gordon.

But would the ice demon be vindictive and wish to destroy him...or would it merely come to say farewell to the son he had never known?

The murky form approached the outer surface of the ice, lumbering and unstoppable. Andrew couldn't tell if it was just his own imagination, a trick of the light. Major Brothers screamed out loud, though, and tumbled backward, falling onto the crumbling ice.

Then he turned around and scrambled away, frantic to return to the meager sanctuary of abandoned Point Tabu...hoping that the Ice Creature wouldn't follow.

When Andrew staggered into the snow-fossilized remnants of the base, he had no recollection of how he had gotten back, how many steps he had taken, or what ordeals he had passed through.

His head seemed empty of the nagging whispers of another man's thoughts, as if Major Brothers were asleep, stunned...or just lurking there. Perhaps the memories he had read from the tape had faded away, no more than an afterimage—or perhaps something had frightened them out of his skull.

The blind eye of the sun gazed through the ever-present mists. Andrew could not tell how much time he had taken, how many hours or days he'd been gone. The rugged mountains of the Hecla Isthmus lay far behind him, and the low buildings of Point Tabu looked like the half-buried bones of an old corpse.

Terror shot down his spine as reality caught up with him. Was he alone here now, stranded? Had the others from the *Polaris* already gone and left him behind?

Then Andrew gazed toward the metal-dark ocean and saw the blocky silhouette of the icebreaker, which had pulled closer to shore amid broken white chunks that drifted away from the coast. The weather had turned warmer, the solid sea crackling and splitting. They would depart soon.

Andrew's hands were numb with a deep burning, and he suspected frostbite. His cheeks were like thick parchment from the exposure. He would get inside and try to assess the damage he had wrought on his body. He would make up some excuse to the others...

He reached the heavy door and fumbled with mittened fingers to get it open. He hammered with a deadened fist to break away a fresh coating of ice from the jamb and suddenly the door was flung open. The broad-shouldered, thick-chested form of Gregor Orlov stood there like a polar bear, a huge grin breaking through his mask of astonishment.

"There you are, comrade! We were worried. I thought you had died." He swept Andrew's heavily wrapped form in a huge hug. Orlov wore only a thick cable-knit sweater, and he smelled of aftershave. "You think a winter in Indiana can prepare you for weather like this? Very foolish of you."

The interior of the base seemed oppressively warm, and Andrew rubbed at the caked frost that covered his scarf, his bristling mustache, and his beard stubble.

Upon seeing the Russian, though, and enduring his familiar embrace, Andrew felt a deep revulsion spring up within him. He pulled himself away, dizzy and out of control, and staggered into the dim hall without saying a word to Orlov. He leaned against the wall to regain his balance, gulping deep breaths.

The Russian meteorologist didn't notice his sudden distaste and continued jabbering. His eyes were bright and dancing. "So, where have you been, Andrew Gordon? I told no one else about your quest and your questions, but the boat is ready to leave in a few hours. We must go! My excuses had run out. I thought we'd have to send out search parties—and you know how the captain would have hated that." The Russian's voice caught, thick with emotion. "I thought we'd find your body dead, frozen meat for the scavengers."

"You were always such a pessimist, Gregor Andreivich," Andrew said, choking out the words. Using the familiar name felt like bile in his mouth, and he fought to control himself. He couldn't understand his gut-level reaction.

"I'd prefer to consider myself a *realist*, comrade," Orlov answered, and then busied himself brushing away the ice caked on the zippers of

Andrew's parka. With a ripping noise, he freed his friend from the cocoon that had kept Andrew warm and alive during the long trek from the Hecla Isthmus.

Inside his head, Major Brothers returned with a vengeance, screaming in revulsion and betrayal. He wanted to leap out and strangle this Soviet spy. Suddenly, questions rattled around in the artificial persona, demands for explanations, why a *Russian* was here on the base, but Major Brothers didn't want to hear the answers.

Finally, Andrew's reaction was strong enough that even Orlov sensed something wrong. The Russian reached forward to clasp the open front of his friend's parka and pull him closer. Andrew/Brothers had a sudden irrational fear that this Soviet monster was a vampire about tear his throat out with yellowed fangs.

Instead, the laugh lines around Orlov's eyes crinkled and became serious. His gaze held nothing but compassion and questions. "In all this time, with all that you have put yourself through...did you find the answers you seek, my friend? About your father and his death?"

Andrew swallowed hard and forced himself to the forefront of his own mind. "I found answers, Gregor. I'm just not sure I can accept them."

Orlov clapped him on the shoulder and propelled him deeper into the dimly lit base. "Come into what we have christened the main hall. There's hot soup and tea, and we're about to have a celebration. We meant to keep this as a surprise from you, but now we have to finish our task. I've even brought some peppered vodka and caviar—the good Sevruga stuff, not those disgusting lumpfish eggs you buy in American grocery stores."

"I don't think the grocery stores in Indiana carried any caviar at all, good or bad," Andrew said, recovering himself, using Orlov's warmhearted friendship as a lifeline.

In a chill underground conference room that defeated the best efforts of the four electric heaters blazing in the corners, the other team members of the auroral expedition set up a toast and a little meal.

"Glad you could join us, Andrew," said one of the engineers with a wry, skeptical smile.

They sipped vodka and munched on small delicacies they had each brought in their personal packs before unveiling a plaque engraved in bronze. Someone had brought it aboard the *Polaris*.

After a brief and dull speech, they mounted the special plaque on the old wall; the words formally declared Point Tabu a historical landmark, through an international agreement. The ruins of the base were to be preserved "as a reminder of a dark time in our world's history that might best be forgotten."

Everyone applauded and congratulated themselves, laughing as the claustrophobic conversation grew louder and louder. But Andrew sat withdrawn, wrestling with his emotions. After what he had been through at the Isthmus, and as he continued to deal with the ominous terrors and suspicions of Major Brothers inside him, the entire ceremony seemed absurd and trivial.

The *Polaris* plowed through the cracking skin of ice with all the finesse of a blunt knife cutting cement. The ship headed north, struggling through the spring fissures in the Arctic Ocean, zig-zagging to find clear water.

The surly Ukrainian captain remained ensconced in the bridge, making his engines roar and whine as if reaching the north magnetic pole were his holy quest, regardless of the fact that he had no scientific stake in the results. Icebergs rammed his prow with sounds like gunshots.

Overhead, the murky air cleared and the mists drew back like a veil. The sky began to glow with the increasing aurora. Solar storms sprayed a fire hose of high-energy particles, dousing the axis of the Earth, which held up its magnetic field lines as a shield. The solar wind struck and ricocheted, splattering against the Van Allen belts and releasing photons as their dying screams.

Andrew Gordon, though—and Major Brothers within him—remained locked in his cabin with heavy storm caps screwed in place over the portholes. He didn't want to look out, nor did he want anyone else to look in at him.

Moving sluggishly, he had washed up, kept himself warm, and applied salve to his frostbitten fingers and toes. Much of the time, though, Andrew slept as if in a coma, hoping that when he retreated inside himself, Major Brothers didn't wake up and run rampant through the ship, operating under his own obsessions.

Gregor Orlov had pounded on his door, only once, but Andrew reflexively cringed back from the big man's pungent Russian accent. He made no answer, and Orlov went away, assuming his friend was sleeping, or at least giving him the benefit of the doubt. He knew what burdens Andrew must be wrestling with after returning from his father's death-place.

Andrew wrapped himself in a warm sweater, but couldn't stop shivering. The memories of Major Brothers felt *cold* inside of him, a frozen presence, thoughts placed in suspended animation and now reawakened...but still not warmed to the new world situation. Andrew stared at his increasingly haggard reflection in the mirror, seeing shadows and angles he'd never before noticed.

Brothers, flaring to full wakefulness and looking through his eyes, saw other evidence of Andrew's crazy story of preserved memories and passing decades—the features that held an echo of the man he'd known as Private Walter Gordon, a terrified face muffled in parka and scarf. Gordon had fallen down into the crevasse...to be left there despite his pleas for help.

Merging his memories with the paranoid Major's, Andrew saw what his father must have looked like. He ransacked Major Brother's leftover recollections for some glimpse of Private Gordon eating in a mess hall, or playing cards with the other soldiers, or just huddled with a book or an old newspaper in the underground buildings. Andrew wanted to see a vision of his father laughing, enjoying himself—but Major Brothers had no such pleasant memories.

In his head, Andrew saw only bursts of static. Either it was continuing degradation from the original magnetic tape in the mind-transfer apparatus, or else the Major had simply cauterized all of those thoughts from his brain. Maybe he wanted to keep Private Gordon as nothing more than a manifestation, a ghost, an ice-encrusted monster intent on vengeance.

Andrew could feel the Major's simmering suspicions and panicked questions as he lurked in the back of Andrew's thoughts. The reality seemed obvious to Andrew, having grown up in a changing world. Why couldn't the other man accept it? Why couldn't Major Brothers *see*?

But the sudden disconnect from Cold War pessimism to world peace seemed impossible for the military man to comprehend. Brothers kept searching for a plot, a grim explanation. He didn't want to believe Andrew's off-handed summary of thirty years' worth of a crumbling and falling Communist empire. The Major clawed for other explanations.

The friendship of Gregor Orlov, the big Russian who called Andrew his *comrade*, and the static-filled gaps in his memory reminded Brothers of what he'd heard about brainwashing, hypnotism, torture. Such things had been so prevalent during the Korean conflict, which seemed to him only a few years ago. Certainly the evil Soviets would have learned lessons from their Southeast Asian brothers? Perhaps this was all an evil trick to convert him into a slave or a mindless robot who could be applied as a double-agent to betray his own country.

Unable to take such outrageous speculations seriously, Andrew tried to shrug them off, attempting to point out how silly and unrealistic those fears were. But Major Brothers was an impenetrable wall of memories inside his mind, and he couldn't get through.

That frightened the young man a great deal.

His further thoughts were interrupted, though, by heavy pounding on his stateroom door. "Andrew, my friend, come! You must come quickly—it is happening!" the Russian bellowed. "All of our years of work have come to fruition. We have triumphed at last. Come, comrade, you must see it with your own eyes."

As Andrew hurried to the door, spurred on by the passion he heard in Orlov's voice, his excitement was trampled under the dread and fury that Major Brothers felt as he drew his own conclusions based on the Russian's words.

The *Polaris* drifted through frozen debris in a black, cold sea at the top of the world. The compasses spun around, but according to satellite charts and GPS locator beacons, they had reached the north magnetic pole. Above, the Earth's field lines captured the incoming solar particles and flashed them into brightness. On deck, the international scientific team looked straight up into the heavens' greatest fireworks show.

Major Brothers, in control now, tugged the fur-lined parka hood to hide his face and his narrow, furtive eyes. He crept up the metal stairs and out onto the frost-slick deck of the *Polaris*.

All of our years of work have finally come to fruition. A group of people clustered near the bow, all dressed in thick clothes. They shouted and pointed at the sky, speaking in guttural foreign languages. Major Brothers felt sure he recognized Russian. *They were all speaking Russian!*

"We have triumphed at last," Orlov had said.

Before stepping out into the brittle wind, Major Brothers passed by a life preserver mounted on the ship's inner wall under the rail. He bent to see an emergency rescue kit filled with survival supplies. He used his mittened hand to crack the ice on the survival kit box, then wrenched the red lid open. And found exactly what he had hoped to find.

Prepared now for anything, ready to die fighting if necessary, he stalked onto the deck. Noticing his arrival, Orlov grinned and waved to him. "Come here, Comrade, and see what we have achieved. Victory at last!" He gestured up to the sky, and finally Major Brothers turned his head up to see why everyone else was so excited.

Huge, blazing curtains of solar radiation, cosmic rays, and nuclear fire streamed in gold and pastel green, deep red, and frigid blue shimmering like burial shrouds for a peacock's funeral.

Major Frank Brothers remembered his training indoctrination back in the late 1950s, the warnings his superiors had given him, and his emergency response instructions. He knew the paths that a Soviet missile attack would take and now he recognized the polar arcs of ICBM launches, distant detonations of hydrogen bombs that ignited the sky.

The holocaust had started while he was being deceived! The long-feared Armageddon. It was all a trick! He must have been taken prisoner and brainwashed to believe a fantastic story of memory transference and the passage of decades. Meanwhile, the Soviets had taken over Point Tabu, sabotaged the DEW Line, and destroyed America's capabilities to fend off a Communist attack.

As Brothers saw the firestorm trapped in the atmosphere above the pole, he pictured multiple warheads exploding on New York, Chicago, Washington DC, Los Angeles, San Francisco. Atomic mushroom clouds, shockwaves obliterating everyone he had ever known, his entire way of life. He knew it was too late.

With a sick, utter certainty, Brothers knew the end of the world had come. Because he had failed to breach the Hecla Isthmus so that American nuclear subs could defend their country, much of the crushing responsibility hung on his shoulders.

His eyes were wild, and he looked up toward the group at the bow, saw the Russians cheering. The Ukrainian captain of the *Polaris* climbed down from the bridge and bellowed to them, grinning from ear to ear, and he too jabbered something that sounded like Russian.

Traitors! Traitors everywhere! Major Brothers went wild. He had to do something, if only to wreak his own revenge, since he had allowed the holocaust to come to pass. They had all deceived him, and he had failed in his duty.

He let out an outraged howl, not even hearing the whispered and frantic pleas of Andrew Gordon deep in the back of his mind. Major Brothers charged forward, rushing the group of smugly satisfied men who stood at their strange and sophisticated instruments. So satisfied, the enemy stared at the atmospheric firestorm that would forever blaze like a cremation pyre for democracy.

Gregor Orlov turned and saw him, grinning as he motioned for Andrew to join the group. The Russian didn't recognize the charging wolverine-taut form of Major Brothers until the man slammed into him. Brothers drove the Russian against the icicle-studded rail. Orlov grunted in surprise, but did not recover enough to fend for himself.

The other auroral researchers scrambled backward, surprised at how their companion had turned on them, still not quite believing what they were seeing. They shouted at him in Russian, demanding explanations. Someone finally stumbled through the same questions in English.

"Stay back!" Brothers screamed, holding the Russian hard against the rail. Spittle flew from his mouth, and his eyes were blazing and bloodshot, ready to explode from the sheer anger kept within him.

"Andrew—comrade," Orlov said, swallowing hard. "What is it? What is wrong with you?"

Major Brothers ripped the heavy flare pistol he had taken from the emergency kit and brought it up, jamming the wide muzzle against the hollow of Orlov's throat. "Don't call me *comrade*, you stinking Red bastard!"

The Russian's eyes widened, and the other scientists backed farther away, leaving their instruments behind.

Major Brothers understood it all now: he could see the plan, the devious Commie propaganda, the way they had corrupted him. "I can't save my world—but I can blow his head off!" He glowered into Orlov's wavering face.

The Russian's expression shifted from terror to deep confusion. "Why, Andrew? Why?"

Major Brothers pictured his hand tightening on the trigger of the flare gun, the explosive launching of a projectile that would plunge into this treacherous man's skull and detonate in a blaze, turning Orlov's head into a comet. The incendiary would peel the flesh away from his bones like a hideous Jack-o-lantern doused in gasoline.

"It's too late!" Major Brothers shouted, pushing the flare gun harder against Orlov's neck. "But none of you can stop me now. Nothing can stop me." He raised his voice higher, like the howl of an arctic storm.

Then he looked back toward the bridge house, past the hesitating scientists...and saw another figure coming toward him, gliding across the deck surrounded by frozen mists. For an instant he thought it was the Ukrainian captain of the *Polaris*, but then fear stabbed him like a sword in the gut.

It was the spectral shape again, the vengeful ghost, the ice-encrusted demon that had awakened from the Hecla Isthmus. The accusing and murderous spirit of Private Walter Gordon had been unleashed from his frozen tomb.

Brothers gave a yell of terror that nearly ripped out his vocal cords. As the spectators watched in terrified silence, seeing nothing, he reeled away, dropping the flare gun from Orlov's chin. He turned and squeezed the trigger, blasting the projectile directly at the Ice Creature that stood on the rear deck. But like a meteor, the flare screamed through the ghost's insubstantial form and flew off low into the Arctic Sea where it detonated into a starfire that overshadowed even the auroral display.

The spectre of Private Gordon drifted closer, extending a mangled gloved hand, his arm bent in odd places, broken and crushed from the avalanche that had killed him long ago. Despite his terrors of nuclear holocaust and his absolute certainty of a Soviet missile attack, in Major Brothers' mind this apparition and its unholy purpose was a thousand times worse.

"No!" he screamed.

The other scientists clustered together, confused and terrified. They knew Andrew had no other flares in the gun, and they began to approach him slowly, surrounding him.

The Major knew these evil Soviet scientists would take him prisoner, they would torture him again—and then the ghost of Private Gordon could come to him in his cell and continue to torment his soul. He was damned forever.

"No!" he screamed again, and backed up until he struck the railing on the prow of the *Polaris*. He realized that he had only one escape. Without another word, he grabbed the railing and slung himself over, plummeting down to the ice-choked black water below. He plunged into the cold, cold liquid ice....

The sudden shock of hitting the incredibly frigid water stunned the memories of Major Brothers, and Andrew Gordon surged back into his own mind, his own body. Just in time to feel himself dying.

He couldn't breathe. The water grabbed him, stopping his heart like a hammer. Chunks of ice floated around him, and he crawled to the nearest one as his vision turned dark. He tried to suck in a mouthful of air, but his lungs were constricted. The freezing intensity of the Arctic Sea squeezed, *squeezed*, and Andrew felt Major Brothers inside him, drifting away, losing his own self-aware consciousness.

Flopping his padded arms, Andrew tried to move, tried to swim—and finally grasped a squarish block of ice that did little more than give him something to hang onto as his muscles seized up. He began to shiver uncontrollably.

Major Brothers came close again, not in despair but in resignation. He had done what he could. He had followed his duty. He knew he was right.

And then, as Andrew clutched the ice, he felt the presence of the paranoid Major flow out of him. Long-dead Frank Brothers had been merely a packet of recorded memories, after all, a truer ghost than anything his twisted imagination had conjured. Nothing alive...nothing that should have deserved an existence of its own. Yet, Andrew felt even more drained as the crazed and suspicious man—a product of his own time and incapable of surviving in another era—seeped out of him.

Andrew just wanted to go to sleep.

Up above, the people on the ship shouted and called to him, screaming his name. Andrew rolled over onto his back and tried to wave weakly, feebly, but he couldn't do anything. The cold was too intense.

Finally, ropes were cast down, life preservers, and Gregor Orlov himself, a man Andrew had never imagined to be the least bit of an athlete, scrambled down a chain ladder hastily thrown over the side of the *Polaris*.

A life preserver struck the ice close to him, and Andrew reached out, putting his dripping mittened hand into the hole. Finally, he got his head and shoulders through. Orlov dropped beside him onto the shifting, rocking raft of ice and grabbed his chest, hugging Andrew. Then the others pulled them up higher.

As Andrew dangled, he looked back down at the flat surface to which he had clung. There, in the translucent blue-white murk he thought he saw another form, a silhouette, the shadowy shape of a man spread-eagled, fallen into the ice and imprisoned there like a ghost...or a memory. He was sure it was just his imagination, his freezing brain offering hallucinations...though another part of him was just as sure that this shadow was all that remained of Major Brothers, now trapped in the ice.

The Northern Lights glared overhead, and as Andrew looked up into the sky, he thought the aurora was the most beautiful sight he had ever seen: shimmering colors, rippling tapestries of ionized radiation—nothing sinister, no echoes of a nuclear holocaust as Major Brothers had believed, but simply a symphony of solar wind and magnetic field lines.

"My friend, I don't know what is wrong with you," Orlov said, leaning close to him and not sure if Andrew could hear.

Andrew croaked, trying to form words. But he couldn't make himself heard.

"I thought you had resolved your mystery, your guilt, whatever it was that drove you, Andrew. I don't know why you decided you had to take it out on me."

"It's...it's all right now," Andrew said. "I've exorcised my demons."

He saw the scowling faces of the captain and the other physicists and meteorologists, their instruments abandoned, the aurora ignored. All were baffled by their colleague's behavior. All were outraged. Some of the meteorologists and physicists seemed most annoyed with the simple fact that he had distracted them from their studies at the moment of greatest importance.

Orlov helped the others haul Andrew over the railing. Hands reached out to grasp his sopping, now ice-rimed clothes. He tried to say something into the cacophony of Russian and German and English expressions of concern and outrage, but he was too weak, too cold, too exhausted.

The Ukrainian captain, more sensible, came forward with an emergency blanket, which he wrapped around the violently shivering man. "Get him down below," he said in clear English, then bellowed again in Russian to make sure everyone understood; he was still the captain, and he expected to be obeyed. "Strip these wet clothes off. Get him a hot shower. Then see him to the infirmary, if there's anything else we have to do."

Andrew shivered and blinked. His vision was failing, and he just wanted to fall into unconsciousness, but as he looked up at the faces that backed away, he saw another form, a horrific vision that Major Brothers had brought to him.

The ghost of long-dead Private Gordon rose up again out of the mists and the glowing spotlights of the auroras.

Andrew's already wavering heart nearly stopped with fright. He thought Major Brothers had gone from him. All the leftover echoes from the memory-transference experiment had faded, shocked out of his system by the arctic water. He should never have seen this spectre that had dwelled in the Major's mind. Yet still the ice-cloaked form rose up, looming taller than the other people on deck. They didn't see the ghost; he was just an apparition...but somehow the phantom had remained behind even after the second death of Major Brothers.

The ghost raised its gloved hand, and Andrew tried to blink. Ice clogged his vision. Frost covered his eyelids, and he couldn't focus clearly on anything. But finally, instead of pointing an accusing finger, the ghost of Private Gordon—Andrew's father—merely raised a hand in *recognition*. In greeting, or farewell?

Andrew's teeth chattered violently, and the scientists jostled him, moving him away to the inner cabins and heated rooms, but Andrew forced his eyes open, tried to focus. He wanted to see. Perhaps his father had a message for him.

Their eyes met. What Major Brothers had seen as demonic torches of fury and accusations, now seemed to hold sadness for Andrew, filled with a deep sense of loss, not just of his own life, but of all the years the man could have spent with his son.

As Andrew stared, feeling consciousness fading away, the spectre shimmered. The aurora shone through his faint and indistinct body. Then the ghost of Private Gordon drifted away, breaking apart...at peace at last.

Andrew could never be sure in the years afterward whether he had truly seen a true vision, or merely a leftover panicked hallucination locked into the transferred memories of the paranoid Major. No matter what, he could not hate Major Brothers, though the man had tried to kill his friend Gregor Orlov, though he had insisted on seeing the worst in the world's situation.

Still, Major Brothers had given Andrew a chance to see his father face to face, for the first and last time in his life. For that, Andrew would have paid almost any price—and he nearly had.

Gregor Orlov bellowed for the others to be careful with his friend, to hurry up and get him warm again. Andrew couldn't say a word as they hustled him into the heated inner cabins of the *Polaris*.

Overhead, shining brighter than any sunrise that had ever graced the Arctic Circle, the magnificent aurora spread a fountain of bright colors over the world.

Introduction to Prisoner of War

ACCORDING TO UNOFFICIAL MILITARY POLICY, the US Air Force knows exactly what it takes to make the best fighter pilot: balls the size of grapefruits, and brains the size of a pea.

Some might say that it requires all the good qualities of a fighter pilot to walk in Harlan Ellison's footsteps. Harlan is always a hard act to follow, and it's daunting even to try.

Since childhood I had always loved *THE OUTER LIMITS*—I never cared about the rubber monsters or the corny special effects—my imagination took care of all that. So, when the publishers asked me to do this book, they found my soft spot. "Pick your favorite episodes, and do anything you want with them," they said.

It didn't take me long to figure that one out. "Even Harlan's episodes?"

A longer pause this time. "Well...if you can get him to agree."

When I first talked with Harlan, he was very skeptical. Given the sheer number of abysmal sequels and bad spinoffs that have graced bookstore racks and theater screens, I suppose he had good reason. "I've never done a sequel to a single one of my stories," he told me. "I never felt the need. If I got it right the first time, I've said all I needed to say."

In the course of my writing career I have gathered a rather impressive (if that's the word) collection of rejection slips—something like 750 at last count—and I never learned to give up when common sense dictates that I should. So, I went back to Harlan. "You've developed a sprawling scenario of a devastating future war, where soldiers are bred and trained to do nothing but fight from birth to death. Are you telling me that there's only *one story* to be told in that whole world?"

Once I'd convinced him that I didn't want to do "the further adventures of Qarlo's ashes" or some other contrived sequel, but rather a *companion piece*, I finally got to play with his toys. This novelette is set in the world of "Soldier", dealing with some of the same themes and ingredients.

PRISONER OF WAR is my tap-dance on Harlan's stage, a story about another set of warriors in a never-ending war, men bred for nothing but the battleground—and how they cope with the horrors of...*peace*.

Prisoner of War

T HE FIRST ENEMY LASER-LANCES BLAZED ACROSS THE BATTLEFIELD at an unknown time of day. No one paid attention to the *hour* during a fire-fight anyway. Neither Barto nor any of his squad-mates could see the sun or moon overhead: too much smoke and haze and blast debris filled the air, along with the smell of blood and burning.

A soldier had to be ready at any time or place. A soldier would fight until the fight was over. An endless *Now* filled their existence, a razor-edged flow of life-for-the-moment, and the slightest distraction or daydream could end the *Now*...forever.

With a clatter of dusty armor and a hum of returned weapons-fire, the defenders charged forward, Barto among them. They had no terrain maps or battle plans, only unseen commanders bellowing instructions into their helmet earpieces.

Greasy fires guttered and smoked from explosions, but as long as a soldier could draw breath, the air always smelled sweet enough. Somehow, the flames still found organic material to burn, though only a few skeletal trees remained standing. The horizon was like broken, jagged teeth. No discernible structures remained, only blistered destruction and the endless bedlam of combat.

To a man who had known no other life, Barto found the landscape familiar and comforting.

"Down!" his point man Arviq screamed loudly enough so that Barto could hear it through the armored helmet. A bolt of white-hot energy seared the ground in front of them, turning the blasted soil into glass. The ricochet stitched a broken-windshield pattern of lethal cuts across the armored chest of one comrade five meters away.

The victim was in a different part of the squad; Barto knew him only by serial number instead of a more personal, chosen name. Now the man was a casualty of war; his serial number would be displayed in fine print on the memorial lists back at the cache—for two days. And then it would be erased forever.

Barto and Arviq both dove to the bottom of the trench as more well-aimed laser-lances embroidered the ground and the slumping walls of the ditch. As he hunched over to shield himself, the helmet's speakers continued to pound commands: "KILL...KILL...KILL..."

The Enemy assault ended with a brief hesitation, like an indrawn breath. The soldiers around Barto paused, regrouped, then scrambled to their feet, leaving the fallen comrade behind. Later, regardless of the battle's outcome, trained bloodhounds would retrieve the body parts and drag them back to HQ in their jaws. After the proper casualty statistics had been recorded, the KIA corpses would be efficiently incinerated.

In the middle of a firefight, Barto and Arviq could not be bothered by such things. They had been trained never to think of fallen comrades; it was beyond the purview of their mission. The voice in the helmet speakers changed, took on a different note: "RETALIATE...RETALIATE...RETALIATE..."

With a howl and a roar enhanced by adrenaline injections from inside the armor suits, Barto and his squad moved as a unit. Programmed endorphins poured into their blood streams at the moment of battle frenzy, and they surged out of the trench. The Enemy encampment could not be far, and they silently swore to unleash a slaughter that would outmatch anything their opponents had ever done...though this most recent attack was assuredly a response to their own previous day's offensive.

Moving as a unit, the squad clambered over debris, around craters, and out into the open. They ran beyond monofilament barricades that would slice the limb off an unwary soldier, then into a sonic minefield whose layout shone on the eye-visor screen inside each helmet.

With a self-assured gait across the no-man's land, the soldiers moved like a pack of killer rats, laser-lances slung in their arms. They bellowed and snarled, pumping each other up. As he ran, Barto studied the sonic minefield grid in his visor, sidestepping instinctively.

From their embankment, the Enemy began to fire again. The smoky air became a lattice of deadly lines in all directions. Barto continued running. Beside him, Arviq pressed the stock of his weapon against his armored breastplate, pumping blast after blast toward the unseen Enemy.

Then a laser-lance seared close to Barto's helmet, blistering the top layer of semi-reflective silver. Static blasted across his eye visor, and he couldn't see. He made one false sidestep and yelled. He could no longer find the grid display, could no longer even see the actual ground.

Just as his foot came down in the wrong place, Arviq grabbed his arm and yanked him aside, using their combined momentum. The sonic mine exploded, vomiting debris and shrapnel with pounding sound waves that fractured the plates of Barto's armor, pulverizing the bones in his leg. But he fell out of the mine's focused kill radius and lay biting back the pain.

He propped himself up and ripped off his slagged helmet, blinking with naked eyes at the real sky. Arviq had saved his life—just as Barto would have done for his squad-mate had their situations been reversed.

Always trust your comrades. Your life is theirs. That was how it had always been.

And even if he did fall to Enemy attack, the bloodhounds would haul his body to HQ, and he would receive an appropriate military farewell before he returned to the earth—mission accomplished. A soldier's duty was to fight, and Barto had been performing that duty for all of his conscious life.

As he activated his rescue transmitter and fumbled for the medpak, the rest of the soldiers charged forward, leaving him behind. Arviq didn't even spare him a backward glance.

Some said the war had gone on forever--and since no one kept track of history anymore, the statement could not be proved false.

Barto knew only the military life. He had emerged from a tank in the soldiers' cache with the programming wired into his brain, fully aware, fully grown, and knowing his assignment. If ever he had any questions or doubts, the command voices in his helmet would answer them.

Barto knew primarily that he had to kill the Enemy. He knew that he had to protect his comrades, that the squad was the sum of his existence. No good soldier could rest until every last Enemy had been eradicated, down to their feline spies, down to the bloodhounds that dragged away Enemy KIAs.

Winning this war might well take an eternity, but Barto was willing to fight for that long. Every moment of his life had encompassed either fighting, or learning new techniques to kill and to survive, or resting so that he could fight again the next day.

There was no time for anything else. There was no need for anything else.

Barto remembered when he'd been younger, not long out of the tank. His muscles were wiry, his body flexible without the stiffness of constant abuse. His skin had been smooth, free of the intaglio of scars from a thousand close dances with death. Barto and his squad-mates—apprentices all—had fought hand-to-hand in the cache gymnasium, occasionally breaking each other's bones or knocking each other unconscious. None of them had yet earned their armor, their protection, or their weapons. They couldn't even call themselves soldiers.

Now consigned to the HQ infirmary and repair shop, as he drifted in a soup of pain and unconsciousness, Barto revisited the long-ago moment he had first grasped a specialized piece of equipment designed to maim and kill. The soldier trainees had learned early on in their drill that any object was a potential weapon—but this was a *spear*, a long rough bar of old steel with a sharpened point that gleamed white and silver in the unforgiving lights. A *weapon*, his own weapon.

He spun it around in his hand, feeling its weight—a deadly impaling device that could be used against the oncoming Enemy.

Later, his advanced training would, of course, include hand-to-hand combat against other soldiers, human opponents, but not at first. All trainees were expendable, but if the young men could be salvaged, then the military programming services would turn them into killers.

For months, Barto received somatic instruction and physical drilling by one of the rare old veterans who had survived years of combat. The veteran had a wealth of experience and survival instincts that could not be matched even by the most sophisticated computers. He made sure that Barto fought to the limit of his abilities.

Swinging the spear against nothing, feeling his body move, Barto reacted to the barked commands of the veteran instructor. Response without thought. He learned how to make the weapon into a part of himself, an extension of his reflexes. *He* was the weapon; the spear was just an augmentation.

Then they gave him a taste of blood, real blood. They wanted him to get in the habit of killing.

The small metal-walled arena was like an echo chamber, a large underground room with simulated rock outcroppings, a fallen tree, and other sharp obstacles. Barto didn't question the reality of the scenario. The environment itself was a tool to be used.

During that exercise, the veteran instructor let him wear his helmet...but nothing else. Stripped naked, he gripped the spear in his hand and glared through the visor. The helmet earphones gave him reassuring commands in his ears, directions, suggestions. Otherwise, Barto felt helpless—but no *soldier* was ever helpless, because a helpless man could not become a soldier.

Underground, the arena door groaned open, and barricade bars moved away. Barto tensed. He gripped the metal shaft of the spear despite the sweat on his palms.

Suddenly, a whirlwind of bristles and scales, sharp hooves and long tusks launched itself like a projectile. An enhanced boar with scarlet eyes snarled and plowed forward, searching for a target, something against which to vent its anger.

And Barto was the only other creature in the room.

On high pedestals in the gallery above, three enhanced cats watched, blinking their gold-green eyes. The feline spy commanders observed for the invisible overlords who wanted to see how the freshly detanked soldiers reacted in their first real life-or-death test.

The boar charged. Barto jabbed with the spear, but he was too tentative. Before, he had only thrust at imaginary opponents and an occasional hologram projected inside his visor. Now, though, the boar came on like a locomotive. The spear glanced off, opening a mere stinging scratch in the creature's skin. Barto had not imagined its hide could be so tough, its bones so hard. He had made the first, terrible mistake in this duel.

The trivial wound enraged the beast.

Barto dove to one side over a synthetic rock, and the boar rammed into the artificial tree trunk. It spun around, shaking its head, tusks gleaming. The ivory spears in its mouth looked much more deadly than Barto's primitive weapon. The boar attacked again.

A moment of panic rose up like an illusion, but he pounded it back, and the fear evaporated, bringing a rush of adrenaline. The chemical and electronic components in his body released the substance, making Barto see red rage of his own.

The enhanced boar recovered itself and snorted. Barto knew he had a better chance of striking the target in motion if he didn't use a tiny pinpoint thrust; instead, he swung the heavy metal bar sideways like a cudgel. The sturdy steel bashed the creature's thick skull. The sound of the impact rang out in the hollow room.

The cats watched from their pedestals.

The boar squealed and thrashed. Barto saw that its eyes held an increased intelligence, like that found in the feline spies and in the daredevil bloodhounds that retrieved bodies from the battlefield. The boar responded with a calculated counterattack, trying to out think this naked human opponent, this would-be soldier. Barto smiled: the boar was the Enemy.

In the frenzy of battle, Barto no longer thought like an intelligent human being. Instead, he relied only on instinct and unbearable bloodlust. He rushed in without forethought, without care, without any sense of self-preservation. After all...he had a spear.

The boar tried to feint, to react, but Barto gave the Enemy no chance. He swung again with the staff, drawing a bright red line of blood and putting out one of the beast's eyes. Crimson and yellow body fluids oozed through smashed skin on the boar's snout. It leapt forward, driven by insanity and pain.

Now, Barto used the spear with finesse.

A great calm flowed through him, as if the rest of the world had slowed down, and he saw exactly what to do, exactly where to hold the spear. The sharpened point neatly plunged through the rib cage of the beast and skewered its lungs and heart. Showering a wet-iron smell in the air, the creature lay quivering, trembling...dying.

When Barto came back to his senses, he saw that his legs had been slashed open by the boar's tusks. The deep gouges left him bleeding, but oddly without any sense of pain or injury. He looked down and studied the corpse of his opponent, the Enemy. Now he had killed. Barto had fresh blood on his hands, real blood from a vanquished opponent.

He liked the sensation.

He knew that this had been no simple exercise. He knew the boar could well have killed him, and that other trainees who had vanished from the barracks must have failed this part of their instruction.

But Barto had succeeded. He was a *killer* now, and he was one step closer to becoming a soldier.

Time didn't matter. For a soldier, time never mattered. He awoke hours, or days, later back in the HQ infirmary and repair shop--patched up, drugged, but fully aware. A hairless chimpanzee tended him, leaning over in a cloud of disinfectant scents and bad breath. The chimp medical techs knew how to bandage and fix battlefield wounds. They could do no surgery that required finesse, but the soldiers required nothing that needed delicacy for cosmetic effect.

Once injured, if a soldier could be fixed, he would be sent back to the battlefield. If his wounds caused the chimp med-techs too much trouble, he would be eliminated. Every surviving member of the squad bore his share of scars, burns, scabs, and callouses. No one paid attention to these trophies of war; they were part of a soldier's life, not a badge of honor or bravery.

Since Barto hadn't been eliminated, he assumed he must have been fixed.

He sat up on the infirmary cot, and the hairless chimpanzees hurried over, uttering quiet reassurances, a few English words, a few soothing grunts. Triggered by his awakening, a signal was automatically sent back to his squad commander.

Barto listened to an assessment of his repaired leg, his stitched muscles and skin, and his bruises and contusions. *Not too bad*, he thought. He'd suffered worse, sometimes even in training with other soldiers (especially during the initial few months, when they'd first been given their own sets of armor). He remembered that back then his comrade Arviq in particular had thought himself invincible.

During downtime before the soldiers crawled into their assigned sleeping bins, the other squad members were required to file through the infirmary to see their injured comrades. Some came only because of orders to do so; most of them would rather have been sleeping.

But the invisible commanders planted instructions to go to the infirmary simply so that other soldiers could see the wounded, could see what could happen to them if they weren't careful...but also so they could see that they just might survive.

Recovering, Barto sat up in the uncomfortable infirmary bed and watched the other soldiers come in. His pain went away with another automatic rush of endorphins to deaden his unpleasant sensations...or perhaps his own determination was enough to quell the nerve-fire of agony.

The fighters filed by. He recognized few of them, all strangers without armor and helmets, though he could have identified each one by the serial numbers displayed on their fatigues. These were soldiers, cogs in a fighting machine. They didn't have time to be individuals.

When Arviq came up at the end of the line, he stood brusque, nodding gruffly. "You'll mend," he said.

"Thank you for saving me," Barto answered. It was the closest thing they'd had to a conversation in a long time.

"It's my duty. I await the day when you can fight with us again." He marched out, and the others followed him. Barto lay back and attempted to sleep, to regain his strength. Through sheer force of will, he growled at his cells and tissues to work harder, to knit the injuries and restore him to full health.

Day after day, lying in the infirmary and *waiting* proved far more difficult than any combat situation Barto had ever encountered. Finally, after a maddening week of intensive recuperation, directed therapy aided by medical technology and powerful drugs, he was released from his hospital prison and sent back to the front.

Where he belonged.

The battlefield screamed with pain and destruction, explosions, fire, and death, but to Barto, after being so long in the sheltered quiet of the infirmary, the tumult was a shout of exuberance. He was glad to be here.

The soldiers raced across the ground, each in his own squad position, weapons drawn. They had already driven back the Enemy, and now the fire of laser-lances grew even thicker around them as the others became desperate. They pressed ahead, deeper into enemy territory than they had ever gone before.

Their helmet locators for sonic mines and shrapnel grenades buzzed constantly, but the reptilian part of Barto's brain reacted without volition, hardwired into fighting and killing. He dodged and wove, keeping himself alive.

His point man, Arviq, jogged close beside him, and Barto extended his peripheral vision behind the dark visor to enfold his comrade into an invisible protective sphere. He would assist his partner if he got into trouble—not out of any sense of payback or obligation, but because it was an automatic response, his own assignment. He would have done the same for any other soldier, any member of his squad, anyone but the Enemy.

Precision-guided mortars scribed parabolas through the air and exploded close to any concentration of soldiers who did not display the proper transponders. Amidst screams and thunder, a massive triple detonation wiped out over half of Barto's squad, but the others did not fall back, did not even pause. They drove onward, continued the push. The fallen comrades would be taken care of somehow, though no one knew how the bloodhounds would ever make it this deep into Enemy-held territory.

This far behind the main battle lines, the Enemy numbers themselves were dwindling, and Barto fired and fired again. The laser-lance thrummed in his gauntleted hands, skewering a distant man's chest plate and leaving a smoking hole.

But it wasn't really a man, after all. It was the Enemy.

The chase continued, and the survivors of Barto's squad ran in the direction of what must have been Enemy HQ. In his dry, dusty mouth he could taste the sweet honey of victory.

But suddenly, unexpectedly, the Enemy triggered a row of booby-traps that did not appear on the helmet sensors. Camouflaged catapults popped up, spraying nearly invisible clouds of netting, monofilament webs as insubstantial as smoke but sharper than the most deadly razor.

The flying webwork engulfed four soldiers near Barto, and they fell into neatly butchered pieces. But oddly enough, so did three of the Enemy men rushing in retreat, as if they themselves hadn't known of these defenses. But their own visor sensors *must* have been keyed to booby-traps they themselves had planted.

Though the question astonished him, Barto did not pause. His job was not to analyze. Paraplegic computer tacticians and the invisible battle-field commanders did all that work. The voices in his helmet told him to push forward, and so he pushed forward.

Arviq ran beside him, still firing his laser-lance and, numbly, Barto realized that most of the other soldiers were dead. His squad had been decimated...but the Enemy was nearly eradicated as well.

War often required sacrifices, and many soldiers died. But a victory would pay the bloody cost ten times over. They had never gone so far.

The thrill of seeing the Enemy nearly exterminated gave Barto all the enthusiasm he needed, even without an adrenaline rush augmented by injectors in his armor. With a shared glance behind opaque visors, he and Arviq both had the same thought, and ran forward with their four remaining companions. They couldn't stop now.

Then large gun emplacements popped out of the ground, more massive than anything he had ever seen before. Barto reeled in unaccustomed confusion. The Enemy had never exhibited technology like this!

Automated fire rained down on them, super powerful laser-lances far more devastating than any of the hand-held rifles.

Soldiers screamed. The blasts were like belts of incinerating flame, vaporizing armor, leaving not even bones for the bloodhounds to retrieve. The firepower pummeled anyone who came close, whether friend or Enemy. They had no chance, no chance at all.

An explosion ripped out a deep crater ten meters from them. Someone screamed, but Barto had no voice. The automated super lasers continued to track across the ground, pinpointing armor, crushing any movement. Barto watched the beams sweep closer, vaporizing everything in the vicinity. His four remaining squad members died in a puff of blood-smoke and molten armor plate.

On impulse he grabbed Arviq and shoved him hard toward the fresh crater. Together, the two dove into the raw trench just as the splash of disintegration passed over them. The voices in his helmet turned to a rainstorm of incomprehensible static.

Within moments the battle stopped. Everyone else was dead.

All of the laser fire and explosions ceased. All the Enemy, all of the squad, every other living thing had been annihilated.

Without saying a word, Arviq hauled himself to his hands and knees and reached over to shake Barto, who also recovered his balance. The two of them sat panting for a moment, stunned but still determined. Neither of them— in fact, no one they knew—had ever been so far behind Enemy lines.

They rose up slowly and carefully into the crackling silence, afraid of other automated target systems. Clods of dry dirt fell from their armor. Dust and crackling ash roiled through the air...but nothing else moved.

"We won?" Barto asked. "Is the war over?"

"I hope not." Arviq turned to him, his mouth a grim line beneath the opaque visor of the helmet. "The war will never be over. But we may have won this battle."

Barto raised his helmet over the rim of the blasted crater. No weapons responded to the motion. The battlefield remained eerily quiet with only the faint sound of coughing fires and settling dust.

"Must be the Enemy encampment," Arviq said with a grunt. "Increased defenses—maybe even HQ." He grinned. "Success!"

But Barto wasn't so sure. Moving with tense caution, he climbed away from the crater. "No, not HQ. The defenses killed as many of them as us. ID transponders useless."

Arviq joined him, sole survivors on the sprawling battlefield. Barto could see where the huge gun emplacements had raised up. Adjusting his visor filters, he spotted different infrared signatures, metallic traces, solid structures and hollow passages beneath the scarred ground.

Amazed, Barto crept forward. "We've discovered something. We're required to investigate."

"No, back to HQ," Arviq said. "We must report. Our squad was wiped out."

But Barto shook him off. He stood determined, looking ahead across the scabbed landscape. "Not until we have hard reconnaissance. This could be important."

Arviq hesitated only a moment. Neither outranked the other, and they had no time for argument, but Arviq quickly came to his own decision. "Yes. Reconnaissance is part of our mission."

Most of the time, sly intelligent cats would creep through the darkness, observing Enemy strongholds and reporting back to HQ. But the squad had gone farther into Enemy territory than any known advance, and they might have new information. That was the most important thing. They weren't doing it for the glory or for a possible promotion, or for any sort of reward. Barto and Arviq would take the risk because it was their duty.

"My head, my thoughts...are empty," Arviq said, tapping his helmet.

Barto adjusted his earphones, but still received no transmission and no commands. An uneasy silence echoed in his head. The speakers growled no more repetitive commands to attack and kill.

"How can you stand it?" Arviq looked at him.

Barto took a deep breath. "No choice. Tolerate it."

Crouched low, they trudged toward the automated gun emplacements, but the motion sensors did not reactivate. The Enemy weapons had gone through their program and wiped out the threat. Somehow, the two comrades had slipped through the cracks. They could move forward.

Barto and Arviq found a metal hatch plate in the half-hidden superstructure of the enormous laser-lances. Barto sat down and pressed his helmet against the hatch, carefully listening for any vibration, fully tense. Any moment now he expected the destructive fire to rain out again.

He tugged on the hatch, looking for access controls. "We can infiltrate," he said. "It's an underground bunker. Maybe weapons storage. We can bring supplies or power packs back to HQ."

Together they wiped off dust and blasted dirt from the plate, used tools at their armor belts to crack open the seals, and finally they lifted the heavy hatch.

Still no voices came to their heads, no instructions. The two soldiers were on their own. Barto didn't like it one bit.

They dropped down into the opening, where a steel ladder led into a maw of shadows. They descended, gripping rung after rung with gauntleted hands. *If this is Enemy HQ*, Barto thought, *it's a much larger complex than anything our squad has ever lived in*.

Finally the ladder ended in an underground tunnel with the hatch cover high above them. Barto paused for a moment to scan the surroundings, then they walked forward into dim silence. The tunnels seemed empty, barely used, abandoned for a long time. Barto realized the Enemy soldiers could not have emerged from this place. No one had walked down these access tunnels in a long, long time.

As point man, Arviq led the way. He strode forward, hands on his weapons, ready for anything. A soldier had to be flexible and determined. The small tunnel lights gave little illumination, but their helmet visors augmented the ambient photons.

Cameras in their helmets recorded everything as reconnaissance files to be downloaded back in HQ. They continued for what seemed like miles, trudging deeper and deeper into the Earth. This place was an important facility, possibly a central complex...but Barto couldn't begin to understand it.

From up ahead came a faint throbbing from generators and heavy machinery. Finally, they saw brighter light, thick windows, rectangular plates that shone through to another world, a subterranean complex that seemed like a mythical land. Inside huge grottoes, pale ethereal people moved about wearing bright colors. Plants of a shockingly lush green, garish hues that Barto had never seen before drew the two of them forward like magnets.

"What is this?" Arviq asked. "Some kind of trick?"

"Paradise."

As the soldiers approached, unable to believe what they were seeing, they crossed an unseen threshold, a booby-trap. They heard a brief hum, a crackle of power-surge. Barto reacted just in time to feel a sinking despair—but not fast enough to get out of the way.

A pressing white light engulfed both of them, swallowing them up. In an instant, Barto's visor turned black, then so did his eyes.

When he awoke, the assault on his senses nearly knocked him back into protective unconsciousness. Sounds, smells, colors bombarded him like weapons fire. His armor and helmet had been stripped away, leaving him vulnerable; without it, he felt helpless, soft-skinned, like a worm.

The bed beneath him was warm and soft, disorienting. A gentle and cozy light surrounded him instead of the familiar garish white to which he was accustomed back in his own barracks. Each breath of the humid air was perfumed with a sweet, flowery scent that nauseated him.

Was this an infirmary? Barto turned his head gently, and a raging pain clamored inside his skull. The place reminded him oddly of the time he had been helpless and healing from his previous injury...but he saw no hairless chimpanzees, no robotic medical attendants. The sheets were soft and slick, vastly different from the usual rough, sterile covering.

Grogginess smothered his mind and body. Barto tried to return to full awareness, but something was wrong. His body remained sluggish and unresponsive, as if the accustomed chemical stimulants were not being released according to program. He needed adrenaline; he needed endorphins.

Arviq lay on another bed beside him, similarly prone, similarly stripped of his armor. When Barto turned his head and directed his gaze in the opposite direction, he was astonished to find another person by his shoulder. Not one of the enhanced animals bred to attend the regiment, but a *woman*, a lovely creature with short, honey-brown hair and a shimmering purple garment so brilliant and dazzling that it made his eyes ache.

Responding with combat readiness, he sat up with a lurch. The woman rushed over and shushed him with a gentle touch. "Quiet now. Everything's all right. You are safe here." Her voice sounded like sweet syrup. *Alien.*

Arviq stirred beside him, groaning in confusion and growing rage.

Then Barto remembered a legend, a story told on the field during the quiet times between battles when some soldiers were more frightened than others. It was a hopeful myth of what happened to brave and dedicated fighters after a death in battle. *Was this...Valhalla?*

He glanced over at Arviq, his face contorted with confusion. His eyes glimmered with dark fires. "Are we dead?"

The woman laughed like tinkling crystal. "No, soldier. We are people like yourselves, human beings."

She didn't look like him, though, or any other person he had ever seen. Barto shook his head, refusing to acknowledge the pain left over inside. He'd had enough experience with pain. "You're not...soldiers."

The woman smiled and leaned closer to him. A warmth radiated from her scrubbed and lotioned skin. He had never noticed a person's physical features before, never paid attention...and he'd never seen anything so beautiful in his life.

"Everyone is a soldier," he said, "either for our side, or the Enemy."

The woman continued to give him a slightly superior smile. "You are soldiers, my friends...but we are not. Not here." She gave a gesture to indicate her entire underground world. "After all, it's a war. You're fighting and dying." Her thin, dark eyebrows rose up in graceful arches on her forehead. "Did it never occur to you to ask exactly what you're fighting...*for*?"

With a sudden burst of energy and an outcry of rage, Arviq lunged up from his bed, reaching out with clawlike hands, his face full of fury. Even without armor or weapons, any soldier knew how to kill with his bare hands. Somehow Barto also found the energy to lash out, to propel himself into a combat frame of mind.

The woman staggered back from the infirmary beds, startled. Barto saw shadows, more people moving behind observation windows, automatic devices activating. There was another flash of white light, and again he lost consciousness.

When Barto awoke once more, he was alone in a room, clad in soft pajamas with more slick sheets wrapped around him. He found his bed too pliant, too yielding, as if it meant to be comfortable with a vengeance.

The gentle sound of running water trickled from speakers embedded in the wall. The white noise had a soothing effect, the opposite of the perpetual, pressuring commands that had droned into his ears from helmet speakers. Now, the image of a soporific, bubbling brook made him want to lie motionless in a stupor.

He no longer even seemed alive.

This room was smaller, the walls painted pastel colors instead of clean white. The illumination was muted and warm, like sunlight through amber. It made his head fuzzy.

Stiffly, Barto rolled over and found that Arviq wasn't with him this time. His comrade had been taken elsewhere. Was this some sort of insidious Enemy plan? Divide and conquer, separate the squad members.

Had he fallen into some new kind of warfare that went beyond violence and destruction to this personality-destroying brainwashing technique? Barto snarled and tried to find a way to escape—a captured soldier's duty was to escape at all costs.

He didn't hear a door open, felt no movement of the air, but suddenly the beautiful woman stood there with him, setting a platter down on a ledge formed out of the substance of the wall. She leaned over his bed, her entire body smelling of gentle flowers and perfumes. She smiled down at him, parting soft lips to reveal even white teeth. Barto started, ready to fight with hand-to-hand techniques even without his armor or his weapons, but she made no threatening move.

"My name is Juliette," she said, then waited as if he was supposed to recognize some significance to the name.

He answered as he had been drilled. "Barto. Corporal. E21TFDN." He rolled off the serial number in a singsong chant, "Eetoowun teeyeff deeyenn." He had spoken it more than any other word in his lifetime. Then he formed his mouth into a grim line. That was all he had been trained to say. The Enemy rarely, if ever, took prisoners. Everyone died on the battlefield.

"I brought food for you...Barto." Juliette picked up a steaming, spicy-smelling bowl from the tray on the ledge. It contained some kind of broth laced with vegetables, even a little meat.

Though he could withstand long periods of fasting, Barto realized how hungry he was. He'd been trained to shut off the hunger pangs and nerve twinges in his digestive system. But he also knew to take nourishment whenever possible, to maintain his strength.

She extended a spoon, and Barto raised his head to accept a mouthful. The spoon was metal with rounded edges. Even such a crude and innocuous weapon could be used in many different ways as a killing instrument. He could have snatched it from her, but he did not, taking the mouthful instead.

The flavors exploded around his tongue, and Barto nearly choked. It was too intense, too spiced, too fresh—experiences his mouth had never had. Back in the barracks all soldiers ate a common meal, a protein-rich gruel that served as sustenance and nothing else. He'd never before dined on a preparation in which someone had cared about its flavors. He didn't find it at all pleasant.

Juliette gave him another mouthful, and he forced himself to eat it. But he did not let down his guard for an instant.

"The stun-field should have no residual effect on you, Barto," she said. "You'll regain your strength in no time." Her voice sounded odd in his ears, pitched with a higher timbre, musical rather than the implacable instructions that had poured into his ears from the helmet's speakers.

"I'm strong enough," Barto said. "Where is my comrade?"

"He's safe and being tended. But we thought it best to separate you." She took the bowl away, then stood back to appraise him. "I'm curious about you, Barto, Corporal, E21TFDN. I want to be your friend, so let's just use our first names, all right?" She brushed her hand along his arm, and he recoiled at her touch; it felt like warm feathers tickling across the skin. "Can you stand up? I'd like to take you for a walk to show you where you are."

Barto did not argue with her. Regardless of her intentions, Juliette's offer would allow him to continue his reconnaissance. She could show him whatever she wished, and he would gather information. Without the helmet visor and its implanted cameras, he would have to observe with his own eyes, and remember details. But it could be done.

As he swung off the bed, the loose-fitting pajamas felt strange on him, not hard enough, not safe. He walked on the balls of his bare feet, every muscle tense, searching for mysterious threats as Juliette led him out of the room. She took him down underground corridors into even richer light. They passed beautiful images of scenery, forgotten forests and lost mountains…waterfalls and lakes unlike anything he had ever seen on the battle-scarred combat fields.

"Who are you people?" Barto said. "What is this place?"

"We're civilians. We went underground centuries ago to escape the fighting, while our armies defended us against the invasion."

Barto tried to assess the information, to fit it like puzzle pieces into the sparse information in his mind. "My squad is…part of the defenders? We fight against the invaders?"

She looked at him with a curious, placid expression. Her pale skin, delicate bone structure, and pointed chin gave her an ethereal, elfin appearance. "No one knows which side is which anymore."

Other people, similarly pale-skinned and soft-looking, observed the pair as they walked by. Some smiled, some drew back in fear. Many regarded him with cold, fish-like interest. Juliette seemed to enjoy the attention she received just by being with him.

Barto scanned his surroundings for a way to escape and return to his squad. But then he remembered that, except for Arviq, all of his comrades were dead, annihilated by the immense gun emplacements that protected this underground shelter. Back at his own HQ, the databases must have already recorded him and his point man as casualties of war.

Juliette talked as they continued, her voice a pleasant melange of words. She told him of their days of peace and shelter down below, how the survivors had made an entire world down here by excavating tunnel after tunnel. Here, the civilians did what she called *the great work of humanity*—composing music, dabbling in art, writing poetry and literature...though, if they remained isolated down here without experiencing the hard edge of life, Barto didn't know how they found any material to incorporate into their creations.

Though she turned at intersections, descended to different levels, walked in circles, Barto never lost his bearings. He imprinted a map of everything they encountered, knowing he might need to use it later. On his own.

Juliette took him to a greenhouse where the smells nearly stifled him: humid air, the odors of vegetation and mulch, flowers bursting forth like explosions from mortar-fire. Pollinating insects flitted from blossom to blossom, and brilliantly ripe vegetables and fruits made his eyes hurt.

He heard the drip of irrigation systems, saw colorful birds hopping from plant to plant, and a shiver went up his spine. Everything was so quiet here, so gentle. It made him feel too full of energy, too restless.

Barto remembered when he'd been forced to recuperate in the HQ infirmary as the hairless chimpanzees tended to him. He had been bored and frustrated...but with a goal—to *heal*, so he could go back and fight. He had managed to wait until his body returned to its optimal condition, when he could go out and serve his purpose in life.

Here, though, these people had a quiet calmness about them, an air of superiority, with nothing else to do. Juliette seemed to enjoy it, seemed proud of being a civilian.

Barto had never experienced such vibrant beauty, the smells, the music, the sense of *peace*. His body rebelled at the thought, but as the hours went by in the beautiful woman's company he began to feel his resistance crumbling. This was all new to him.

As she showed him their underground paradise, Barto followed her and listened. Finally, in exasperation, he turned to Juliette and asked, "So there's no war here?" He couldn't believe it. Such a concept had never occurred to him. "No battles?"

"Oh, we have a little." Juliette smiled, then gestured him forward. "Here, let me show you. Maybe you'll find it comforting."

She led him down smooth passages where the temperature grew cooler, the smell more metallic. They walked down glass-walled hallways until they reached a control center.

Battle plans. Tactical maps. Troop movement displays.

"This is how we maintain our edge, Barto, and our window on the outside world." Juliette's people sat at stations in front of the shifting screens, their fingers raised across control panels. Terrain grids spread out in front of them in bristling colors.

High-resolution panels showed other soldiers, people in familiar armor and helmets, jittery point-of-view images transmitted from visor cameras. Civilian men and women leaned over, punching in commands and speaking into microphones.

"Move left. Open fire."

Another man with a deep voice droned, "Kill the Enemy. Kill the Enemy. Kill the Enemy." He sounded bored. The others looked very relaxed in their positions.

Barto stared with shock as he realized that *these* were the voices he'd heard in his helmet all his life: directing him, helping him plan his attack. *These* were his ultimate commanders in the war.

Astonished, Barto looked over to see Arviq also standing inside the control room, chaperoned by a civilian man, also dressed in a loose jumpsuit. His point man's chaperone demonstrated the workings of the controls. Arviq's eyes were wide as he watched the battle.

Sensing the new arrivals, Arviq looked up to see Barto. Their eyes met, and hot understanding flashed between them. *This* was the ultimate headquarters of their army. Arviq reeled from the revelation, but Barto felt a nagging question in the back of his mind. He wondered if other civilians in this control room might be directing the *Enemy* troops in a similar fashion.

Safe in their protected bunkers, these isolated civilians played the deadly war like a game, an exercise. They'd lived here for so long, so comfortably, they seemed uninterested in winning the conflict or ending the crisis...merely in maintaining what they already had.

"So you see, Barto," Juliette said, touching his arm again; this time he did not withdraw so quickly, "we understand what you go through. We're familiar with the war, we're there with you inside your head during even the most terrible missions. We know how difficult it is for the soldiers." She smiled. "That's why I'm very glad to offer you asylum here. Stay with us." Now she sounded coy. "I'd be...very interested in getting to know you better."

Arviq glowered, out of his element. The chaperone next to him nodded toward Juliette, and she said, "You see, Gunnar is also taking good care of your comrade. Stay here. Consider it well-deserved R&R."

Barto looked around, saw the controllers, heard the familiar command voices. He answered gruffly, "I'm a soldier. I follow orders." Even if it meant he must stop fighting for a while.

Once the two prisoners had resigned themselves to their situation, they were allowed to speak with each other, though neither Barto nor Arviq had ever had much use for conversation. For a week they had made no violent gestures and learned to *behave themselves*—as Juliette described it. As a reward, Barto and Arviq were allowed to sit next to each other in the dining hall.

The room was a large chamber with plush seats and long tables. Lights sparkled from prisms overhead, and the air was redolent with the rich smells of exotic dishes. Various salads and broiled fishes and interesting soups were spread before them. The hall echoed with a murmur of voices.

In his training sessions, Barto had learned about the horrors of being a POW, should such a fate ever befall him. But he was now confused, not sure which orders to follow, what was the proper course of action. Juliette had insisted he was their honored guest, not a prisoner. Should he still try to escape? These civilians had given him food and shelter, and a soft bed, though he desperately wanted his narrow basket-bunk back. He longed for the decisive voice in his ears that commanded him to do his duty—but Barto no longer knew exactly what his duty was.

Arviq looked at his plate and poked at the gaudy, frilly dishes that had been served to him. Soft-skinned civilians walked by, staring at them, whispering to each other. One reached out to touch Arviq on the shoulder, as if on a dare; the soldier lashed out like a python, and the two observers scampered away giggling, as if titillated by the thrill they'd just received.

Barto felt as if he and his point man were on display, specimens for a zoo...or humiliated members of a captured Enemy force, dragged before the public as trophies. Shrouded in silence, Arviq seemed to be doing a slow burn as he sat staring at his food, glaring at the other people.

Barto tried to calm himself. His own emotions seemed so much *flatter* since he'd been brought underground, his mind dulled—as if the adrenaline pump, endorphin enhancers, even his root survival instincts had been neutralized. Listening to the muted drone of conversation and music around them, he thought back longingly to the cacophony in the mess hall at his old barracks.

He remembered the clatter of metal trays, the crash of armor plates as soldiers jostled each other. With wordless camaraderie, the squad members sat on hard benches, grabbed their utensils, and gobbled their tasteless food. Together, they recharged their batteries and stoked the fires that they would need for combat in their next mission.

While none of the soldiers knew each other very well, each knew his place in life, his purpose...and his Enemy. These underground civilians had nothing to compare with that.

Juliette sauntered up to them, her elfin features positively glowing, as if Barto's presence had increased her own standing among her people. She walked with her tall friend, Gunnar, who had spent days escorting Arviq. She looked down at the food on Barto's plate, and clucked in a mock scolding tone that he should eat more.

Barto felt a strange sensation in his stomach and heart, as if he were basking in the sunlight of her presence. How could Juliette make him feel proud that she had chosen *him* for her special attentions? He had never been singled out for anything before.

On the days when Juliette brought him to the breakfast hall, Barto was glad to see her, eager to hear her voice, just to look upon her face. As his senses had become accustomed to his environment, his tongue relished the taste of fresh fruits and breads. The flower scents in the air smelled sweet, and he didn't flinch when Juliette touched him this time, taking him by the elbow. He liked the softness of her fingertips, the way they moved up and down his arm. He felt that he wanted to be even closer to her, to allow her into the walled fortress of himself.

"Do you like it with us here?" Juliette said with a hopeful, even plaintive, lilt to her voice. Ignoring Arviq, she touched the lumpy intaglio of scars on Barto's forearm, tracing patterns and imagining his terrible wounds, as if she had never seen such marks before. "I'd like for you to stay with us, Barto...with me." She reached to clasp his hand, and he felt the urge to withdraw. What was she doing?

Gunnar's narrow face seemed drawn and concerned. He shook his head gravely. "You know how he's been trained. You know what this man has been through. He's not a toy for you, Juliette."

"I know exactly what he is," she answered. They both talked as if Barto wasn't even there. "And that doesn't change my wishes one bit."

With intent, flicking eyes, Barto followed the conversation, the conflict. If Juliette wanted him to stay here—and he vehemently wished that she did—then he would stay.

He'd seen the control chambers, the computer screens. He knew that these were the ultimate commanders of the war, the people who issued the instructions through his helmet speakers. His job had been to defend these civilians, to protect them...and if Juliette should happen to give him leave to stop the fighting and stay here, with her, then he would follow orders.

Moving around behind him at the dining table, Juliette held out a large purple flower, its petals like a soft starburst. With particular care, she slid it into the close-cropped dark hair behind his right ear. Then she clapped at her audacity and at the spectacle she had made. He flushed.

Barto did not remove the flower, knowing it was somehow special to Juliette. The other civilians in the dining hall spoke to each other, pleased and entertained. Then Juliette danced away with tall Gunnar beside her, leaving the two soldiers to continue eating under the scrutiny of the curious observers.

Arviq looked across the table at him, scowling at his comrade's behavior. He narrowed his flinty eyes at the flower in Barto's hair. "You look like a fool," he growled, and snatched it away.

Back in his too-peaceful quarters with the door sealed and locked from the outside, Barto lay on his too-comfortable bed and then finally curled up on the hard floor. He would sleep better that way.

He dreamed of other times, when there hadn't been so much peace, when he had felt alive and useful and necessary. Where he had known his place in the world.

After one particularly furious foray, he, Arviq, and five other squad members crept ahead, continuing to approach the blasted Enemy territory even after the main conflict was over. They followed trails of blood and footprints, drag marks left by the bloodhounds that had come to retrieve the bodies of Enemy soldiers.

In the dream Barto increased his visor's sensitivity to search for infrared traces of organic waste or warm blood droplets. The enhanced bloodhounds were not trained to cover their trails, and with their heavy, mangled burdens, they left a path that was easy to follow, even across the blistered landscape.

The squad followed the trail back to a shielded Enemy encampment. Barto and his comrades prided themselves on their bravery (or foolhardiness), and they charged into the bunkers with their weapons drawn, their adrenaline packs tuned to full output. Their laser-lances blasted the hinges off the doors and made short work of the plasrock bricks that shored up the damaged buildings.

Within moments, Barto's squad had breached the outer defenses and came in firing. *No mercy.* Many Enemy soldiers were still in their armor, but their weapons were locked in recharging racks. Others fought hand-to-hand, never giving up.

Barto's team suffered heavy losses, but during the fight he was dizzy with exhilaration. By himself, he vanquished fifteen of the Enemy soldiers; altogether, his squad destroyed the entire outpost. *Total victory.*

Throughout the combat, during the screams and explosions, the violence and death, Barto had felt a sure camaraderie between his fellow soldiers. He never let doubt enter his mind, never a question. He knew exactly what he was doing here.

The Enemy bloodhounds, locked in their small home-kennels, bayed until Arviq cut them all down. The dogs seemed to know they had been responsible for betraying their masters' location.

With a resounding cheer of triumph, the survivors of Barto's team gave a shout to celebrate the defeat of the Enemy. Then, as part of a ritual for such infrequent but absolute victories, the men reached down to tear the helmets off the Enemy corpses, taking them for souvenirs.

Barto removed the helmet from the soldier he had just killed, then looked down to see the visage of the Enemy.

In his dream, the face belonged to Juliette.

As days of contained rage and frustration built within him, Arviq found that he didn't even need the supplemental adrenaline pump from his dismantled armor. This was all *wrong!* His blood boiled, his anger rose into a thunderstorm of fury, and he unleashed it upon the walls, the bed, anything in his room. *His cell.*

Arviq didn't want to be a prisoner of war. He wanted to fight, to kill the Enemy. He had been bred and trained for nothing else.

The quiet stillness of this underground civilian world, the soft fabrics, the perfumes, and the too-tasteful food…all pushed him into a frenzy. He tore the coverings off his bed and thrashed about, ripping the sheets to shreds. He howled and screamed without words, a bestial cry of damnation. He pounded on the door, but it only rattled in its grooves. Then he threw himself upon the bedframe itself, yanking and pulling, until finally he uprooted it from the walls.

He didn't know if anyone was watching him, nor did he care.

Arviq hurled himself against the metal wall, battering his shoulders, bruising his muscles, but feeling no pain. His body was accustomed to running on the ragged edge of energy, and he had been resting here for days, storing up power in his muscles. Now he released it all in his frenzy.

His attack made marks on the wall, left some smears of his own blood. His fists caused dents. The sealed door rattled again in its tracks; it seemed looser now. He pounded and pounded, receiving no answer.

Finally, Arviq returned to the ruined bedframe, wrenching free a strip of metal that he could use as a crowbar. He had to escape. He had to get back. He didn't belong here.

He wedged the ragged end of torn metal into the door track and *pushed*, prying…bending. The door began to buckle, and Arviq worked even harder.

After his nightmares had left him like exorcised demons, Barto fell into a deep slumber and awoke incredibly refreshed. Sometime in the middle of the night he had crawled back into his bed and rested peacefully.

A soldier had to be flexible, had to adapt to new circumstances. At last, he had begun to do just that.

When Gunnar and Juliette came to fetch him, he sensed their strain. The other civilians continued to stare at him, as they had done for days, but now they held a greater glint of fear in their eyes, a more uncertain look on their faces. Barto couldn't understand it, because for the first time since he'd come to this place of sanctuary, he felt more relaxed, more at ease, as if his life had indeed changed.

Seeing how the underground people had changed, how their attitude toward him had shifted, Barto knew something must have occurred. He could sense it. "What has happened?"

Gunnar looked at him and answered crisply, "Your friend Arviq has gone on a rampage. He broke out of his room, and he's escaped."

Barto bolted to his feet. He understood Arviq's impulses. He had felt them himself, and now alarm bells rang out in his head. "What has he done?"

Juliette took a deep breath and blinked her deep brown eyes, as if the subject itself made her uncomfortable. "He broke his way out of the room. He smashed some windows in the corridors, destroyed one of our greenhouses. That was an hour or so ago. No one has seen him since."

Barto pushed his half-finished breakfast away and stood tall and strong. *Called back to active duty.* He didn't need any more sustenance, no more food to distract him. His mind became focused again, delving into the old hunter/survival mentality.

"I know how he thinks, and I know what he's doing," Barto said. "You cannot let him get away."

"We can't stop him," Gunnar said. "He'd kill all of us if we tried."

Barto shook his head. "You don't understand what Arviq can do, or what will happen if he gets away from this place. You can't just ignore him." Then he looked over at Juliette again. He finally admitted to himself that she was beautiful.

"Can *you* stop him?" Juliette said, "It would be to protect us."

"I will need my armor and my helmet if I'm going to do this right."

At first the armor felt rough and strange, but rapidly Barto adopted it as a second skin. The protective covering *belonged*, as much a part of him as his bones and muscles.

Looking at her soldier, Juliette wore a concerned expression, as if he had too easily stepped over the brink. Barto saw something unreadable deep within her brown eyes, a flush on her elfin face, as he picked up the helmet. He looked at her uncertainly one last time, then seated it firmly on his head. He pressed the side speakers against his ears, lowering the visor in place so that he looked at her through filters and scanning devices instead of his own eyes.

Barto drew a deep breath, stretching his chest against the breastplate armor plate. He flexed his arms against the hard biceps plates, the forearm protections, the gauntlets. His torso was solid and impenetrable. His legs and back, shoulders, hips, everything could withstand the worst that Arviq threw against him.

Barto was invincible.

"I must stop him before he leaves," he said. "He'll report the location of this place to HQ."

Juliette hesitated, moved forward and then stopped, as if she wanted to embrace him but was afraid to. Barto was glad she didn't. He didn't want to get close to her, like this.

The tall chaperone Gunnar stood beside her, his face grim, and he drew her back. "Let him go now, Juliette. He has a mission."

Barto turned and marched out of the room, summoning up his mental map of the underground civilian sanctuary. He would begin in Arviq's quarters, where the point man had smashed his own room and broken loose. It would not be too difficult to pick up his former comrade's trail. Barto knew how to track down a quarry.

Leaving the other inhabitants behind, he followed the tunnels. Most of the civilians reacted with fear when they saw him now. They hid within their own quarters or clustered together in the communal halls. Though only one unarmed soldier had gone on a rampage, it was all beyond their experience.

All of these people cowered down here, helpless. And Barto was the only one who could protect them.

Though Arviq had not been able to retrieve his armor or his weapons, Barto did not underestimate him. A properly trained soldier could fashion defensive materials out of just about anything.

At the pried-open door, Barto stood motionless, assessing Arviq's damaged room, saw how his comrade had wrenched open the barricade using a piece of the bedframe as a lever, how he had battered the walls with his bare hands. Barto saw blood, but knew that Arviq would pay no attention to such minor cuts and bruises. Not Arviq.

Barto had seen him through much worse.

One time on a reconnaissance and destruction mission, Barto and his point man had ventured into the crumbling ruins of what must have been an impossibly large building, now scarred, empty, and blasted. The structure had fallen into rubble with haphazard girders and broken glass protruding from poured stone walls.

They had chased several Enemies into the wreckage. Their senses screamed that it was probably an ambush, but still the two soldiers had followed, weapons drawn, confident that they could defeat their opponents. He and Arviq separated and traveled along different passageways, using their scanners to pick up infrared footprint traces.

Barto had proceeded cautiously, but Arviq, incensed and determined, charged through the darkened halls, knocking wreckage aside. Finally he had crashed down a rickety iron staircase that shattered into rust as he stepped on it. And he dropped through to the under levels.

When Barto had found him later, he saw that Arviq had broken his left leg in two places and had sprained his right ankle. His helmet visor was cracked and damaged—yet still Arviq had pulled himself along to find the Enemy. He certainly had. Though severely injured and at an extreme disadvantage, Arviq had slaughtered both of the Enemy soldiers.

From their missions together, Barto knew that his comrade was utterly relentless, feeling no pain and no fatigue. Nothing would stop him from escaping the underground enclave. He would never give up.

And neither would Barto give up. He was the only thing that could keep this civilian paradise protected and intact.

He strode out and moved briskly along the corridors. His bootsteps ricocheted off the metal walls. Arviq had smashed windows and thrown loose objects from side to side, leaving a painfully clear trail until he had learned better and sensibly stopped his rampage.

Then tracking him became more of a challenge. Barto called up a detailed implanted map of all the underground corridors, which Juliette had added to the information systems in his helmet.

Arviq was running blind, by instinct, just trying to escape, but his movements displayed a pattern. On the map gleaming inside his visor, Barto could see the best paths, learn where to go, where to intercede.

Arviq didn't have a chance against a fully armed, fully outfitted soldier, like Barto.

He marched along, his senses tuned to a high pitch. He moved carefully in case the other soldier had set up some kind of booby-trap or ambush. That was to be expected. Arviq must know Barto would come after him.

Because Arviq was without his armor, his bare feet left a trail of infrared images on the clean floor plates. The marks were old and fading, but still identifiable with Arviq's genetic signature: droplets of sweat, skin particles, even stride length gave evidence of his passage. The other soldier was still bleeding from one of the cuts he'd inflicted upon himself in escaping from the room; occasionally a telltale crimson droplet reinforced Barto's tracking.

The control voice returned, insistent and self-confident. It comforted Barto, who had lived his conscious life hearing the words: "KILL THE ENEMY! KILL THE ENEMY! KILL THE ENEMY!" He no longer felt so alone.

According to the map display, Arviq had made it to within several hundred meters of the long access ladder that led up a shaft to the outside—to the battleground where their squad had been killed.

But Barto also knew he had cornered his quarry.

At an intersection of the dimly lit corridors, a framework of girders and support beams held up the ceiling. The place had been long-abandoned by the underground civilians.

Barto's visor-sensors detected a large smear of blood at floor level in a corner, as if Arviq had rested there, or as if he had encountered an Enemy, and they had struggled, hand-to-hand. The blood was fresh, wet, warm in IR—like a sign emblazoned there to draw Barto's attention.

Too late, he realized the ambush. From the shadowed support girders above, Arviq let out a loud cry and dropped on top of him. Though he had no armor and no weapons, the other soldier crashed down upon Barto with brute force. Barto might have found the conflict absurd if Arviq hadn't been so determined, so passionate—if the other man hadn't been his own comrade for so long.

Arviq wrapped his left arm in a vice-lock around Barto's neck, trying to wrench the helmet off his head. With his other hand he tried to grab one of the ID-locked weapons sealed in armored holsters on Barto's hips.

Barto rose up like a tank, as if his armor gave him stimulus and energy, though Juliette had told him his artificial adrenaline pumps were disconnected from the suit.

Inside his ears, the helmet commanders shouted, "KILL THE ENEMY! KILL THE ENEMY! DON'T LET HIM ESCAPE!" With a weird disorientation, Barto thought the voice sounded like Gunnar's.

Without letting go, Arviq fought like a wild thing, clamping his knees on either side of Barto's armored chest, trying to tear the helmet off. When Barto staggered backward, slamming his comrade against the metal wall, Arviq let out an explosive exhale of pain and surprise. Barto recovered his balance and slammed him against the wall a second time.

Arviq struggled, but would not let go. He continued pounding with naked fists against the impenetrable armor.

"Come with me!" Arviq shouted loudly enough to penetrate the heavy ear coverings, to break through the harsh command voice. "Let's go back to HQ. Back to our lives, Barto! We don't belong here."

Barto bent over and butted him against the wall, hearing ribs crack this time. Arviq's grip finally loosened. He wheezed in pain, coughed blood. "Let me go then. Just let me run from here. I'll leave." Arviq slumped to one side and scrambled to his feet. Blood from his raw wounds smeared Barto's scuffed armor.

"Can't let you do that," Barto answered. "You must stay here. The commanders gave their orders. Defy them, and you're a traitor."

Arviq stood up, glaring at him. His face was uncovered, his emotions unmasked. "This isn't what we were made for. We are soldiers. War is our life. Not this...where we're pets on display." Barto had never really studied his comrade's face before. "What happens when they get bored with us?"

Barto pressed his gloved palm against the hilt of his ID-coded blaster weapon. The device detected its proper owner and released its grip in the holster. Barto yanked the weapon free, held it in his hand.

Not far down the corridor, he could see the tarnished rungs that rose up the dark shaft. It would take so little for Arviq to scramble up the ladder, pop the heavy hatch and be out, all alone on the blasted battlefield. Without armor or weapons, he didn't have much chance of survival, but Arviq seemed desperate enough to take that option.

Arviq gathered himself up, glared at his former comrade and stepped away. "I know what I am, and what to do." With the back of his hand, he wiped a smear of blood from his mouth. "Which one of us is the traitor, truly?" He turned and, moving slowly, not threateningly, took a step toward the ladder, the escape.

Barto raised the weapon. "Halt."

Arviq turned to look at him with flinty, determined eyes. "I'm dead down here anyway. If I can't get back onto the battlefield, then you may as well blast me now."

Barto powered up his weapon.

The other soldier took two more steps down the corridor.

Inside the helmet, Gunnar's voice shouted, "KILL THE ENEMY! DON'T LET HIM ESCAPE. YOU MUST PROTECT US. KILL HIM!" Barto leveled the blaster at the target.

Then he heard another voice—Juliette's—muffled and distant, but coming closer. She cried out, running down the long-abandoned corridors toward him. "Don't shoot, Barto. You must learn not to kill if you're going to stay here."

"Kill! Kill!" Gunnar's voice bellowed.

Arviq turned as Juliette appeared, all alone, her elfin face distraught. Then he used the moment of distraction to dash toward the rungs.

"KILL!" shouted the voice in Barto's ears again. And he did.

Depressing the firing stud, he blasted his former comrade in the back as he ran. Arviq had no armor, no protection whatsoever. The bolt flared out and incinerated him, turning the him into a smoking pile of burned bones and cooked flesh that fell in a heap on the floor, as if still trying to run.

"No!" Juliette cried out, but it sounded like a pout. Barto turned to see her standing there. Her expression was stricken, and then even more terrified as he faced her, the charged weapon still in his hand. "I wanted you to stay here with me," she said. "It's a better life, but you've got to learn not to kill. Stay away from violence. You've earned it. You could live here with me in peace and enjoy your life, escape the horrors of war."

"They're not horrors," Barto said in a flat voice. He refused to take off his helmet. He was a soldier now, fully armed, ready to fight. "It's the only thing I know." He holstered the warm blaster. "I can't stay here as a prisoner of war."

"But you're a free man among us," Juliette pleaded, refusing to come closer. She seemed as much confused as saddened. She couldn't understand why he would make this choice.

"I am still a prisoner," he said. "War holds me prisoner." He stood at attention, as if the feline spies were watching him from the shadows. "I must live by fighting, and I must die by fighting. I have no way to escape that."

He understood now that this place, despite its comforts and its new experiences, could not possibly be for him. Not for a soldier.

He didn't begrudge Juliette her civilian life, her pampered existence. And if these people were indeed the commanders in the war, if he was a soldier charged with protecting them, then he must go back and do his duty until death inevitably claimed him on the battlefield. And if he should happen to survive, then he would grow old and train other soldiers until the war was won and the Enemy completely vanquished.

There was nothing else for him to do.

Juliette watched him with despair, then a flash of anger in her brown eyes. Finally, her slender shoulders drooped in defeat. She said nothing else, just watched him with a flush in her cheeks.

Barto didn't know what he had really meant to her...whether he had merely been a trophy from the battlefield, something that increased her prestige among her people or if she had really cared for him, in a way.

At the moment it didn't matter. It was irrelevant information.

Leaving his dead comrade behind, sad that the bloodhounds could never retrieve Arviq and take him back to where he could be buried with full military honors, Barto climbed the rungs of the ladder.

It was a long way to the surface, but when he released the hatch and climbed out under the open, bruised sky, he stared for a long moment. He breathed the burnt air, studied the roiling dust from distant explosions.

He lifted his visor to stare out across the stricken field with his own eyes, then he shut the hatch behind him, sealing Juliette and her world underground, keeping her secret safe. And then he strode off, heading in the direction of his HQ.

It would feel good to get back to the business of fighting once again.

Soldier

THE OUTER LIMITS

"Soldier"

written by

HARLAN ELLISON

FADE IN:

1   BATTLEFIELD - ESTABLISHING - NIGHT

<u>LONG HIGH SHOT</u>

A nightmare landscape seen in chiaroscuro--shadows and light sharp and distinct. Illuminated from moment to moment by a spiderwork tracery of light-beams across the sky. They might seem to be searchlights, were it not for the SIZZLE as they flicker on, and their pulsing irregularity. They form a lattice against the blackness of the sky. Piles of rubble bulk huge against the skyline, unidentifiable; twisted members of strange machines rise up like imploring arms; smoking shells of bombed-out structures line the horizon. Nothing moves on this battlefield, though the sounds of warfare--the SIZZLING of the beams, the DISTANT WHUMP of explosions--comes through dimly. CAMERA COMES DOWN toward a dark figure hunched over in a shallow foxhole as VOICE OVER:

> NARRATOR
> (softly)
> Night comes too soon on the battlefield. For some men it comes permanently, their eyes never open to the light of day.
> (beat)
> But for <u>this</u> man, fighting <u>this</u> war, there is never total darkness: the spidery beams of light in the sky are the descendants of the modern laser beam. Heat rays that sear thru tungsten-steel and flesh as though they were cheesecloth.

CAMERA COMES DOWN to MED. CLOSEUP of the soldier. He wears an odd helmet, equipped with antenna and night-vision glasses and padded earpieces that deaden sound. We see his heavy cape that he has pulled around himself as protection against the cold. The metal harness over his chest from which hangs a wicked-looking, strangely-constructed rifle. He pulls a cigarette from a metal tin and, holding it like a kitchen match,

he scratches the end of the cigarette on the side
of the pack. It ignites as CAMERA MOVES INTO EX-
TREME CLOSEUP and we see his face clearly, the
pattern of radiation burns that mars one side of
his handsomely brutal face. He smokes, waiting,
as VOICE OVER CONTINUES:

                    NARRATOR
     And this soldier must go against those
     weapons. His name is Qarlo (pronounced:
     Kw<u>ahr</u>-lo), and he is a foot-soldier, the
     ultimate infantryman. Trained from birth
     by the state, he has never known love, or
     closeness, or warmth… he is geared for
     only one purpose: to kill The Enemy.

During narration camera moves around Qarlo, showing us his almost bovine calm, as he waits.
Abruptly, there is the SOUND of a TINNY VOICE ON
FILTER and an ELECTRICAL BUZZING, both in his
helmet. Qarlo's free hand presses to the ear
piece as the voice repeats in his ear.

            HELMET VOICE (FILTER)
                  (urgent)
     Attack! Kill! Attack! Kill! Attack!
     Kill…

The cigarette drops from Qarlo's mouth, unnoticed, as his eyes seem to re-focus.

2   TRUCKING SHOT - WITH QARLO - AEROFLEX

OVER HIS SHOULDER as he leaps out of the foxhole,
rifle at the ready, as he sprints forward, charging into the dark.

3   EXTREMELY HIGH SHOT

DOWN ANGLE ON THE BATTLEFIELD. Empty save for
Qarlo running full-out from the right-hand side
of frame, toward center of frame; and suddenly,
THE ENEMY running at top speed from the left-hand
side of frame toward center. Two broken-field
attackers charging dead-on for each other, destined to meet at some central point in the middle

of the frame, illuminated by the heat rays that
now seem to have increased in number.

4   MED. LONG SHOT - ON QARLO & ENEMY

as they near each other, still separated by empty
space, each man lifts his rifle to fire as we
SHARP CUT TO:

5   ANOTHER EXTREMELY HIGH SHOT

angle on the men as two thick laser beams spear
down out of the sky ONE FROM EITHER SIDE, and
zero down, directly on Qarlo and his Enemy. They
are instantly bathed in a coruscating aurora of
flickering light that SIZZLES and POPS. There is
an insane ELECTRICAL CACKLE, like a thousand arc
lights burning out all at once.

6   CLOSEUP - QARLO

arms flung up as though being crucified, still
gripping the strange rifle in one hand, he
SCREAMS SOUNDLESSLY, writhing, twisting, tor-
mented, in the flickering eerie light-bath.

7   CLOSEUP - THE ENEMY

as the same happens to him, he contorts, huddles,
tries to wring himself free from the insane
forces that grip him.

8   MED. LONG 2-SHOT - THE MEN

as CAMERA PULLS RAPIDLY BACK to give us a WIDER
ANGLE of the SCENE, the two men twisting in their
light-bath, they suddenly VANISH! They SNAP OUT
OF EXISTENCE like two balloons popping. They are
gone. The light-rays flicker a moment longer,
then dissipate, and the battlefield is empty and
dark once more as CAMERA CONTINUES TO PULL BACK
and we abruptly

                              SHARP CUT THRU:

9   SPECIAL PROCESS SHOTS
&
10

of reversed images against a grey background,
flickering, indistinct, warped, indicating dimen-

sions and times being traversed, strange polarities and effects spinning eternity for us, a weird melange of special effects with no pattern.

                              SHARP CUT TO:

11   INT. MODERN SUBWAY - ESTABLISHING - NIGHT

MED. SHOT on an OLD MAN, with a cane, putting a penny in a gum-ball machine attached to a stanchion of the subway platform. Signs indicate one side of platform is EXPRESS TRAINS and the other side is LOCAL TRAINS. The subway is obviously modern-day, as opposed to the strangeness of the battlefield we have just seen. There are clots of commuters standing around, though most of them are on the other side of the platform, turned away from the old man. Their clothes and mannerisms are typically contemporary (it is essential that this be stressed immediately).

CAMERA HOLDS several beats as the Old Man inserts his penny.

12   ANOTHER SHOT - PAST OLD MAN

as SUDDENLY QARLO WINKS INTO EXISTENCE! Pop! A flickering of light as his insubstantial shape takes form, then totally, as the warrior with rifle aimed straight ahead materializes completely in our world. CAMERA MOVES QUICKLY AROUND to show us the Old Man's eyes widen in surprise and terror and CAMERA PULLS BACK as he clutches his heart, this face twists with the strain of a coronary thrombosis and he falls dead almost at Qarlo's feet. A WOMAN SCREAMS.

                              BLURRED PAN TO:

13   MED. CLOSEUP - WOMAN COMMUTER

CAMERA PANS TO SHARP STOP on face of woman just turning to see Qarlo and the Old Man dying. CAMERA HOLDS A BEAT as she SCREAMS, then PULLS RAPIDLY BACK for WIDE SHOT of the scene: the platform with its throng of commuters, suddenly turning to see the weird soldier, and the dead man at his feet.

                    WOMAN
                 (hysterically)
          He killed him! He shot him!

There is SCREAMING and confusion as the soldier's
head whips back and forth like a caged animal's,
and he hefts the futuristic rifle menacingly. It
hangs from his harness but he holds it tightly.
Two men with attaché cases start toward Qarlo.
They are both burly, wearing hats, and in the
grey-flannel uniform of the young executive.

14   MED. SHOT - PAST QARLO

TO THE GREY-FLANNELS as they advance on him from
opposite sides, dropping their attaché cases.
Qarlo looks from one to the other, shakes his
head, obviously trying to decide who they are,
what they want, if they are the Enemy or not.

15   FULL SHOT - PAST GREY-FLANNELS

as they suddenly jump Qarlo. He lunges out in a
smooth catlike movement and smashes the first one
across the jaw with the butt of the rifle. The
man is literally hurled backward by the force of
the blow and skids across the platform in a dis-
jointed heap, unconscious, bleeding. Qarlo grabs
the second Young Executive by the neck as he
leaps at the soldier, and seemingly without effort lifts him in the air, by the neck, and hurls
him away as though he were tossing a coat onto a
hat-rack. The man flails through the air, hits a
stanchion, still a few feet off the platform, and
crumbles to the floor unconscious. The SCREAMS of
the CROWD mount. Panic!

16   FULL SHOT - THE CROWD

as it panics, breaks and tries to run in all directions at once, people being trampled under-
foot.

17   CLOSEUP - QARLO

with a wide-eyed panic of his own. It is a panic
based in confusion at his surroundings, the
noise, the crowd activity. He wakes one after an-

other false moves, to jump this way or that, but in trembling anxiety stays where he is.

18   PANNING SHOT - THE CROWD

As CAMERA PANS RIGHT TO LEFT the scene passes across utter confusion, screaming men and women, and CAMERA STOPS at a sudden point of immobility: a COP. The uniformed officer standing stock-still in the forefront of the crowd as CAMERA PULLS BACK to show us the bluecoat pulling his re-volver. CAMERA CONTINUES TO PULL BACK as the cop herds people behind him, and advances toward the soldier.

19   CLOSEUP - QARLO

as he recognizes a man in uniform, a potential enemy, if not The Enemy. The rifle comes up into firing position.

20   CLOSEUP - THE COP

as his eyes widen with fear, the rifle aimed at him. He brings his revolver up quickly to fire.

21   LONG SHOT

as Qarlo fires. A beam of SIZZLING LIGHT erupts from the mouth of the strange weapon, the Cop ducks, and the beam spears at an up-angle over his head. The crowd has begun to surge up a flight of stairs labeled EXIT TO 42nd ST. and as the beam hits the steel supports

QUICK CUT TO:

22   INSERT - THE GIRDERS

as they are momentarily bathed in a light-bath, then vanish.

23   ANOTHER MED. LONG SHOT - THE CROWD

as the steel·supports under the stairs vanish, the entire stairway collapses, tumbling people back down onto the platform in a writhing, tan-gled, screaming mass of humanity. Instant panic as the crowd still struggling over the bodies tries to get out of the way of the melee and the

SCREAM OF TORTURED METAL as the structure falls
on them. They flow back toward Qarlo and the Cop.

24   MED. SHOT - ON QARLO

as he falls back, searching for a pattern to this
madness. He stumbles up against a stanchion, and
his helmet is knocked off. We see he has a sort
of hearing aid in one ear, but as the helmet
falls THE NOISE LEVEL RISES TREMENDOUSLY and his
eyes widen in horror. At that moment CAMERA PULLS
RAPIDLY BACK PAST QARLO so we can see DOWN THE
TRACKS as an express subway train roars, screaming insanely, into the station. The NOISE is
DEAFENING.

                              QUICK CUT TO:

25   CLOSEUP - ON QARLO - ANOTHER ANGLE

as his mouth opens in a SOUNDLESS SCREAM and he
falls to one knee, his hands clapped to his ears
to shut out the noise. His face is twisted in
pain, and it is obvious the noise is literally
destroying him. The rifle swings unnoticed on his
harness.

26   MED. SHOT - ON COP

as he sees Qarlo fall to one knee, the train
plunging thru, still shrieking a METALLIC CACOPH-
ONY. The Cop charges, as CAMERA GOES WITH him.
And as CAMERA MOVES INTO TIGHT 2-SHOT the Cop
brings the barrel of the revolver down viciously
hard across the back of Qarlo's neck. The soldier
crumples to the platform, lying flat on his back,
the rifle useless on his chest.

27   ANOTHER SHOT - MED. LONG - ANGLE ON COP

as the crowd moves in to look at the strange man
unconscious on the platform. The Cop holsters his
gun, bends to slip cuffs on the soldier.

28   HIGH SHOT - ON QARLO

90° ANGLE DOWN ON QARLO'S FACE. CAMERA COMES DOWN
for EXTREME CLOSEUP of his unconscious face, as
dimly, from the tiny hearing aid in his ear we

continue to hear the WHISPERING METALLIC COMMAND,
Over and over:

                    HELMET VOICE (FILTER)
                         (monotonous)
           Kill! Kill! Kill! Kill! Kill...

CAMERA HOLDS on Qarlo's face, the mental command,
as we

                                   SLOW FADE TO BLACK

                                             and

                              FADE OUT.

          (COMMERCIAL INSERT)

<u>ACT ONE</u>

FADE IN:

29   LONG PERSPECTIVE SHOT - COUNTRYSIDE - NIGHT - ES-
     TABLISHING

<u>HIGH ANGLE ON HIGHWAY</u>

stretching out endlessly between desolate hills.
No buildings, no movement as CAMERA HOLDS on the
empty road. Then, two headlight beams scythe out
of the darkness, far down the road. A car coming
toward CAMERA. HOLD several beats as the car
races toward us.

                                       CUT TO:

30   INT. CAR (PROCESS) - NIGHT

MED. SHOT on IRA & JEANNIE. She is very crab-
grass/suburban housewifey with a pleasant face,
and her husband is greying at the temples from
too many stock debentures. They watch the road;
he a bit more intensely than her, as he grips the
wheel.

                  JEANNIE
  Don't drive so fast, Ira. The plane
  doesn't leave till eleven-fifteen.

                    IRA
                 (smiles)
  If I can close this deal, it means a bo-
  nus, Jeannie. And <u>that</u> means a new car,
  not to mention some clothes for <u>you</u>, so
  let me make that flight.

She smiles back, and idly glances out the window.
THUNDER ROLLS in the distance. A <u>light flickers
on a hill</u>.

                  JEANNIE
  Hmmm, heat lightning. Perhaps rain.

He continues watching the road ahead, murmurs:

                  IRA
  Perhaps.

31 EXT. COUNTRYSIDE - EYE LEVEL WIDE SHOT - NIGHT

EXTREME CLOSEUP ON CAR as it whips PAST CAMERA
and CAMERA HOLDS as it vanishes with a ROAR down
the road, and is gone. CAMERA PANS ACROSS highway
to the hills and MOVES FORWARD as we

LAP DISSOLVE THRU:

32 EXT. COUNTRYSIDE - TRUCKING SHOT/EYE LEVEL -
NIGHT

CAMERA MOVES MEASUREDLY, SUSPENSEFULLY across
desolate hillsides toward the light that we now
see flicking and flickering irregularly on the
high rise, and we

LAP DISSOLVE THRU TO:

33 EXT. COUNTRYSIDE - THE HILL - NIGHT

as CAMERA MOVES IN on the source of that light.
As CAMERA COMES IN FOR MED. CLOSEUP we see it is
The Enemy. Bathed in a coruscating glow of eerie
light. But only <u>half</u> of him is visible. As though
a cheese-cutter had neatly sliced him off at the
waist, only his top half is visible, hanging four
feet above the ground, emptiness below and around
him. He has been pulled only <u>halfway</u> through the
time-warp. He clutches his weapon and struggles
futilely with the invisible trap that has closed
around him, locking him in stasis between the
worlds.

As CAMERA MOVES IN TIGHT he flails around himself
helplessly, at empty air. For a moment he is silent and in that silence we hear a soft, insistent, mechanical voice:

HELMET VOICE (FILTER)
Attack! Attack! Attack! Attack!

Then, in insane fury at his helplessness, he begins to BELLOW almost like a rabid animal, a
deep-toned, frightening SHRIEKING torn from inside him as CAMERA MOVES IN FOR EXTREME CLOSEUP
of his screaming face; and we

MATCH CUT TO:

34   INT. CELL - CLOSEUP ON QARLO

<u>90° ANGLE LOOKING STRAIGHT DOWN ON HIS SLEEPING FACE</u>

MATCHING SHOT OF FACE as Qarlo sits bolt upright
DIRECTLY INTO CAMERA CLOSEUP and like his Enemy,
he HOWLS.

35   INT. CELL - ESTABLISHING - NIGHT

It is a drunk tank cell. Bare and grey steel save
for a mattressless metal trough in which Qarlo
was lying, a toilet with no seat, a sink with one
push-in faucet and a naked light bulb in the
ceiling, protected by a wire jacket.

Qarlo leaps off the metal bunk-trough, flattens
himself against the rear wall of the cell and
looks about wildly as CAMERA PULLS BACK to give
us a WIDER ANGLE. His harness and helmet and rifle and cape are gone. He is clothed from head to
toe in a metallic garment of unusual but simple
design, and in the light we can see the terrible
radiation scars that cover one side of his face.

36   REVERSE ANGLE - THRU BARS - QARLO'S POV

WHAT HE SEES is the drunk tank itself. A long
empty room lined down both sides by cells, the
doors of which all stand open, save his. In the
center of this corridor, there is a huge wooden
table with benches joined to it, like a picnic
table. And around it sit DERELICTS, smoking and
reading girlie magazines, talking in coarse
voices. Abruptly, one of them turns, stares INTO
CAMERA.

1st DERELICT
Hey! Sleepin' Beauty's awake!

They rise, and half a dozen of the seedy, filthy
drunks—Negro and white—come toward the closed
cell door. CAMERA MOVES AROUND THEM as they near
the cage. They stand very close to the bars,
staring in at the unusual prisoner.

37   INTERCUT - QARLO

as he stares at them, warily, his cunning eyes
flicking back and forth and around. He is not exactly afraid, but there is an element of fear in
his restrained power.

38   CLOSEUPS - THE DERELICTS
thru
40   as they stand in front of the cell, very close,
taunting Qarlo.

ALTERNATING WITH:

41   CLOSEUPS - QARLO
thru
43

as the NOISE from the drunk tank begins to climb
higher and higher, and the taunters yell their
epithets, and he claps his hands to his ears, and
screams.

> 1st DERELICT
> The screwball's wearin' a tin suit!

> 2nd DERELICT
> Hey, man, you be cool an' I go get you a
> can-pener, so's you c'n change your un-
> ner'wear!

They all laugh loudly. Qarlo shies from the
noise.

> 3rd DERELICT
> OoooeeeeMomma! Lookit that jazz on that
> boy's face! You been cut up, baby?

> 1st DERELICT
> No, he just uses a live razor, you know,
> that beep-beep kind!

They laugh and clap their hands together. Qarlo
flat to the wall, his eyes wide with pain at the
noise, and some other fear...he is shivering.
Their taunting gets louder and louder.

> 4th DERELICT
>
> We're sure gettin' class in this
> tank...puttin' us in with uptown action
> like this monkey. You escape from a mas-
> querade, Monkey?

> 2nd DERELICT
>
> He ain't no monkey, daddy. He the <u>king</u> of
> the monkeys...he's King Kong hisself.

He leans in close and ROARS at the top of his
lungs. Qarlo slides across the wall into the corner at the onslaught of noise, clapping his hands
to his ears. They all start the ape-like ROARING.
The sound BUILDS and BUILDS as CAMERA COMES IN
CLOSE on QARLO and WE HEAR THE NOISE AS HE HEARS
IT—deafeningly, reverberatingly, maddeningly! He
screams.

44   MED. SHOT - THE CELL - THRU BARS

PAST DERELICTS as they SCREAM AND ROAR and Qarlo
begins beating on the steel wall of the cell, and
abruptly flings himself around the tiny cubicle,
bouncing off walls, with no regard for the pain
of hitting the bulkheads. He SCREAMS in unintelligible frenzy, and rushes to the bars, trying to
reach thru to get at the derelicts taunting him.
They fall back, afraid, but still MAKING A GREAT
DEAL OF NOISE. Qarlo shrieks in some strange
tongue, GIBBERISH SOUNDS, and with teeth bared
smashes again and again and again on the bars as
his HOWLING RISES;

                                          CUT TO:

45   INT. POLICE SQUAD ROOM - ESTABLISHING - NIGHT

<u>MED. SHOT ON POLICE SGT. AT HIGH DESK:</u>

An intelligent, beefy man of middle-age in uniform. He looks up from making a note in his desk
book as the SOUND of QARLO HOWLING O.S. reverber-
ates through the building.

CAMERA MOVES IN SLOWLY as a pair of beat cops
walk up to the chest-high Desk. One of them holds

Qarlo's strange rifle. As they talk, two more
cops sign in. Then another.

                1st COP
Sounds like our friend's back with us.

                DESK SGT.
Zimmerman! Stop playing with that weapon.
Don't you know that's impounded
goods...gimme it.

The cop hands it up to the Desk Sgt., who begins
examining it, turning it this way and that, as
they talk fiddling with first one dial, then another.

                1st COP
You ever seen anything like that, Sarge?

                DESK SGT.
            (shakes head)
Probably some foreign jobbie. That guy
looks like he comes from somewhere else,
I wouldn't be surprised if he was—-
        (pauses meaningfully)
—from you know where.

                2nd COP
Oh, come <u>on</u>, Sarge! Down in the <u>sub</u>way?

                1st COP
Don't knock it, Mencken; could be. He
might be in town to assassinate one of
the candidates; we got elections pretty
soon, y'know.

                DESK SGT.
           (brusquely)
You two got nothing better than to stand
around growing moss on your North sides?

                2nd COP
Just interested in the weapon, Sarge...

The Desk Sgt. fiddles with the rifle.

46   WIDE ANGLE - PAST DESK SGT.

over the top of the high desk we can see the two
cops' heads and several other uniformed cops
through the squad room, as the Desk Sgt. touches
a knob on the rifle.

> Desk SGT.
> Yeah, well, go on, you got rounds to
> make. Let _me_ worry about this--

As he touches the knob, a SIZZLING BOLT OF ENERGY
spears from the mouth of the rifle, over the
heads of the cops, and disintegrates a gigantic
hole in the wall opposite. Cops turn...

47 INSERT - THE WALL

as it vaporizes, leaving a gaping, neatly-melted
hole in the wall, so we can see the street outside.

48 ANGLE ON DESK - MED. CLOSE

the two uniform cops have fallen back, eyes bug-
ging, staring INTO CAMERA as if they are staring
at the wall. The Desk Sgt. above and behind them,
still holding the rifle limply, stunned at what
he has done. Their voices are hushed, awestruck.
Terror and confusion, but soft awe!

> DESK SGT.
> (reverently)
> Oh...my...God...

The cops turn to him. The Desk Sgt. sets the rifle down very gingerly, withdraws his hands as
though it is alive. He turns his head slightly,
speaks to a cop on the switchboard to his right,
behind the desk.

> DESK SGT.
> (continues)
> Thompson. Get me the local office of the
> F.B.I.

He turns back to stare into CAMERA as CAMERA
MOVES IN on their three faces, white, terrified,
bug-eyed.

DISSOLVE TO:

49   INT. CELL BLOCK - ESTABLISHING - NIGHT

<u>CLOSEUP PAST F.B.I. MAN'S'S BACK TO QARLO THRU BARS:</u>
CAMERA HOLDS A BEAT then MOVES AROUND & PULLS
BACK as he turns to the Desk Sgt. standing behind
him. The FBI man—Tanner—is tall and icy-eyed.
Sharp features and utter competence. His jaw muscles work as he looks at the Sgt. for a long moment, as though acknowledging by silence the
strangeness of the man in the cell. They move off
down the drunk tank, derelicts staring, as CAMERA
FOLLOWS. As they approach the drunk tank door, a
guard opens it for them.

50   INT. POLICE SQUAD ROOM - ON DOOR

as the FBI Man and Desk Sgt. come through, close
it tightly behind them. They walk TOWARD CAMERA
and stop.

TANNER
> I don't know what you've got in there,
> Sergeant, but whatever it is, <u>I'm</u> not
> about to fool with it. I'd like to use
> your phone.

He moves toward the switchboard and the phone as
we

DISSOLVE THRU:

51   EXT. ANGLE ON SKY - ESTABLISHING (STOCK) - DAY

as a large plane circles Washington, D.C.

DISSOLVE THRU:

52   EXT. AIRFIELD - ESTABLISHING (STOCK) - DAY

as the plane comes in for a landing, jets streaming.

DISSOLVE THRU TO:

53   MED. LONG SHOT AIRPORT DEBARKATION GATE - ESTAB-
LISHING

PAST KAGAN staring out at the hustle and bustle
of the airfield, to TANNER, striding toward the
glass doors with attaché case in hand, snapbrim
on head, determination in eyes. He shoves through
the doors, walks up to Kagan and CAMERA.

54 2-SHOT - KAGAN & TANNER

Kagan is a short, intense man who looks as though
he's been sleeping in his clothes for several
months. But there is a silent power in his features, a perceptivity, and even— if you care to
look hard enough—a kindness. He extends his hand
to Tanner, and it is like a pair of prizefighters
gauging each other. The FBI man is the very an-
tithesis of Kagan: tall, dapper, restrained, in
every sense of the word "cool".

                    KAGAN
   Mr. Tanner? I'm Tom Kagan, the philologist your office sent down.

                    TANNER
                 (confused)
   Philologist?

                    KAGAN
             (smiles tolerantly)
   Right. Language expert. I read your report. He seems to be speaking some sort
   of strange dialect. They decided I was
   the one to unravel it.

Tanner sets his attaché case down with a bang,
shakes his head in shocked annoyance.

                    TANNER
   You've <u>got</u> to be kidding.
                   (beat)
   Right? You're putting me on.

                    KAGAN
   What's <u>that</u> supposed to mean?

                    TANNER
   I'll <u>tell</u> you what that's supposed to
   mean, friend. Right now they're wheeling
   something out of that plane that is guar-

anteed to stand your hair on end. It took
six beefy men to get him into the two
strait jackets he's wearing...and they
send down a...a phil<u>ol</u>ogist!

                    KAGAN
                 (lightly)
     I know a little karate...

                    TANNER
                 (not amused)
     Oh, say, Kagan you are a real knee-
     slapper. What's the matter, didn't I make
     my report strong enough?

Kagan is about to answer, but a SOUND of opening
doors stops him.

55   LONGER SHOT - THE SCENE

as Kagan and Tanner move apart, two MPs wearing
white helmets and armbands, pistol belts supporting unsnapped holsters, wheel a mobile stretcher
through the glass doors. CAMERA MOVES IN over Kagan's shoulder as the stretcher rolls between
them, pausing a moment as Kagan and Tanner look
down at Qarlo, mummy-wrapped crossarm in two
straitjackets, and strapped to the stretcher. He
is shaking with restrained fury, his teeth bared,
the radiation scars livid. Kagan stares dumbly as
the stretcher rolls away, and he turns INTO CAM-
ERA with Tanner in B.G. Kagan's voice is raw and
soft.

                    KAGAN
                 (awed)
     No...I don't...think...you...did...

CAMERA HOLDS on their faces, Kagan finally realizing what Tanner has brought in, and Tanner,
concerned yet amused by Kagan's confusion as we

                              DISSOLVE TO:

56   INT. OBSERVATION CHAMBER - ESTABLISHING - NIGHT

<u>CAMERA LOOKING STRAIGHT DOWN</u> through a square
glass window set in the floor of the observation

room. We are looking down from a high ceiling
into a padded cell. Below us, Qarlo paces back
and forth like a caged animal. There is the SOUND
of a HIGH WHINING NOISE as a FREIGHT ELEVATOR
starts. Qarlo claps both hands to his head, falls
against a wall, thrashes about. He comes off the
wall, plunges across the room, slamming his fists
against the unfeeling wall-pads. CAMERA PULLS
BACK.

57   ANOTHER SHOT - OBSERVATION CHAMBER

It is almost totally dark, with only the illuminated square of the one-way observation window in
the floor throwing a radiance up from below,
casting light on the faces of Kagan and Tanner,
staring down at the soldier. Their faces have an
eerie underlit effect and they don't look at each
other as they talk softly, but continue to stare
down at what we know is the padded cell and
Qarlo.

                    KAGAN
  What was that noise?

                    TANNER
  Freight elevator.

                    KAGAN
  Have them shut it off.

                    TANNER
  What for?

                    KAGAN
  Sharp sounds drive him wild. Apparently
  his hearing is on a more sensitive
  threshold than ours. That helmet you
  showed me: there were sound baffles built
  in, to deaden outside noise.

                    TANNER
  So we'll give him back the helmet.

                    KAGAN
  I wouldn't, if I were you.

                    TANNER
What harm can it do?

                    KAGAN
That's the point. I don't know.

                    TANNER
I think you're scared, Kagan.

                    KAGAN
That's the name of the game.

                    TANNER
So that calm exterior is just a pose. I'm
glad to know there's somebody else in
this boat with me.

                    KAGAN
Mmm. Up the crick, minus paddles.

                    TANNER
                 (offering)
Want a piece of gum?

Kagan nods, takes it, unwraps it, and folding it,
begins to chew it.

                    KAGAN
Those scars...radiation burns, I'd say.
But I can't be certain, it's outside my
field.

                    TANNER
                 (agreeing)
Radiation all right. Johns Hopkins had
him for five days. But it's outside <u>their</u>
field, too. Whatever caused those burns,
we haven't seen anything like it around
here.

                    KAGAN
He's shouting something! Hit that switch!

Tanner reaches over, flicks a switch on the wall.
From a grille beside the switch comes the hollow
SOUND of Qarlo yelling. (NOTE: the following is
written phonetically for the benefit of the play-
ers.)

                    QARLO'S VOICE O.S. (FILTER)
M'nemzz Kwahr-loe Klo-breg-knee, pryte,
sihz-fi-wun-oh-too-too-nyne, damm-
meeooooo!

                    KAGAN
Cut it.

Tanner hits the switch, the voice stops.

                    KAGAN
                  (continues)
Same speech over and over. It's all he
ever says.

                    TANNER
So what's it mean? What language is it?

                    KAGAN
I'm warning you, Tanner: ask a nitwit
question, I'm going to give you a nitwit
answer.

                    TANNER
Get smart with me, boy, and I take back
your choon gum.

                    KAGAN
I'm not clowning, Tanner. I hear that
line of gibberish in my sleep. There's
something familiar about it, but I can't
place the dialect.

                    TANNER
Have you been able to make anything from
the tapes?

                    KAGAN
                  (shakes head)
Random sounds mostly. Anger, frenzy, a
few scattered word-groups I can't decipher. Taking tapes of his mumblings
locked in a padded cell aren't going to
help me. I've got to go down in there
with him.

> TANNER
> (shocked)
> Oh, now wait just a <u>second</u>, friend. Have
> you lost your mind? That isn't some or-
> dinary psycho down there...he's the most
> dangerous piece of equipment I've ever
> seen. He'll take you and tear along the
> dotted line!

58   CLOSEUP - KAGAN & TANNER

as he looks across at Tanner for the first time,
seriously.

> KAGAN
> Tanner, you're not a scientist. That man
> down there is something we've never seen
> before. He's from somewhere or some<u>when</u>
> outside our knowledge. He's a walking
> challenge.

> TANNER
> He's a walking <u>bomb</u>, you mean!

> KAGAN
> Six of one, half a dozen of another.

> TANNER
> It's entirely possible we've put the
> wrong man in that padded cell.

> KAGAN
> Do I get the permission?

> TANNER
> Not a chance.

> KAGAN
> Can I try to persuade you? Logically?

> TANNER
> You can try till you grow webbed feet,
> Kagan. You'll never convince me.

CAMERA HOLDS a long beat as Tanner sits smugly
staring at the vaguely smiling little Kagan.

CUT TO:

59   CLOSEUP ON DOOR TO PADDED CELL

as the latch is thrown, and a guard opens the
cell. CAMERA PULLS BACK to show Tanner and a
GUARD with drawn pistol, standing behind Kagan as
the door opens and CAMERA SHOOTS THRU OPEN DOOR
to the INT. PADDED CELL with Qarlo tensed against
the far wall, framed by the doorway, ready to
spring. Kagan moves into the room, stops, stares
at Qarlo.

60   INT. PADDED CELL - 2-SHOT ON KAGAN & QARLO

as they face each other. Behind Kagan, through
the open door, we see the Guard leveling his pistol. Tanner tensed.

The man from the present and the man from the future stare at each other across an abyss of time
and each other's natures. Qarlo looks as though
he might leap at any moment. Then, slowly, Kagan
reaches for a pack of cigarettes. Qarlo tenses.
Kagan pulls out a cigarette, puts one in his
mouth. Qarlo's eyes widen. He bites his lip. He
recognizes tobacco! Kagan sees the recognition,
offers the pack, shaking the cigarettes up for
Qarlo to see. For a long beat Qarlo stares at
him, then cautiously reaches out to the full
length of his arm.

61   INTERCUT - THEIR HANDS

across the open space between the offered pack
and the hard, brutal-looking reaching hand of the
soldier. There is long hesitation, then the hand
grabs the pack!

SHARP CUT TO:

62   ANOTHER ANGLE - THE SCENE

as Qarlo jumps back, the pack in his hand. Kagan
watches as the soldier pulls a cigarette from the
pack deftly. He tries to strike it on the side of
the pack as we saw him do in the first scene. It
crumbles into paper and bits. He looks surprised,
then angry. He bares his teeth, snarling at Kagan
for tormenting him with a smoke. Kagan dimly realizes what is going on. He pulls out a lighter,

lights his own cigarette, draws deeply, exhales
smoke. Qarlo watches. Kagan moves toward him with
the flickering flame. Qarlo tenses. Kagan stops,
extending the flame. Qarlo hesitantly moves forward, eyes always on Kagan. He puts another cigarette in his mouth and, still watching, gets a
light. Then he moves smoothly back to the wall,
drawing deeply.

63   MED. SHOT - ON KAGAN

as he makes his next move. He walks slowly to the
side wall and sits down on the padded floor. He
moves very slowly, very studiedly, so as not to
alarm the soldier. Kagan smokes for a moment,
studying Qarlo. Then he makes a fist, the thumb
pointing back at himself. He taps himself lightly
on the chest with the thumb-tip. He names himself.

                    KAGAN
     Kagan. Kagan.

Qarlo stares at him. Kagan points to the soldier,
makes a helpless hands-open gesture, then points
to himself again.

                    KAGAN
                 (continues)
     Kagan? Hmmm? Kagan?

Qarlo stares. He understands. We <u>know</u>, by his
expression, that he understands. But he isn't
giving an inch. This is not—we should realize at
this point—a dumb brute, but a thinking entity. A
man with a mind. But what the nature of that
locked mind may be, we do <u>not</u> know. Kagan tries
again.

                    KAGAN
                 (taps himself)
     Kagan. Come on, man, confound it, <u>Kaye-
     gannn</u>! Kagan!

He points to Qarlo, who smirks softly. Then the
soldier speaks. It is all run together, and totally unintelligible. But what he says is:

                    QARLO
M'nemzz Kwahr-loe Klo-breg-knee, pryte,
sihz-fyfe-wun-oh-too-too-nyne...

CAMERA HOLDS A BEAT on Qarlo, then PANS RAPIDLY
to Kagan, who smiles, draws on his cigarette, and
settles back against the wall in a relaxed position. He has broken through.

                    KAGAN
            (softly, prayerlike)
You can say _that_ again, brother...

HOLD ON THEM smoking—together—for a moment as we

                                    DISSOLVE TO:

64   INT. OBSERVATION ROOM - ESTABLISHING - DAY

The room is lit now, and a portable protective
railing surrounds the observation window in the
floor. Kagan, Tanner and a SECRETARY taking notes
on a courtroom stenographic transcriber. She sits
as Kagan paces, a cigarette hanging from his
mouth, ashes falling on his jacket-front. Tanner
sits at the other side, listening, as Kagan dictates to the girl.

                    KAGAN
                 (dictating)
Brown hair, clipped so short you can see
the scalp. Brown...no, _black_ eyes. Six
feet, three inches. Radiation scars,
right cheek. Smaller scars, above the
eyes.
                    (MORE)

             KAGAN (CONT.)
Three parallel scars, left temple, running down cheek almost to chin; very
faint, not like right cheek burns.
                    (beat)
Something else. It may mean nothing, but
his forehead seems higher than normal,
with a peculiar bulging, as though he'd
been smacked with something hard, and the
forehead's swelling.

                    (beat)
That's all, Karen.

The girl stops typing, gathers her little machine, and leaves quickly. Kagan has continued
pacing, and Tanner has sat through the entire
scene without a word. It is apparent he is trying
to be patient, though bugged.

                    TANNER
Well?

                    KAGAN
Well _what_?

                    TANNER
Seven days and you ask me "well what?"

                    KAGAN
                    (smiles)
He's a soldier.

                    TANNER
          (throws up his hands)
Any other late bulletins? I spent three
years in the Rangers, Kagan, I _know_ a
soldier when I see one.

                    KAGAN
No, I mean he's _really_ a soldier. There's
but nothing about him _not_ a soldier. The
ultimate, perfect infantryman. I don't
think he knows anything else.

                    TANNER
And what makes you think that?

                    KAGAN
That gibberish he's been spouting.

                    TANNER
Which is...?

                    KAGAN
                    (lightly).
English.

                    TANNER
                  (annoyed)
English? Come <u>on</u>, Kagan, I'm not the most
fluent speaker in the world, but I know
English when I hear it. The guy is obviously a foreigner of some kind.

                    KAGAN
Wrong word. Not foreigner. Try alien.

                    TANNER
               (incredulously)
Alien? From another planet?

                    KAGAN
                (shakes head)
No, from <u>this</u> planet.

                    TANNER
The Department wants facts, Kagan, not
wild conjectures. Who is he, and what
country is he from?

                    KAGAN
I'm not sure yet.

                    TANNER
Not sure? How the devil long does it
take, man?

                    KAGAN
It takes time. Lots of time. I have to
break down his speech syllable by syllable. It seems to be a corrupted form of
American English, degenerated the way
Canterbury English became the Cockney
dialect.

                    TANNER
Lovely, but what do I tell them upstairs?

Kagan spins on him, furiously; he is tired and
involved.

                    KAGAN
Tell them not to press me! Tell them I'm
just starting to break through. Tell them

he has to trust me implicitly. One slip
and it may lose us the game!

Tanner, snapped back by this sudden irrational
tirade, realizes Kagan has been pushing himself
to the edge. Kagan slumps down into the chair.
Tanner uses a softer tone.

                    TANNER
Hey...take it easy, Tom...

                    KAGAN
                (wearily)
I'm just a little bushed, is all. It's
like holding onto fog. One moment I think
I've got it, and the next it's gone. He's
by no means stupid...that's a strange,
peculiar item we've got down there, but
not a stupid one.

                    TANNER
You think you can hack it, Tom?

                    KAGAN
                (nods)
Keep them off my back, let me handle it
my way, and I think I can get thru to
him. Trusting me is the key.

                    TANNER
                (nods resignedly)
Okay, I'll do the best I can to run interference for you. But I just wish you
could give me <u>some</u>thing to placate The
Men Upstairs.

                    KAGAN
                (nods agreement)
All right. I'll give you something.
                (beat)
You want to know what he keeps saying,
over and over, without any change? He's
saying, "My name is Qarlo Clobregnny,
private, six-five-one-oh-two-two-nine."
His name, rank, and serial number.

CAMERA HOLDS on Tanner's startled face as we

DISSOLVE TO:

65   EXT. COUNTRYSIDE - ESTABLISHING - NIGHT

that hillside out there, in the darkness, with
the light of The Enemy, still flickering, flickering, ominously as we

FADE OUT.

ACT TWO

FADE IN:

66   INT. PADDED CELL – ESTABLISHING – DAY

<u>EXT. CLOSEUP ON PICTURE BOOK:</u>

It is of the Giant Golden Book variety, patently
for a child. A hand is pointing to a picture of a
dog, a very large picture of a dog. And Kagan is
speaking.

> KAGAN
> (repeating)
> Dog. D-O-G. Dog. It's a dog, Qarlo, a
> dog. You know it, you <u>must</u> know it, a
> <u>dog</u>!

CAMERA PULLS BACK to show us Kagan with the book
on his lap, tapping the dog picture over and
over, as Qarlo sits on his haunches near him,
smoking. It is obvious Qarlo is merely tolerating
what Kagan is doing. He smiles, just an edge of a
smile. Kagan is infuriated.

> KAGAN
> (continues)
> Dog! Stop playing dumb! <u>DOG</u>!

Qarlo claps his hands to his ears as Kagan
shouts. His teeth bare. He tears the cigarette
from his mouth and grabs the book. He holds it
up, smashes his finger into the picture.

> QARLO
> Dogizzadog! Dog! Dogdogdogdogdog...!

He tears the book in half, flings the pieces
against the wall, stares defiantly at Kagan. Then
he shrugs bitterly, smiles as though it were
spitting, and walks to the other side of the
room, where he slides down to a sitting position.

> KAGAN
> (wearily)
> I give up.

Qarlo snickers. Kagan looks up, angry. Qarlo sneers. And then as CAMERA HOLDS ON KAGAN he realizes: Qarlo understands! He has reached him.

67   PERSPECTIVE SHOT

FROM QARLO FAR ACROSS THE ROOM TO KAGAN with their faces very distinct, every expression catalogued.

                    KAGAN
     You know, don't you? You understand everything I'm saying and doing, don't you? Not in my words, or yours, but you know! And you won't give me an inch will you? Will you, damn it!

Qarlo says nothing.

                    KAGAN
                 (continues)
     Where you come from, who you are, you'll tell me; yes, you will; soon enough. But not till I tell you where you are, who I am--right?

Qarlo snickers deprecatingly. His face tells it all.

                    KAGAN
                 (continues)
     How could they have thought you were a dumb brute. You're quicker than I'd be in your place, soldier. Qarlo. Private. 6-5-1-0-2-2-9.

                    QARLO
     Dogdogdogdogdogdogdog...!

                    KAGAN
     A-B-C-D-E-1.2-3-4-5-6!

                    QARLO
     DogaKaganaDogaKaganaDog... dammit!

CAMERA COMES IN SLOWLY on Qarlo's face as he spits out the words rapidly one after another,

like a machine gun spitting bullets, bambambam-
bambambam as we

SHARP CUT TO:

68   EXT. TARGET RANGE - ESTABLISHING - DAY

EXTREME CLOSEUP on the muzzle of a machine gun,
firing, bambambambambam, SYNCHED IN TO MATCH QAR-
LO'S LAST WORD. CAMERA PULLS BACK to show FBI men
up and downrange, firing machine guns, rifles,
pistols, at various targets. CAMERA TRUCKS BACK
ALONG LINE till we get CLOSEUP of Tanner, with
Qarlo's rifle, aiming it downrange at a stack of
vertical 3" thick steel bulkheads. He presses the
knob, there is a SIZZLING CRACK and the bulkheads
are neatly melted to slag, Tanner turns INTO CAM-
ERA, dazed.

69   ANOTHER ANGLE - MED. SHOT - PAST TANNER TO KAGAN

as Kagan approaches him. Tanner hefts the rifle,
shakes head.

                    KAGAN
          They told me you were out here testing
          his rifle again. I've got to talk to you.

                    TANNER
                   (stunned)
          Kagan, this weapon is incredible!
          There's no power source, none at all.
          It's inexhaustible. I could fire it
          steadily for a month and its power
          wouldn't decrease by a kilowatt.

                    KAGAN
          Tanner, listen--

                    TANNER
                  (cuts him off)
          Do you know they took this thing apart in
          the lab, disassembled every piece, and it
          has only three moving parts.
                   (½ beat)
          And they tried leaving out half a dozen
          pieces, and it <u>still</u> worked! And we don't
          know how, not the faintest idea!

                    KAGAN
                  (sharply)
Tanner! I broke through this morning. I
think we talked.

                    TANNER
You _think_ you talked?

                    KAGAN
                  (softly)
He's from the future, Paul. Eighteen hundred years in Earth's future.

Tanner stares at him incredulously. CAMERA HOLDS
for several long beats as Tanner reorganizes his
thinking. He shakes himself physically, draws a
deep breath:

                    TANNER
Come on. We can talk in the car.

CAMERA HOLDS ON THEM as they walk away into B.G.
to a car parked on the low ridge in center frame.

70   LONG SHOT - PAST EXTREME CLOSEUP OF CAR IN F.G.
     TO MEN

as they approach the car in F.G. and Tanner puts
the rifle in the rear seat, and they get in the
front. CAMERA HOLDS ON THEM as they talk.

                    TANNER
Now tell me...

                    KAGAN
It's only rudimentary conversation. I
think he's been able to decipher what
I've been saying all along. It must sound
to him like a phonograph record of English as spoken by—say— Chaucer, played at
the wrong speed, a slower speed, would
sound to us.

                    TANNER
Then it _is_ English he's speaking.

                    KAGAN
Not really. Not entirely. It's what I
thought, gutter English, vastly speeded-
up, and filled with slang from his time.

                    TANNER
Eighteen <u>hundred</u> years...

                    KAGAN
...in the future. Exactly.

                    TANNER
How did you get <u>that</u> out of him?

                    KAGAN
I wasn't certain he was even from this
planet, so I--

                              SHARP CUT TO:

71   INT. PADDED CELL - ESTABLISHING - DAY

EXTREME CLOSEUP ON STAR MAP spread on floor. CAM-
ERA PULLS BACK TO SHOW Qarlo and Kagan looking at
the map.

                    KAGAN
   This is our galaxy. These stars here.
   This is our sun, light, up there... and
   here: one, two, three. Third from the
   sun...Earth...

Qarlo follows his fingers as they point out nebulae, white dots on the blue starmap, the larger
blowup of the Solar System. Kagan talks, but
mostly to himself, knowing Qarlo cannot understand him.

                    KAGAN
                (tapping Earth)
   Here. Here. Earth...
       (makes wide arm movement in air)
   Us. This dot. The Earth. Now...
           (he taps Qarlo)
   Which one is yours. Which star. Which
   planet. Qarlo...which...?

Qarlo shakes his head as though Kagan was a dull-
ard. He wipes his hand across the star map, finally settles on the same point Kagan had
touched. The Earth.

                    KAGAN
                  (wearily)
      No, man that's the <u>Earth</u>! Which planet
      is <u>yours</u>...?

Qarlo taps the paper again. Same spot. Kagan reg-
isters a dawning realization. He pulls a large
tablet of writing paper from his briefcase lying
on the floor nearby, and with a ball-point pen
quickly sketches the solar system, circling Earth
heavily. He gives the pen to Qarlo.

72   CLOSEUP - ON QARLO

as he looks at the pen. He turns it over and
over, examining it as though it were the rarest
jewel he had ever seen. Then Kagan urges him,
tearing off the top sheet, and indicating Qarlo
should write. Qarlo quickly bends to the task,
and though at first he uses the pen incorrectly,
he masters it in a few moments and draws the same
thing Kagan drew.

                    KAGAN
      Great! Imitation is the sincerest form of
      flattery, but it doesn't help us much--

Qarlo cuts him off with a rapid wave of his hand.
He pulls the star map to him, indicates the Milky
Way, the galaxy in which Earth spins around its
sun.

                    KAGAN
      flight. Our solar system. Our galaxy.
      Okay. Now what?

Qarlo begins sketching, faster and faster, making
dots in concentric patterns. Kagan studies them.
Finally Qarlo stops. He taps the Milky Way on the
star map, then his own drawing. Kagan picks up
Qarlo's drawing. He stares at it.

                    KAGAN
     It's our galaxy. The same as the star
     map, the same as--

CAMERA COMES IN FOR EXTREME CLOSEUP as Kagan's
eyes widen. His mouth opens in astonishment as
we

                                   SHARP CUT TO:

73   MATCHING SHOT - ON CAR - TANNER & KAGAN

SAME SHOT AS SCENE 70 when we cut away. We have
been in a <u>flashback</u> as we can see from the fact
that Tanner and Kagan are in the same exact positions as when we left them in Scene 70.

                    KAGAN
     Except it <u>wasn't</u> our galaxy. At least not
     the way it is today.
                    (beat)
     I took that drawing to a friend of mine
     at the Naval Observatory. He thought it
     was an amusing sketch. But it took him
     four hours to plot it correctly.

                    TANNER
     Well? What was it?

                    KAGAN
                    (flat)
     The position the stars of our galaxy will
     be in...in eighteen hundred years.

Tanner's eyes widen. He wipes his mouth which is
suddenly dry. He pulls out a pack of gum. Anti-
climactically:

                    TANNER
     Have a piece of gum...

CAMERA HOLDS on them as Kagan takes the gum, and
they stare at each other across a dawning abyss
of fear and anxiety.

                                   DISSOLVE TO:

74   INT. PADDED CELL - ESTABLISHING - NIGHT

CLOSEUP ON MOVIE SCREEN set up at one end of the dark cell. The WHIRR of a MOVIE PROJECTOR is heard O.S. as the screen flashes brief scene after scene. As each scene flashes, Kagan speaks forcefully, O. S. (STOCK SHOTS)

The first scene: a mother affectionately holding child.

                    KAGAN
  Love. Love. Love.

The scene flashes: war; a shot of incredible violence.

                    KAGAN
  Hate. Hate. Hate.

New scene: man and woman walking through forest, kissing.

                    KAGAN
  Love. Love. Love.

CAMERA HAS PULLED BACK to show Kagan running the projector, Qarlo watching. Now, as the scene of war flashes, Qarlo slides up the wall, watching with fascinated face. As the scenes of love flash, he looks confused, does not understand.

New scene: an attacker, teeth bared, sword raised, large in the frame, bearing down on them.

Qarlo suddenly leaps forward, throws himself at the screen, rips it to shreds, literally snaps the steel legs of the instrument, spins on Kagan, stops and, pulsing like a furnace about to explode, clenches his fists.

                    QARLO
                  (furious)
  Why'dja'yoo peep me thiz?

His speech is still slurred, run together, and dotted with slang from his own time, but we can now understand what he says without translation. Kagan tries to placate him.

                    KAGAN
           (shuts off projector)
I want you to know. I want you to understand.

                    QARLO
           (aims sharp finger)
I catch. You! You're'da drumbum. Send me
home'a'ways. Now! Doncha know thereza
war-ron?

Kagan comes toward Qarlo. The soldier backs up.
He is obviously restraining himself from tearing
Kagan in half.

                    KAGAN
              (helplessly)
I can't send you home, Qarlo. I don't
know how; no one knows how. Your home
doesn't exist yet.

                    QARLO
Lovehate, lovehate, fret it.

                    KAGAN
I can't forget it.

                    QARLO
Fret it. Thinkspeek'll pull me.

                    KAGAN
I don't understand that. I'm sorry.

Qarlo snarls, He shakes his head. He taps his
head several times, trying to get his meaning
across to Kagan.

                    QARLO
Thinkspeek! Thinkspeek! C.O. See-Oh!
See-Oh! Ah, fret it!

He turns away, leans against the wall, and suddenly—but quietly—pounds his fist into the wall
pads. His fury is a controlled thing, but the
passion is there. Kagan moves in to touch him on
the shoulder, a compassionate gesture. QARLO
WHIRLS and with one catlike movement literally
LIFTS KAGAN off the floor, pins him against the

wall, his feet dangling. The fires that have burned low in Qarlo suddenly blaze forth. He is the kill-machine.

75   CLOSEUP 2-SHOT - QARLO & KAGAN

THEIR FACES close together as Qarlo hisses into his face.

                    QARLO
     Donnever...touch...me!

He is banging Kagan against the wall mercilessly, repeating "don't ever touch me" over and over and over. The SOUND of the DOOR SLAMMING OPEN.

76   WIDE ANGLE - THE SCENE

as two MP's rush in, grapple with Qarlo; Kagan drops, clutching his neck; the MP's are tossed this way and that, finally club Qarlo into uncon- sciousness. They help Kagan up. He stumbles to Qarlo, looks at his wound. He shakes his head sadly as we

                                   DISSOLVE TO:

77   INT. DISPENSARY - ESTABLISHING - NIGHT

CLOSEUP ON A BARE CHEST BEING TAPED UP. As CAMERA ANGLE WIDENS we see Kagan being attended by a DOCTOR who is neatly taping up his ribs in wide, white swaths of tape. Tanner sits nearby, one foot on a small stool, watching.

                    TANNER
     Well, how does it feel to be dribbled
     like a basketball?

                    KAGAN
     It was my fault.

                    TANNER
     Oh, cut it out, Kagan.

                    KAGAN
     It was _my_ fault!

TANNER

You just can't admit it when you fail,
can you? Well get it straight, Tom, that
soldier is only a half a step up from a
wild animal, and he has to be treated
that way. Caged!

KAGAN

Listen, Tanner... ouch!

DOCTOR

Stop twisting.

TANNER

Five weeks, and what've you got to show?
Nothing but a set of staved-in ribs and
one helluva headache from having your
skull bounced off a wall.

KAGAN

And I've got him speaking our language.

TANNER

Not so's I noticed. Every third word's
gibberish.

KAGAN

Not gibberish...common usage from his own
time. And have you stopped to think how
valuable even <u>those</u> clues are to our own
future?

TANNER

Tom, we can't let you go back in there
with him. He can't be controlled, he
can't be predicted...he's--

KAGAN

He's a man!

TANNER

He's not a man, he's something else. Just
look in his eyes, man, at the hate in
them, you can see he was born to be a
killer!

                    KAGAN

That's the point, He <u>was</u> born to be a
killer; and <u>trained</u> to be a killer; and
if he hadn't found his way into our time,
he'd <u>die</u> a killer. But he doesn't hate,
Paul! He doesn't understand hate...or
love...or compassion.

                    TANNER

And you think you can teach him what
they mean?

                    KAGAN

Not in that cell...

                    TANNER
                 (suspiciously)

Kagan...

                    KAGAN

I want you to release him.

                    TANNER
                 (to Doctor)

Doc, you'd better get a pulmotor. He's
obviously suffering from oxygen starva-
tion.

                    KAGAN

I mean it, Paul. I want to take him home
with me.

                    TANNER

<u>Home with you</u>! Oh, now come <u>on</u>!

Kagan grabs Tanner's arm, he speaks with intensity. He <u>has</u> to convince him.

                    KAGAN

Paul, he hasn't <u>done</u> anything to keep him
penned up like a criminal. That old man
in the subway died of a heart attack, and
he was only defending himself in a
strange situation when he fired at that
crowd.

                    TANNER
Don't you think we've considered that?
It's not just a fine legal point, Tom.
It's his freedom, I know that, they know
it Upstairs. But we can't turn him loose,
ready to go off at any moment.

                    KAGAN
So let me try and teach him what it means
to be a functioning human being. He can
adapt; he's quick; he can fit in.

                    TANNER
Tom, it's lunacy.

                    KAGAN
But I can try.

                    TANNER
It's too risky.

                    KAGAN
But I can try!

                    TANNER

I don't know...I don't think they'll go
for it...Upstairs.

                    KAGAN
Paul, think about it. Trust me. I can
control him. I know I can. We're making
more progress every day.

The Doctor slaps Kagan gently on the back. Kagan
gets up, starts to put his shirt on. Tanner is
thinking.

                    TANNER
What about your family? How are they going to like the idea of a potential killer in the same house with them?

                    KAGAN
I've already talked to them about it.

                    TANNER
And...?

KAGAN

Abby's not sure. But both the kids are
fascinated.

TANNER

Your wife has more sense than all three
of you put together.

KAGAN

And what about you? How're you fixed for
sense?

Tanner spreads his hands helplessly. He shakes
his bead.

TANNER

You're making an old man of me, Kagan.

KAGAN

But you'll do it.

TANNER

I'll _talk_ to them Upstairs. That's all I
guarantee. But after I do, you'll probably be having conferences with me in the
cell next to Qarlo's.

Kagan fumbles in his pocket, pulls out a pack,
extends it.

KAGAN

Have a piece of gum...

Tanner smiles helplessly. Kagan could get around
a plaster saint. They start toward the door as we

DISSOLVE TO:

78   INT. CONSULTATION ROOM - ESTABLISHING - DAY

HIGH SHOT LOOKING DOWN into a room without furniture. It is white, all white, the only opening a
white door in one wall. The light comes from
above, a hidden source and the shadows are stark
in the room. And in the center of the room,
standing fairly close to each other, talking, are
Qarlo and Kagan. As they talk, CAMERA COMES DOWN

and this scene plays importantly on their faces,
and the bond between them.

                    KAGAN
On the other side of that door is the
world, Qarlo.

                    QARLO
Springin' out.

                    KAGAN
Yes, you're going home with me.

                    QARLO
Home? Define it.

                    KAGAN
A place to live, a house, a place where
you can rest, where no one locks you in.

                    QARLO
                 (understands)
Barracks. C.O.?

                    KAGAN
No, there's no C.O. No Commanding Officer, no other troops, no war, nothing but
freedom. Do you know what I mean? I've
told you about freedom.

                    QARLO
Where I come from, everyone lives alone.

                    KAGAN
Alone?

                    QARLO
No one comes up to each other...
     (indicates Kagan and himself)
like this. We don't mouthtalk.

                    KAGAN
Then how do you communicate?

CAMERA COMES DOWN to 2-SHOT and MOVES AROUND
THEM, gauging their expressions, dark against the
stark-white of the room.

                    QARLO
                  (taps head)
        In here... Thinkspeek. When the C.O.
        wants us, he orders us. In here.

                    KAGAN
        You'll be close to people now, Qarlo. My
        wife, my son and daughter. And me.

                    QARLO
        I don't grasp. I'll have to see.

                    KAGAN
        Yes. You'll have to see.
                  (beat)
        We'd better go now.

They stare at each other a moment. Kagan seems
frightened suddenly. They start toward door, Kagan stops Qarlo, without touching him.

                    KAGAN
                  (continues)
        Qarlo...would you hurt me. The way you
        did when I touched you?

                    QARLO
        You aren't The Enemy.

                    KAGAN
        But...could I be an enemy?

                    QARLO
                  (it says it all)
        You aren't The Enemy.

Kagan nods. He looks uncertain. They walk out the
door. The door closes as CAMERA PULLS BACK FROM
IT, PANS TO EXTREMELY WHITE WALL and MOVES IN ON
WHITE as we
                    RAPID LAP DISSOLVE TO:

79   EXT. COUNTRYSIDE - ESTABLISHING - DAY

The hillside and the WHITE LIGHT that encases the
Enemy. We see him as before, trapped halfway between tomorrow and today. It is RAINING. LIGHT-

NING FLASHES in the sky and THUNDER ROLLS heavily
as CAMERA MOVES BACK from the white.

80   EXT. COUNTRYSIDE - ANOTHER SHOT

ON THE ENEMY as a sudden bolt of lightning arcs
down out of the sky and CRACKLES AROUND HIM. It
touches his metal uniform, there is a BLINDING
FLASH OF LIGHT and when we can see again, the Enemy is free, completely seen now, for he has been
pulled completely through by the lightning. CAM-
ERA COMES IN RAPIDLY on his killer face, a
frightening face. His eyes widen in pleasure, and
he laughs at the sky, turning his face up into
the rain. We hear a steady ELECTRICAL IMPULSE in
his helmet and he touches one dial on a small machine strapped to his left forearm. The SOUND
grows louder, a spaced, metronomic BEAT BEAT BEAT
that matches the voice we hear faintly in his
helmet.

                HELMET VOICE O.S. (FILTER)
     Find your Enemy! Find your Enemy!
     Kill him...kill him...kill--

As the call grows louder and matches the BEAT
BEAT BEAT of the electrical impulse from the ma-
chine on his arm, he turns and sets out as CAMERA
HOLDS on the rainswept hill. He GOES AWAY and
CAMERA RISES to clock his progress down the hill,
getting smaller, smaller, smaller...stalking the
Soldier. As we

                                    FADE OUT.

        (COMMERCIAL INSERT)

<u>ACT THREE</u>

FADE IN:

81   INT. KAGAN LIVING ROOM - ESTABLISHING - DAY

<u>CLOSEUP ON BLACK CAT IN F.G. WITH ROOM IN PERSPECTIVE</u>
<u>ANGLE:</u>
we are up—looking from the cat bulking huge in
F.G. to the action taking place at the far end of
the room in B.G. At the open door stands Kagan
and Qarlo. The soldier fills the doorway, and despite the fact that the people at that end of the
room seem small in comparison to the cat, it is
obvious Qarlo towers over the group. Greeting Kagan and Qarlo at the door is ABBY KAGAN, Tom's
wife, a handsome woman who is a trifle too sophisticated and warm to be considered the Momma
type. With her are TONI KAGAN, an extremely-
attractive 20-year-old girl with long hair and a
fine figure, and LOREN KAGAN, 13 years old and
very wide-eyed. They stand in a semi-circle, awkwardly, as Kagan allows Qarlo to enter the room
before him.

                    KAGAN
     Qarlo, this is my wife, Abby; our daugh-
     ter, Toni, and the little one is Loren.
     He's--

Qarlo has not been listening. He ignores the people, stalks between them and COMES TO CAMERA,
kneeling down to look directly at the cat and
CAMERA. He talks to the animal. The cat tenses.
Qarlo speaks in future tongue.

                    QARLO
     See-Oh! Kwahr-loe Klo-breg-knee, pryte,
     sihz-fi-wun-oh-too-too-nyne. Reporting.

The cat stares. Qarlo looks as though he is expecting the animal to answer. It bolts and runs
away. Qarlo stares DIRECTLY INTO CAMERA and we
see his face, which has been hard, crumble. He is
lost. He has expected something to happen, and it
hasn't, and he is mystified by this new world

once more. He starts to rise as the Kagan's come
toward him from across the room.

82   GROUP SHOT - ON QARLO

as he rises, and the family comes up to him. All
but Kagan himself are looking at Qarlo strangely.
Kagan is confused, but there is curiosity and a
desire to understand in his face.

> KAGAN
>
> Cat. Remember? The book? What did you
> want from the cat, Qarlo?

> QARLO
> (bitterly)
> Nothing's same.

> KAGAN
>
> Cats are different where you come from?

> QARLO
>
> Different. C.O. prowler thinkspeek.

> KAGAN
>
> I don't understand that, Qarlo. The Com-
> manding Officer, the C.O., uses cats?

> QARLO
>
> On patrol, troopers, cats tied together
> by thinkspeek; cats do prowl, spot the
> Enemy, troopers jump.

The family is attentive, but their eyes widen at
the strangeness of what Qarlo is saying. Kagan
explains to them.

> KAGAN
>
> I think what he means is that somehow, by
> some technique we don't even suspect,
> wars in the future are fought by men and
> animals...the cats used to do reconnais-
> sance work, and by telepathy, they relay
> their messages.

                    LOREN
                   (excited)
And...and he thought he could get in
touch with his Commanding Officer by
talking through Macbeth!

                    KAGAN
It makes sense. What a fine patrol
prowler a silent cat would make.
                 (beat, to Qarlo)
It's not like that here, Qarlo. Macbeth
is just a cat.

                    QARLO
                   (wearily)
Nothing'z here are like war zone.

                    ABBY
But we'll do our best to see that things
are pleasant for you here, Qarlo.

                    QARLO
                  (to Kagan)
Camp follower? Joy-girl?

                    KAGAN
                   (archly)
Not so's you'd notice, Qarlo. Wife. Family unit, female C.O. Mother. Like your
mother.

Qarlo stares at him oddly.

                    QARLO
Mother? My mother?

                    TONI
You have a mother, don't you?

Qarlo looks superior for a moment, then recites:

                    QARLO
Clobregnny. Creche Hatchery 559. I am the
State, the State is All.

They look at him uncomprehending. All but Kagan,
who goes white, and who looks as though he may be
sick.

                    KAGAN
          Loren, take Qarlo up to his room.

Loren looks bugged, but turns and smiling, indicates Qarlo should follow him. They climb the stairs to the upper floor as CAMERA MOWS PAST KAGAN, TONI & ABBY to their passage. Kagan turns to his women when Qarlo is gone.

83   3-SHOT - ON KAGAN

as he wipes a hand across his forehead. There is infinite sadness in his face.

                    KAGAN
          Now I understand why he didn't respond to
          a film I showed him of a mother and
          child. He has no mother, he never knew a
          mother.
                    (beat)
          A creche is a day nursery, a foundling
          hospital. He's a product of artificial
          birth... he has no real parents...he was
          born and raised in a hatchery, like an
          egg.

                    TONI
          And that, about "the State"...?

                    KAGAN
          The State: his mother, his father, his
          everything.

                    ABBY
          How pathetic.

                    KAGAN
          He knew about the position of the stars,
          because a foot-soldier always knows how
          to navigate by the stars...but he never
          knew the most elemental kind of love...

                    ABBY
          Tom, can we help him...he seems so...so
          lost, so confused. And from what you've
          said, he's capable of—of—anything.

> KAGAN

We can help him.

> ABBY

But are you <u>sure</u>, Tom. Loren and Toni—

> KAGAN
> (intensely)

We've <u>got</u> to help him, Abby. And not just
for him, either.

He turns and walks toward the stairs as CAMERA
HOLDS on the faces of his wife and daughter, following with their eyes. They don't understand,
but they think they should.

> DISSOLVE TO:

84   INT. KAGAN DINING ROOM - ESTABLISHING - NIGHT

Qarlo sits next to Kagan, who is at the head of
the table. Loren sits across from Qarlo, and Toni
next to Loren. The young boy obviously is en-
thralled by the soldier.

> LOREN

Hey, Qarlo, in the future they got baseball and football and the World Series,
huh?

> KAGAN

I don't think Qarlo under--

> QARLO

Don't you know there's a war on?

He has said it almost by rote, as though it were
an explanation of <u>every</u>thing.

> LOREN

Yeah, I know. But I mean, when you <u>ain't</u>
fighting.

> KAGAN

<u>Aren't</u> fighting.

> LOREN

<u>Aren't</u> fighting. Huh, Qarlo?

                    QARLO
Why do you peep me drumdum questions?

                    LOREN
Peep? Drumdum? Huh?

                    KAGAN
"Peep" is a slang word for ask, or show,
or anything that informs him. Drumdum
means just what it sounds like...I think
your word is "square" or "dopey".

                    LOREN
Hey! That's wild! Peep and drumdum. I
gotta use that.

                    KAGAN
(smiles amusedly at Loren, turns to Qarlo)
  Isn't there a time when you aren't at
  war, Qarlo. It isn't drumdum of me...I
  just don't grasp...I want to know.

As Qarlo speaks, Abby comes in from the kitchen,
with a tureen of something steaming. She stands
listening for a long moment, worry on her face.

                    QARLO
When I had not as many time as him--
                (points to Loren)
my Drillmaster gave me my first weapon. I
had twelve by the time I killed my first
Enemy.
                    (beat)
The War has been fighting from before my
hatch-time. One hundred eighty.

                    TONI
Years? The war has been on for one hundred and eighty years?

Qarlo nods. They are thunderstruck. Abby brings
the tureen, sets it down in front of Kagan, next
to Qarlo. Before Kagan can ladle out the soup
from the tureen into the soup bowls stacked beside him, Qarlo seizes the bowl and shoves away
from the table. He smoothly walks around the table, and into the living room. The SOUND of him

GOING UPSTAIRS lingers in the room as they stare open-mouthed.

                    TONI
                 (ruefully)
     I've heard of lousy manners, but that's a
     bit much.

                    KAGAN
     I forgot. In his time, it's considered
     obscene to eat in front of anyone else.
     Not so strange, really; there are primi-
     tive tribes that have the same custom.
     And when you think about it, watching
     some people eat is rather sickening.

                    ABBY
     That's grand, just grand. But what do we
     do for soup?

                    KAGAN
     I'll talk to him. We can pass on the
     soup tonight, and I'll have a long talk
     with him about table manners...but I
     suspect he'll think we're terrible
     boors.

They stare at Kagan wide-eyed. He grins, enjoying
the reversal of social protocol.
                              DISSOLVE TO:

85   INT. KAGAN HALLWAY & BATHROOM- ESTABLISHING -
     NIGHT

Toni, in bathrobe, stands with toothbrush in
hand, by the half-open door of the bathroom,
talking to Abby. CAMERA MED. CLOSE on them as
they talk softly.

                    TONI
     Mother, you're getting hysterical. Daddy
     would never have brought him home if he
     thought we were in danger.

                    ABBY
     Your father was born type-cast as the
     trusting scientist. All he knows is

that--that creature may give him clues to
the future.

                    TONI
Oh, I don't know. He's not Tony Curtis,
but in a way he has a certain charm...

                    ABBY
Charm?!!

                    TONI
          (another suggestion)
Sex appeal?

                    ABBY
          (trapped)
I'm beginning to wonder who has what to
fear from <u>whom</u>!

                    TONI
          (lightly)
I'm just a jazz-mad baby, livin' a life
of sin.

Abby throws up her hands in exasperation, turns
and goes into another doorway, obviously a bedroom. Toni grins, and opens the bathroom door.
CAMERA SHOOTS PAST HER as she thrusts open the
door suddenly and QARLO SPINS AROUND his arms up-
thrust as though to strike her with a vicious ka-
rate chop. She gasps, falls back against the
wall.

86   INT. BATHROOM - ON QARLO TO TONI

the water in the sink is running, and his face is
wet, as is the floor and the front of his metal
suit. His hands drop water as he speaks.

                    QARLO
Get out!

She doesn't get out. Her fear drains away and is
replaced by temper and surprising verve.

                    TONI
I'll do no such thing. I live here, too,
you know.

                    QARLO
Sleeptime is for aloners.

                    TONI
I feel the same way about it, friend,
but I <u>still</u> have to brush my teeth, and
right now you're blocking the water.
                    (beat)
Say, what're you doing?

                    QARLO
Drinking.

                    TONI
Haven't you ever heard of a glass?

Qarlo stares at her uncomprehending. Obviously he
hasn't.

                    TONI
                 (continues)
Forget it.

They stare at each other silently for a moment.
The girl is obviously appraising him, and Qarlo,
for his part, is interested, but suspicious. <u>Very</u>
suspicious.

                    TONI
                 (continues)
Anything I can help you with?

                    QARLO
Help me?

                    TONI
Yes, do you have a towel, a wash
cloth...a partridge in a pear tree?

                    QARLO
                (suspiciously)
What do you want from me?

                    TONI
What do <u>I</u> want from <u>you</u>? Oh, brother,
how it saddens me to know men haven't
changed a bit, even eighteen hundred
years from now.

Qarlo backs away from her. He becomes wary.

> QARLO
>
> You're'a one more danger to me than Ka-
> gan. What do you want from me?

> TONI
>
> Don't you trust <u>any</u>one? Can't you even
> see we're trying to help you? Didn't you
> ever want to get near someone, talk to
> someone?

> QARLO
>
> That isn't possible. We can't close to
> each other, anyone can't. Thinkspeek
> comes best, not to touch.

> TONI
>
> You don't know what you're missing,
> friend.
> >   (then, soberly)
> And I thought <u>this</u> was the worst of all
> possible worlds, because <u>nations</u> can't
> get together.
> >   (beat)
> What a lousy, lonely life you must lead.

> QARLO
>
> That's my world. It's fine.

> TONI
>
> Mm-hmm. Just fine. And I guess if you're
> blind from birth you don't miss the
> color red.

> QARLO
>
> I don't grasp.

> TONI
>
> Forget it.

> QARLO
>
> Fret it.

> TONI
>
> I'll do that little thing.

He stares at her a moment, passes her and goes
out. She stands tipped onto one hip, tapping her
toothbrush against her palm. She shakes her head
wearily.

CAMERA COMES IN on Toni. CLOSEUP

                    TONI
  You'll never make it, Tiger.   I
  hope...but I don't think so.

CAMERA HOLDS on Toni as we

                                        CUT TO:

87   INT. LOREN'S BEDROOM - ESTABLISHING - NIGHT

CLOSEUP ON LOREN as his eyes widen and he looks
about to shout something loud and nasty. CAMERA
PULLS BACK TO WIDE ANGLE as he speaks.

                    LOREN
  Hey, what's <u>this</u>?

WIDE ANGLE OF ROOM shows all the furniture jum-
bled and piled in one corner. There is a desk and
several chairs and a toy box and all manner of
other kid's things on the bed, leaving a wide
empty space in the middle of the room. The walls
are pennant-covered, teen-style. Qarlo is lying
in the middle of the floor, and as Loren comes in
through the door, and speaks, Qarlo rises up, a
heavy brass bookend ready to smash.

                    LOREN
                 (anxiously)
  Hey, hold it, stop, wait a minute!

                    QARLO
  Sleeptime's for aloners.

                    LOREN
  I Just came in to get a comic book. They
  got me bunkin' in with Toni, I didn't
  mean to disturb you.

                    QARLO
  Get out!

> LOREN

Sure, sure...
>> (interested)
Hey, how come you're sleepin' on the floor? And all the stuff piled outta the way?

> QARLO

Clear the perimeter. No Enemy gets past. Troopers can Jump.

> LOREN

Hey, that's cool. You sleep on the floor in the future?

> QARLO

Sleeptime is anywhere. When a trooper hasta jump...he jumps!

> LOREN

<u>That</u> figures. Geez, you must have a great time, just soldier'n all the time. But don't worry, Qarlo, there ain't—aren't—isn't any Enemy here. You're in the past now, remember?

He smiles, grabs a comic book from a stack, and leaves, shutting the door behind him. Qarlo sinks back down, with the bookend in his hand, as CAMERA COMES IN for CLOSEUP.

> QARLO

No. No Enemy here. Another time...a past time. No Enemy.

His face seems to relax. He shoves the bookend away, and lies down. His eyes close as we

SHARP CUT TO:

88   EXT. STREET - ESTABLISHING - NIGHT

EXTREME CLOSEUP on the ELECTRICAL IMPULSE MACHINE on the Enemy's arm. It BEEP BEEP BEEPs for a moment, then suddenly begins to CRACKLE & WHINE as though interference is jamming it. As we realize it has gone out of kilter CAMERA RISES UP AND AWAY RAPIDLY giving us a LONG HIGH SHOT of The

Enemy, standing in shadows on a street of silent buildings, as though they were warehouses or large-industry structures. He spins around, look-ing, looking, and suddenly stops. He sees some-thing.

89   FULL SHOT - ENEMY'S POV - WHAT HE SEES

INSERT SHOT of a GIANT TRANSMITTING TOWER and the SOUND of that JAMMING.

90   EXT. STREET - ON ENEMY

as he starts toward the CONTROL SHACK serving the tower. CAMERA GOES WITH HIM as he hefts his ri-fle, and silently stalks through shadows to the building. CAMERA PANS WITH HIM as he circles the building and peers into a lighted window. PAST HIM & THRU WINDOW we see an old man with a rail-roader's cap and pipe, operating a huge bank of machinery. The JAMMING IS STRONGER NOW. The old man looks up at the sound.

91   INT. CONTROL SHACK ESTABLISHING - NIGHT

as the door MELTS AND BURNS AWAY with a SIZZLING CRACKLE. The old man falls back in terror as The Enemy comes through, his weapon raised. His eyes open in stark terror and he starts to scream, raising a Stillson wrench as he does.

The Enemy fires point-blank.

The old man vanishes in a BLAZE OF LIGHT from the death-ray, and The Enemy plays the beam over the machinery, melting it to slag. CAMERA HOLDS ON THE DESTRUCTION and then pans in for CLOSEUP as the JAMMING CEASES and the BEEP BEEP BEEP RE-SUMES.

CAMERA RISES to CLOSEUP of the Enemy's face, and the voice in his helmet that produces an evil smile on his strange face.

> HELMET VOICE O.S. (FILTER)
> Find your Enemy! Find your Enemy!
> Kill...kill...kill...

CAMERA PULLS BACK as The Enemy moves out through
the slag and destruction, through the melted
doorframe. SHOT THRU THE DOOR, into the darkness,
as he stealthily stalks his prey. CAMERA HOLDS
THRU DOOR ON HIS DEPARTING FORM as we

                              FADE TO BLACK

                                        and

                        FADE OUT.

                    (COMMERCIAL INSERT)

<u>ACT FOUR</u>

FADE IN:

92   INT. KAGAN LIVING ROOM - ESTABLISHING - DAY

CLOSEUP ON KAGAN using a tape recorder, speaking
into a microphone. He is reading from notes. A
phone sits near at hand on the desk. Dimly, we
can hear the SOUND of Loren in the yard, yelling
baseball-type remarks ad lib (e.g.: "Put it in
there, Qarlo! Toss it here! Good catch!" etc.)
Kagan looks up from time to time, and smiles.

                    KAGAN
     ...the words <u>love</u> and <u>hate</u> still have no
     meaning for subject. Though he has fit-
     ted--no, make that--<u>adapted</u> to the fam-
     ily unit's needs and structure, it now
     seems apparent from a two month perspec-
     tive, with a week in controlled situa-
     tion, that subject can <u>never</u> grasp these
     concepts...

PHONE RINGS. Kagan picks it up.

                    KAGAN
     Hello?
                    (beat)
     Paul! How are you? I was just preparing
     the weekly for you.
                    (beat)
     They what?

93   INTERCUT - PAUL TANNER

He sits behind a desk, receiver in hand.

                    TANNER
     They've made a dispensation in Qarlo's
     case, Tom. They feel he's made as much
     progress as can be expected...
                    (beat)
     I <u>know</u> that's for you to decide...
                    (MORE)

                    TANNER (CONT.)
but the papers have gotten wind of the
experiment, and there's a chance
there'll be repercussions —and they've
been talking about Civil Obligations and
Danger To The Community...
                    (beat)
I know, I know! But they won't listen to
that. All they know is he's a psycho-
pathic killer by our standards, and he's
on the loose.

94   SAME AS 92

                    KAGAN
So what have they decided?

            TANNER'S VOICE (FILTER)
He'll be remanded to my custody, and be
put under protective surveillance in a
maximum security pri--

                    KAGAN
         (cuts him off, furiously)
—prison! A bloody prison, right? The man
hasn't <u>done</u> anything, Paul! He's merely
bewildered, lost, out of joint with his
Times. That's no crime, so sin...he
didn't <u>ask</u> to be warped into the past.

            TANNER"S 'S VOICE (FILTER)
I'm sorry, Tom. That's the way it is.

                    KAGAN
                (defeated)
When?

            TANNER'S VOICE (FILTER)
As soon as possible. Tonight, at the
latest tomorrow. Can you get him ready?

                    KAGAN
Physically.. or emotionally?

            TANNER'S VOICE (FILTER)
Tom, don't take it out on me, for crine
out loud, I'm only--

                    KAGAN
                  (bitterly)
     I know: you're only doing your job!
     That's rapidly becoming the slimiest al-
     ibi of our times.

He slams the receiver down on the deskset, buries
his head in his hands for a moment, then rises
and CAMERA GOES WITH HIM as he goes to the window. He looks out.

95   KAGAN'S POV - WHAT HE SEES

EXT. YARD with Qarlo and Loren playing ball:
Qarlo tossing baseball awkwardly, and Loren popping bunts and flys into his area. Qarlo goes
about the business without a smile or seeming understanding of what is going on. But he does it,
the way he might empty garbage or peel potatoes.

96   INT. KAGAN LIVING ROOM - ON KAGAN

as he turns from the window. Abby comes into the
room. He turns to her.

                    KAGAN
     They've decided to put him away. Tonight
     or tomorrow.

                    ABBY
                 (mixed emotions)
     I can't say I'm sorry, Tom. It's been
     terrifying.

                    KAGAN
     Abby, cut it out. You're dramatizing
     again.

                    ABBY
     You see what you want to see, <u>only</u> what
     you want to see. And not that Toni has
     been spending more and more time with
     him... that Loren is beginning to idol-
     ize him...that...

KAGAN
Isn't that what we wanted, for him to
fit in, to adjust, to learn what caring
means?

Abby is getting worked up now. There is a note of
hysteria in her voice.

ABBY
But he doesn't care! He's just as he was
when he came here. He's playing with us,
Tom, letting us think he understands,
that he wants to make the best of it.

KAGAN
I think you're seeing shadows.

ABBY
From the future, Tom. Shadows from the
future. That man is a killer... he was
trained from birth for only one thing!
To kill! Do you think a week here with
us is going to erase all that?

KAGAN
I hoped it would...

ABBY
I'm afraid, Tom. Afraid of him... and
afraid of the future he comes from.

Kagan turns to the window. His voice is filled
with sadness as, back turned, he speaks to
her--and himself.

KAGAN
(distantly)
Jung (pronounced: Yoong) once said: "The
only thing Man has to fear on this
planet--is himself."

CAMERA HOLDS on Kagan's back, and Abby staring at
him with helplessness, and the SOUNDS of Qarlo
and Loren playing ball outside as we

SLOW DISSOLVE TO:

97   EXT. FOREST - ESTABLISHING - NIGHT

the Enemy, moving among the shrubs and trees. A forest, a park perhaps; a place of fog and shadows, eerie, dark, and trembling with his presence, as he follows the impulse BEEP BEEP BEEP of his wrist-machine. He stops, listens, there is a SOUND of movement behind him. He spins.

98   ANOTHER ANGLE - WIDE SHOT

PAST A WILD DOG TO ENEMY. Or perhaps it is a wolf. Whatever it is, there is no doubt it's dangerous. Jaws slavering, it crouches low, its growl a deep rumble in the night. Past it, we see another, and another, all closing in on the Enemy, and the only sound to match their GROWLING is the ELECTRICAL IMPULSE from the machine the Enemy wears. He drops back, lifts the rifle, and they spring as we

                              SHARP CUT TO:

99   HIGH ANGLE DOWN ON SCENE

as the wolves, dogs, beasts attack. The rifle spits a stream of light and one of the animals vaporizes in mid-leap. Then the others are on him, and the rifle is useless, wrenched from his grasp as he swings it to club a second beast. The creature goes down, its head staved in, and the Enemy grapples with the third one without the weapon's aid. He lifts the creature, and with seemingly unstraining ease, breaks its back and hurls the carcass away. CAMERA COMES DOWN to CLOSEUP of the bleeding Enemy. His face is marked by deep furrows where claws have ripped at him. But he stumbles to the rifle and, breathing hard, retrieves it. The BEEP BEEP BEEP continues as he staggers away from the scene of carnage.

                              DISSOLVE TO:

100   INT. KAGAN LIVING ROOM - ESTABLISHING - NIGHT

Kagan and Qarlo sit talking.

                    KAGAN
          They've decided you can't stay here.

                    QARLO
Who? Who has decided?

                    KAGAN
Some men who make decisions for the rest
of us, because we let them.

                    QARLO
C.O.?

                    KAGAN
In a way, yes. They've decided you might
hurt someone...that you have to be--sent
to a place.

Qarlo's face suddenly goes cold and hard. This
he understands.

                    QARLO
Pee-owe-dubbel-yoo. I peeped that'd happen. I knew you troops would jump.

                    KAGAN
                 (hastily).
Not a prisoner of war camp, Qarlo. Nothing like that. It's a—a—

                    QARLO
                 (intensely)
Liar!

                    KAGAN
It wasn't my idea...I tried to keep them
from doing it...but these men, they--

                    QARLO
Qarlo Clobregnny. Private. Six five one
oh two two nine.

                    KAGAN
Listen--

                    QARLO
                 (bitterly)
Where I come from, it's true, it's
right. No two ways. Us and them. The Enemy. We know who they are, they know us.

No two-ways troopers who jump sometimes
one way, sometimes the other.

                KAGAN
It's better here, Qarlo, if you could
only understand...if you could only
grasp—

                QARLO
Grasp? Your words, your drumbum empty
words, love, hate, dog, mother...?

                KAGAN
Yes, yes!

                QARLO
No, I want my time, my world.

                KAGAN
It's better here, now, Qarlo. We don't
have the War...

                QARLO.
                (sneers)
You have worse. In my world we don't
grasp these love, hate, all of them. We
never <u>know</u>, so we don't want. Here, you
peep love...then take it away.

The doorbell RINGS. We hear a woman's footsteps
going across the tiled hallway, and a MURMURING
VOICE admitting someone.

                KAGAN
It's Tanner, Qarlo. He's here to get
you.

Qarlo gets up, drops back into a striking position. If they want him, they'll have to take him
by force. He watches the front hall as Tanner en-
ters, with PROFESSOR CHARNEY, a smallish, dapper
man with bright little marmoset eyes.

                TANNER
Tom...something unexpected's happened.

                KAGAN
Professor Charney...

                    CHARNEY
Mr. Kagan, I think...no, I'm <u>sure</u> I can
send this soldier back to his future...

                    KAGAN
                 (astounded)
Whaaat?!!

                    QARLO
              (can't believe it)
Back? I can jump back?

101 ANOTHER SHOT - THE GROUP

     as they gather around Charney, and he explains,
     with a vast, reflexive, expansive and Continental
     use of his hands to illustrate his speech. The
     others listen in awe.

                    CHARNEY
     We've been experimenting with the
     cross-polarization of laser beams. From
     what this man told us, we think we've
     got the answer.

                    KAGAN
     And you can actually warp him back
     through? Safely?

                    CHARNEY
     It's a matter or time...
                    (chuckles)
     excuse my pun. What I mean is, by util-
     izing the correct vector of a positively
     charged, and a negatively charged, laser
     beam...with the correct refractive index
     of each, we can pinpoint him into any
     year we choose.

                    TANNER
     The Men Upstairs reversed their decision,
     Tom. They've decided to let him stay
     here till the Professor's team works it
     out.

                    CHARNEY
     It may be as soon as a week, or as much
     as a year...we have six thousand to the

tenth power combinations of refractive
index to rotate. But one of them will
prove out. We're certain.

                    KAGAN
                 (to Tanner)
Thanks.. Paul...

                    TANNER
Forget it....just doing my job.

He has said it archly, Kagan catches the message.
He looks suitably quashed. Qarlo has listened to
all this, and now he speaks, with the first thing
approaching joy we've yet seen.

                    QARLO
Back? I'll jump back! My time, my
world...yeahhh!

102 2-SHOT - CHARNEY & QARLO

who look like Mutt and Jeff.

                    CHARNEY
Oh, now don't get all fired up, this is
all still very much hypothetical. We
have many preliminary experiments —in-
animate objects, various metals, guinea
pigs--before we can even think of send-
ing a man through, with any degree of
certainty for success.

                    QARLO
But back! I can jump back! To my War, to
my C.O. A new weapon!

A voice breaks in from O.S. It is Loren, who has
come in, unnoticed.

              LOREN'S VOICE O.S.
What do you wanna go back for? I thought
you liked it here, I thought we were
friends! Why do you wanna go to that
place, where everybody kills everybody?

103 FULL SHOT - THE SCENE

as everyone turns to see the boy, with baseball
mitt and ball, standing just inside the hall entrance to the living room.

                    QARLO
    My time is the best! For me! I <u>need</u> to
    jump! Find my unit, boy. Don't t you
    know there's a war on?

                    LOREN
               (disillusioned)
    You just like to kill people! You're not
    like us you was just pretending, you
    only wanna kill people and hurt'em.
                  (beat)
    Well, g'wan then, g'wan back to there..
    nobody cares...you can kill everybody
    for all we care...you stink!

He turns and runs from the room. Qarlo's jaw muscles jump. There is silence. No one knows what to
say.

104 ANOTHER SHOT - THE GROUP - ON TANNER

He coughs nervously. They each move a little, as
though breaking free of an invisible spiderweb of
emotion that has held them immobile, locked in
their own thoughts.

                    TANNER
    We'll be going, Tom. We're on our way to
    an Executive Meeting. Just stopped by so
    I could tell you myself.

                    KAGAN
        (distracted, staring after Loren)
    Hmmm? What? Oh, yes, thanks, Paul. I'll
    talk to you later. Professor. Thank you.

The Professor nods his understanding, and quietly, he and Tanner leave. Qarlo has not moved.
Kagan moves to him.

105 2-SHOT - QARLO & KAGAN

there is concern on Kagan's face. Concern for the
huge, bewildered creature ripped out of the future.

> KAGAN
> (softly)
He's a child. He doesn't know. He
doesn't understand.

> QARLO
He grasps more than you, Kagan.   He
knows. He knows what I am.

> KAGAN
It isn't true, Qarlo. You've seen yourself. In just the short time you've been
here, you've changed tremendously...

> QARLO
> (coldly)
I am what I am. He knows, and I know.
Why do you dream, Kagan?   I know how to
do one thing, be a trooper. I'll do it
again...you know that's true.

> KAGAN
> (fervently)
Dear God, I hope not...if that's all we
have to look forward to, then we're
lost, every one of us.

CAMERA HOLDS on his frightened face as we

> DISSOLVE TO:

106 EXT. KAGAN HOUSE – ESTABLISHING HIGH SHOT –
(STOCK) – NIGHT

A VERY HIGH SHOT looking down on the house. It is
raining. A dark, moonless night. Lightning splits
up the sky every few seconds. THUNDER ROLLS in
the distance. A night for witches to think twice
before mounting brooms. CAMERA COMES DOWN SLOWLY
as we

> DISSOLVE THRU TO:

107 INT. KAGAN DINING ROOM – ESTABLISHING – NIGHT

The Scene: in the F.G. is the empty end of the
dining table. At the far end, the head, sits Kagan himself, Toni to his right, Abby to his left,
Loren next to Toni, nearest to us. The empty
place across from Loren shows signs of someone
having been in the process of eating. Qarlo, obviously. Abby yells into the kitchen, which is
directly behind Tom Kagan.

                    ABBY

  Qarlo...as long as you're in the
  kitchen, would you bring the coffee,
  please?

No answer. Abby looks at Tom.

                   KAGAN
He heard you. He'll do it.

                   TONI
Why has he started helping with chores,
Daddy? It's so—so strange. Like having
a pet gorilla that sniffs flowers.

                   KAGAN
He's learning about us...I think he
wants to remember, when he goes back.

                   LOREN
                (kid-vicious)
He's just fakin'. He wants you to think
he's a good guy. All he wants to do is
kill people.

                   KAGAN
Stop it, Loren!

                   TONI
Yes, knock it off, cockroach. Pretend
you have manners.

Loren stands up abruptly, the perfect model of an
angry child. He throws his napkin on the table.

                    LOREN
     Yeah, well you watch...he's   gonna beat
     in your brains with a baseball bat when
     you're not watchin' him.

                    KAGAN
     All right, Loren. That's it.   Go to your
     room!

                    LOREN
     I don't ca--

                    KAGAN
                  (angry)
     I said: go to your room! Now!

The boy is hurt and frightened, and shoves his
chair away. He starts away from the table as we

                              SHARP CUT TO:

108 REVERSE ANGLE – PAST KAGAN TO LOREN

and the outside wall of the house behind him. As
the wall glows red, then white, there is a WEIRD
CRACKLING SIZZLING SOUND and the wall slags away
to melted mush, a gigantic hole appears as if by
magic, and thru the hole we see the dark,
rainswept night. As Abby and Toni SCREAM, the Enemy leaps thru the hole in the wall, his hideous
face alert and teeth bared, the rifle tilted up
and aiming at them. We hear the BEEP BEEP BEEP of
his tracking machine and the SOFT WHISPERING
VOICE in his helmet saying "Kill, Kill, Kill,
Kill..." as he advances slowly, menacingly, into
the room.

Loren falls back against the table. He is directly in the line between the Enemy and the family, the table, the kitchen door, and behind
it—Qarlo.

The Enemy's head turns. Holding the rifle with
one hand, he aims the machine on his wrist. As it
points to the kitchen door the BEEP BEEP BEEP
climbs to insane loudness. His face sets in an
evil, determined leer, a twisted expression that
embodies all the murder in the universe.

He starts toward them. Kagan's family falls back
to Kagan himself. They are grouped in front of
the kitchen door. The Enemy must go through them
to get the soldier.

109   EXTREME CLOSEUP - THE ENEMY

as he advances. CAMERA TILTS FROM HIS FACE TO
THE MUZZLE OF THE WEAPON and his hand, tightening
on the firing knob.

110   ZOOM SHOT - KAGAN & FAMILY

CAMERA ZOOMS IN MED. FAST on their terrified
faces, as they realize:

                    ABBY
     He...he's come...for...

                    KAGAN
           (suddenly shouts)
     Qarlo! Jump!

111   CLOSEUP - KITCHEN DOOR

as it bangs open and Qarlo stands there as CAMERA
PULLS BACK RAPIDLY to show us THE ENTIRE SCENE.
The soldier, with the steaming pot of coffee in
his hand. His eyes widen. The SOUND of the KILL
VOICE has GROWN LOUDER over and over and over...

112   EXTREME CLOSEUP - QARLO

as his face becomes something terribly alien. He
is the ultimate killer now, as he was when first
we saw him. The softness that has been in his
face for most of the last scenes, is gone. He
BELLOWS IN FURY.

113   ACTION SEQUENCE - WITH QARLO ALL THE WAY - AERO-
      FLEX!
thru

116

as he hurls the coffee pot at the Enemy, just as
the beam of light spears out of the weapon, as
Qarlo viciously rams the family out of the way.

He upsteps almost effortlessly, is on the dining room table, and running the length or it, hurls himself on the Enemy just as the weapon spurts another beam of light. It goes wild, melts half of another wall.

They grapple, tumble, vicious, cries of animal power and frenzy fill the room, and the BEEP BEEP BEEP and the KILL VOICE now almost OVERPOWERINGLY LOUD. Qarlo on top of the Enemy, strangling him, literally choking the life out of him as the Enemy manages to jack the weapon up into Qarlo's stomach, and presses the stud. There is a SHORT SHARP SPIT OF POWER and Qarlo throws back his head and SCREAMSSSSS a final death-scream, without letting go of the Enemy's throat. He falls atop the Enemy. They are both dead. Silence fills the room, except for the soft voice now helplessly, sadly saying:

      HELMET VOICE O.S. (FILTER)
  Kill… kill… kill… kill…

                        FADE OUT.

<u>EPILOGUE</u>

FADE IN:

117   INT. KAGAN LIVING ROOM – ESTABLISHING – NIGHT

HIGH SHOT looking down on what must be two bodies, under blankets. A hand protrudes from under
one edge of one of the blankets. The hand disap-
pears under the blanket at a point well up the
wrist, we see it is Qarlo's metal suit. No one is
in the room, but we HEAR VOICES as though there
were people talking in a hushed tone, in a
church, or a morgue, or any room where death has
come to stay for a while. It is important that we
see no one, but easily recognize their voices.

> TANNER'S VOICE O.S.
So he finally reverted. He was born a
killer, and he died a killer.

> KAGAN'S VOICE O.S.
Perhaps.

> LOREN'S VOICE
He wanted to go away from us, so's he
could kill people...

> ABBY'S VOICE O.S.
And the future came to him, as if he had
never been away. He died what he was.

> TONI'S VOICE O.S.
Daddy, was that how it was? Didn't we do
any good at all...didn't he see...

> KAGAN'S VOICE O.S.
Didn't he learn what it was to care?
> (beat)
I don't know. I don't think so.

> TANNER'S VOICE O.S.
And this is what we have to look forward
to. A world of men who are machines,
trained for murder...

CAMERA COMES DOWN SLOWLY on Qarlo's blanketed
body.

                    TONI'S VOICE O.S.
I don't believe it...I think he knew. I
think something in him was still human.
He saved us.

                    KAGAN'S VOICE O.S.
But because he cared what happened to
us...or because that was all he knew to
do...to kill His Enemy?

                    ABBY'S VOICE O.S.
Tom, is...is there still time to
change...for all of us...?

                    KAGAN'S VOICE O.S.
Time? There's all the time in the
world...

CAMERA HAS COME DOWN to EXTREME CLOSEUP of Qarlo's hand. It is a fist. Even in death, he is
ready to fight.

                    KAGAN'S VOICE
                     (continues)
But God help us...that may not be
enough...

CAMERA HOLDS on the clenched fist of the soldier
as we

                              SLOWLY FADE TO BLACK

                                                and

                              FADE OUT.

                    <u>THE END</u>